To my dear niece, Lia

BLOOD STONE

BLOOD STONE

MICHAEL ALLEGRETTO

AVON BOOKS ◆ NEW YORK

AVON BOOKS
A division of
The Hearst Corporation
105 Madison Avenue
New York, New York 10016

For their generosity and patience in telling me what's what, I wish to thank Charles J. Onofrio, attorney-at-law; Mel Apodaca, investigator for the Denver coroner's office; and Kim Knox, rock climber. Any errors are certainly mine.

BLOOD STONE

1

Lloyd Fontaine coughed smoke across my desk and said he could make me rich.

"I'm on a case," he said, "and I want you for my partner."

"I'm pretty busy now, Lloyd." I wasn't.

"Look, Jake, there's millions involved here. Believe me."

I didn't believe him. When you're talking about money, it's tough to trust a guy who's wearing a brown-checked coat, green polyester pants, black shoes, and white socks. He tugged at his flowery tie and looked at me with rheumy eyes.

"At least let me tell you about it," he said.

Fontaine's voice was as whiny as it had been the last time I'd seen him, four years ago. He'd looked the same then, too—tired face, thinning hair, and a mustache like a plucked eyebrow. He'd been down on his luck. A mutual acquaintance, an attorney, had sent him to me for work because Fontaine was in the business and at that time I had one or two more cases than I could handle. It was no big deal, and I didn't expect to be paid back. Hell, I didn't *want* to be paid back.

Lloyd Fontaine wanted to pay me back.

"Sure, Lloyd, tell me about it," I said, and a few of the wrinkles went out of his face.

"It was twenty years ago," he said, coughing. He lit a cigarette from the one he had going and dropped the old butt in his coffee cup. "Lochemont Jewelers in downtown Denver was knocked over by four gunmen for two-point-one million in jewelry and loose stones plus a necklace on loan from the state historical society that was worth another six hundred grand. You probably read about it."

"Lloyd, twenty years ago the only things I read were dirty magazines and the instructions on tubes of acne cream."

"Oh. Anyway, the guys shot up the place, wounding a guard and accidentally killing a little girl. Then they took off with the store manager, a guy named Charles Soames, who, it turned out, had been in on the robbery. He'd disabled the alarm system and opened the safe for his pals. To make a long—"

Fontaine coughed a few times and wiped his hand across his mouth. Then he brushed ashes from his lapel to his lap.

"To make a long story short," he said, "most of the robbers wound up dead. One got away and one got caught—the store manager, Soames. The jewels were never recovered. Soames stood trial for the felony murder of the little girl and went to prison without revealing the location of the jewels."

"Wait a minute. You said one of the robbers got away."

"Yep."

"Didn't he take the jewels with him?" I asked.

"Nope, even though that's what everyone thinks."

"Everyone being—"

"Everyone," he said. "The cops, the insurance company, the newspapers."

Everyone but the deluded private eye, Lloyd Fontaine.

"Everyone but you," I said.

"You don't believe me, do you?"

"Sure, Lloyd, I guess, it's just that—"

"Jake, let me explain something to you. The jewels were insured by National, and back then I was their chief investigator. This was *my* case, you understand? I've been living with this thing for twenty years."

He made it sound like a disease.

"You're not working for National Insurance now, are you?"

Fontaine started to answer, then coughed to remind himself his cigarette was almost gone. He lit another with the butt. The smoke was starting to get to me. I got up and opened a window and breathed in mid-September smog. One floor below me, the afternoon traffic on Broadway was thickening as the downtown office workers tried to beat the rush back to the suburbs. At least they had real jobs.

"Hell no, I don't work for them," Fontaine said, calling me back. "The motherfuckers. But that's neither here nor there."

Seen from behind, Fontaine was so skinny and slumped over that he looked ninety years old. There was a sprinkling of ashes on the floor and on his clothes and on the thick manila envelope he held in his lap. The ashtray I'd put in front of him was still clean. I went back to my swivel chair.

"The point is," he said, "the jewels are about to surface and I intend to be there when they do."

"Surface? And why, after twenty years?"

"You still don't believe me, do you, Jake?"

What I believed was that Fontaine didn't have both feet in the batter's box. What I also believed, from the little I'd heard, was the majority view: The robber who got away, got away with the jewels, and was now living comfortably in Brazil or Australia— that is, if he hadn't yet died from overindulgence. On the other hand . . .

"Keep talking, Lloyd."

"Well, the ex-manager of Lochemont Jewelers just got out of prison and I've been keeping a close eye on him. He's going to lead me to those jewels. Hell, I've already got a general idea of where they are."

Fontaine scratched under his tie, dropping more ashes on himself.

"And if you get the jewels, what, you head for South America?"

Fontaine tried to laugh, but it threw him into a coughing fit. I got a glass of water from the tiny bathroom and set it in front of him. Then I poured myself some bourbon from the bottle in the bottom drawer. I'd gone two whole weeks without having my first drink before six, but if I had to put up with this obsessed SOB I deserved one now, four-thirty or not.

Fontaine drank his water. "I'm not going to *steal* the jewels, Jake, I'm going to turn them over to National Insurance and collect their ten percent reward." He reached for my bottle and poured three fingers into his water glass. His eyes gleamed behind crusty lids. "With inflation boosting the price of gems," he said, "that ten percent should be in the neighborhood of half a million bucks." He chugged my booze and sucked his cancer stick.

"You know, Lloyd, you really ought to cut down."

"On what?" he said and coughed smoke in my face.

"Nothing."

He waved his hand, scattering ashes on my desk. "That'll get their fucking goat, you know, those jerks at National, when I walk in there with the Lochemont jewels. After all these years, too. Old Lloyd Fontaine will have the last laugh." He reached for my bottle.

I was beginning to wonder if Fontaine might really know something. Or maybe it was just my greed disguising itself as professional curiosity.

"Why do you think Soames knows where the jewels are?" I asked. "Since no one else thinks he does."

"Not everyone has my nose for the truth," he said, slamming back his whiskey. "When I interviewed Soames after his trial, I could tell from the tone of his voice and the look in his eye that he knew exactly where that fortune was hidden. That's why I'm a professional. I have a *feel* for these things."

"Did Soames tell you he hid the jewels?"

"No."

"Do you have any evidence that he did?"

"I don't need evidence, Jake." He touched the side of his nose. It was as runny as a puppy's. "I've got this."

What pissed me off was that I'd been ready to believe that this clown could lead me to a fortune. He reminded me of a lottery ticket, promising riches until you scratched the surface and found nothing but a worthless piece of cardboard. At least he hadn't cost me a buck.

"Uh, Lloyd, I appreciate your asking me to—"

"Hey, I'm not asking you to work free, Jake, believe me. I'll cut you in on thirty percent of what I realize—say, a hundred and fifty grand. And I promise you won't have to shoot anybody." He coughed a laugh.

"Gee, Lloyd, I don't know—"

"Okay, make it thirty-five."

Thirty-five percent of a Fontaine fantasy would be exactly nothing.

"Really, Jake, I want you in with me on this. I need someone I can trust. We're talking about a lot of money here, the kind some people would kill for."

"What makes you think I wouldn't?" I asked, trying to discourage him.

"What a kidder," he said. Then he checked his gold-toned throwaway plastic digital watch, lit a fresh cigarette, and dropped the smoking butt in his coffee cup. My cup, dammit.

"All I need is for you to help me follow a few people. Plus, I could use a guy your size—I might have to show them some muscle."

I didn't know who Fontaine was talking about now and I didn't care. It wasn't that I hated confrontations, for chrissake, and I certainly had nothing against money, if there really was any—in fact, I was getting pretty low on funds. But what I did hate was chasing after make-believe fortunes. And what I *really* hated was tagging along with a guy who had his head stuck up his you-know-what.

"I'd like to help you, Lloyd, but—"

"I know, I know, you want all the details. That's why I brought this along." Fontaine dropped his fat manila envelope on my desk. It was smudged with fingerprints and flecked with ash. "Background information. You can look through it later." He checked his watch again. "But right now I want you to come with me and meet some of the players. It'll give you a better idea of what's going on."

"I can't, Lloyd," I lied, "I'm seeing a client at five."

"Oh. Okay, well, how about I come back later after I've talked to these people and you've looked through this stuff and you can give me your answer."

I already knew my answer.

He opened the envelope, which appeared to be stuffed mostly with old newspaper clippings, removed two black-and-white photographs, and shoved them in his jacket. I caught a glimpse of the pictures—two men standing by a car.

"A little leverage for my meeting," he said, patting his jacket. Then he winked and stood up. "You sure you can't come with me? I could use your presence."

"I'm sure."

"Hey, no problem. I'll be back in a couple of hours—say, around seven."

"Great."

"Don't lose that, okay?" he said, tapping the envelope with nicotine-yellow fingers. Then he inhaled a lungful of smoke to make it across the room, coughed good-bye, and closed the door.

I opened the other window, washed out the cups in the small bathroom sink, and swept Fontaine's ashes under the desk. Then I locked up the office and went to a bar down the street to socialize with four or five of my old pals, all named Bud. They helped me wash down a cheap steak. When I got back, it was nearly seven. Fontaine's envelope full of clippings was still on my desk, waiting to be read. I reread the morning paper instead. At eight-thirty he still hadn't shown up. I looked up his number in the book. No answer. I stayed in the office until ten.

Lloyd Fontaine never came back.

2

The next morning I drove to Lloyd Fontaine's office. I figured he hadn't shown up last night because he'd become preoccupied with something important, like a bottle of gin.

I'd shuffled through the contents of his manila envelope during my morning coffee to see if the light of day made any difference. It hadn't. Old news clippings of a forgotten robbery plus photos of two men by a car plus a scribbled-in spiral notebook plus Fontaine's half-ass story did not add up to a fortune. When I'd phoned, he hadn't answered, so I planned on shoving the envelope under his door with a note: Thanks, but no thanks.

His office was near Twenty-second and Arapahoe, beyond the shadows of the tall buildings, in the nether region of downtown Denver. The area featured warehouses, gin mills, and pawnshops, all built with grimy bricks and wire-mesh windows. It was inhabited by people with hidden pasts and no future, who lived on the street, slept in doorways or abandoned buildings, and dined at the Salvation Army. Some businesses operated in this area precisely because of the depressed environment, which brought with it rock-bottom rent.

I parked the old Olds in the street and went into Fontaine's building.

The hallway was a narrow stretch of grimy linoleum between two rows of locked doors. Light bulbs hung overhead like dusty, dead plants. Fontaine's office was at the end. I knocked, and the sound echoed in the hall. Through the frosted glass door panel I could see someone's silhouette—either a very short, fat person or somebody sitting in a chair. I knocked again.

"Fontaine?"

The figure didn't move, so I tried the knob. It wasn't locked. I really didn't want to go in there, but I pushed open the door anyway.

The air was filled with the sickly sweet odor of death.

The office had been ransacked—file cabinets tipped over, desk drawers on the floor, and papers and folders strewn about. Pieces of musty carpet had been ripped away from the floorboards, and sections of wallpaper were torn and hung down like peeled skin. The one padded chair in the room had been slashed open and its stuffing pulled out. Fontaine sat in a hardbacked chair, tied there with the phone cord.

I went over to him without touching anything and tried to breathe through my mouth. No good. He stunk of voided bowels and scorched flesh. His shirt was off and his scrawny yellow-white chest looked like a plucked chicken's. Ugly cigarette burns peppered the skin on his chest and neck. His head was bowed, as if in apology, and his tie had been wrapped around his mouth for a gag. There was a pair of neat, round, reddish-black holes in the center of his forehead, one above the other.

I backed out of the room, drove three blocks to a bar with a pay phone, and tossed whiskey on my unsettled stomach. Then I went back to Fontaine's building and stood in the hall, waiting for the cops.

A few minutes later, tires screeched to a stop out front. Two uniforms entered the building—a tall white guy and a short Chicano. They were both young and quick and alert and had their hands on their holstered weapons.

"Are you the man who phoned?"

I nodded. "The body's inside."

The short cop went into Fontaine's office. The tall cop kept me company.

"What's your name, sir?"

"Jacob Lomax."

"May I see some identification, Mr. Lomax?" He was very polite. So was I. I gave him my driver's license. Then my PI card. He wasn't impressed.

The short cop came out of the office. "One dead," he said. "I'll call Homicide." He went out to the squad car.

The tall cop asked me who was the dead guy and when did I find him and how did I know him and what was I doing here and who if anyone did I see leaving the building and who did I suppose could do such a thing and he wrote down all my answers with precise penmanship in his notebook. When the short cop came back, we all three stood around and waited for the homicide investigators. We passed the time by them asking me more questions and me answering.

Eventually, an unmarked city car pulled up in front.

I had two, maybe three friends on the police department, and one of them was in Homicide. If I was lucky, he'd be the one leading this group.

I wasn't lucky. It was Lieutenant Dalrymple. A couple of detectives trailed in his wake, then followed the short cop into Fontaine's office.

Dalrymple stopped and looked at me the way a forest ranger looks at a cigar butt. He was a big man, a bit taller than I was but a lot heavier, and it wasn't all fat. He had short, pale hair and a wide, freckled face. Running across his right ear and through his sideburn and halfway across his chunky, muscled cheek was a thin scar. I'd been with him the day he'd acquired it. We'd both been in uniform then. Which was about the only thing we had in common. Which was partly why I was off the force and he was a big-deal homicide lieutenant, pushing forty and working hard to keep his weight down—weights, handball, punching bag. From what I'd heard he mainly wanted to stay in shape because he hadn't lost his fondness for beating the hell out of suspects. Aside from that, his only character flaw was he hated my guts.

"Well if it ain't Lomax, ace private eye." He squinched his eyes nearly closed and gave me what passed for a grin. "I was wondering when I'd get the chance to bust your ass. Is this man under arrest, officer?"

"No, sir. He phoned it in."

"Too bad. Wait here." He went into Fontaine's office.

The tall cop and I stood in the hallway and waited for Dalrymple to tell us what to do.

A while later a guy with a camera showed up and went in the office and began clicking away. Then the coroner arrived and declared Lloyd Fontaine officially dead. The man with the camera left and was replaced by a couple of police technicians. They went to work with tweezers and vacuum cleaners and put their tiny treasures in plastic bags. One of them began dusting everything in sight with fine black powder.

Dalrymple came out to the hallway.

"You know him?"

"His name is Lloyd Fontaine," I said. "He's a private detective."

"He looks like one. Pal of yours?"

"Not exactly."

"Any idea who shot him?"

"Not really."

"What the fuck does that mean?"

"I don't know who shot him."

"What were you doing here?"

I told Dalrymple about Fontaine's visit last night. Most of it, anyway. If it were anyone else but Dalrymple, I would have told him everything. I'm sure that's why I held some of it back. Pretty sure.

"He was on a case and he wanted me to follow some people," I said.

"Follow who?"

"One guy was an ex-con named Charles Soames."

"And the others?"

"I don't know."

"Why did Fontaine want you to follow these people?"

"He thought they might dig up some buried treasure."

"Some what? Are you trying to be funny, Lomax?"

"Not to my knowledge."

The police technicians came out of the office. "We're through here, Lieutenant," one of them said, a skinny dude with rimless glasses.

Dalrymple nodded at them and they left.

"Whoever iced your pal in there," he said, "what do you suppose he was after?"

"How should I know?"

"From the looks of things, your buddy was reluctant to tell the guy where it is, or was, whatever it is. One thing, though, the guy wasn't just after petty cash—there's still twelve bucks in your pal's wallet, which, come to think of it, is kind of a lot of money for a PI to be carrying around."

"Are we through here?"

I wasn't in the mood now for Dalrymple's jokes, not that I ever was. But especially not with a dead man in the next room, a man who had come to me for help. The double shot I'd had an hour ago had turned sour and I could feel sweat on my upper lip. Dalrymple didn't budge. His eyes moved around my face, like a pair of wasps searching for a way in.

"Did Fontaine have any enemies you know of?" he asked. "I mean, besides the public at large, which knows each and every. one of you private eyes is a horse's ass."

"I hardly knew the man. Before last night, I hadn't seen him in years."

"Really," Dalrymple said. "And here I thought all you play-cops hung out together and swapped dirty pictures you took of cheating wives."

"Does she want copies?"

Dalrymple blinked once, then shoved his big jaw close to my face. I smelled Aqua Velva.

"Get smart with me, Lomax, and I'll haul your ass in right now on suspicion."

"Then do it," I said, louder than I meant to—the short cop turned to look at me from Fontaine's doorway. "Otherwise, I'm out of here."

I took a step and Dalrymple put his hand on my shoulder. I shrugged it off.

"What's the rush, Lomax?"

"I don't like hanging around dead people."

"Is that why you drank your breakfast?" he asked. "You know, you're beginning to *smell* like a private eye."

I said nothing.

"I may want to talk to you again," he said.

"I'll rush right home and sit by the phone."

Before I left, the body people arrived—a man-and-wife team. They were independents, contracted by the city, a special form of waste removal. The husband unrolled a rubber sheet the color of old blood, then he and the little woman laid Fontaine on it, wrapped him up, and hauled him onto their collapsible gurney. I followed them outside. They dumped the bag of trash that used to be Lloyd Fontaine into the rear of their station wagon and took off for the morgue. A cop car trailed behind.

I climbed in the Olds and drove to my office, Fontaine's manila envelope on the seat beside me.

3

I tried to shake the feeling that I was responsible for Lloyd Fontaine's death. I couldn't. Guilt, with fur sleek and claws sharp and appetite whetted, had pounced squarely on my back, making me hunch my shoulders and scrunch my neck. I couldn't escape it now any more than I could when I'd been a child.

"You *should* feel guilty, Jacob," my Catholic mother, God rest her soul, used to say. "You do wrong and God gives you guilt to remind you about it. If He didn't, everyone would be stepping on everyone's toes and no one would be saying they were sorry. We'd all have to wear combat boots. Guilt keeps us in soft shoes."

Soft shoes or not, Fontaine had asked for my help last night and I'd turned him down for no reason other than that he was a burned-out lush who irritated the hell out of me. If I'd gone along, I probably could have saved him. Of course, I might have found myself tied up in his other chair.

I parked in the street and went upstairs to my office.

I'm on the second floor of a two-story building on Broadway. Street level is storefronts—liquor store; pawnshop; café; and the Zodiac Bookstore, which caters to literati fond of interstellar philosophies and satanic trivia. Upstairs with me was a dentist, who I wouldn't let clean my socket wrenches, let alone my teeth; a vacancy; and Acme, Inc. I didn't know what kind of business Acme was. I'd never seen the guy who ran it, but I'd often heard him—he was always on the phone. He was on it now as I walked past his door.

". . . are the goddamn handles, Murray? You ship me twelve thousand and not one with a handle. What do you think, my customers have suction cups for fingers? You have killed me with this shipment, Murray, killed. I am dead. At least my casket will have goddamn handles. . . ."

Fontaine's stale cigarette smoke still permeated my office. His story had sounded unbelievable when he'd sat in here telling it to me. But his death made it more convincing.

I opened a window, then dumped the contents of his envelope on my desk: clippings, photographs, notebook. I'd glanced through this stuff before. It didn't look like much to die for. Apparently, though, it was enough for someone to kill for.

I thumbed through the spiral notebook. It was filled with pencil scribbles in an indecipherable hand, possibly in code. I could make nothing out of it.

There were five photographs. Four of them were eight-by-ten black-and-whites that showed two men arguing by an old car. I could see now that one was a civilian and one was a cop. There was a passenger in the car, mostly hidden by the doorpost. I couldn't tell if it was a man or a woman. The fifth photo was actually thirty-six separate pictures—a contact sheet of thirty-five-millimeter prints. But it was so overexposed that the individual prints were difficult to make out. Most of them appeared to show a two-story house in increasing stages of consumption by fire. The cop and the angry guy and the passenger in the car were featured in the last six shots on the contact sheet, four of which I had as blowups. My guess was the blowups of the other two frames had been in Fontaine's jacket when he'd left my office yesterday. I wondered if he'd also had the negatives.

I flipped over the photographs. On the back of each there was a faded red stamp:

The GAZETTE
—
H. R. Witherspoon

The newspaper clippings, most of which were from the *Rocky Mountain News* and the *Denver Post*, dealt with the robbery twenty years ago of Lochemont Jewelers.

On that fine spring morning four men—Ed Teague, Rueben Archuleta, Robert Knox, and Buddy Meacham—entered the store before business hours. Charles Soames, the store manager, had shut off the alarm and unlocked the door. The robbers were armed with pistols and shotguns and had little trouble convincing everyone present to do exactly what they asked. Everyone, that is, except a store guard, who drew his gun and was immediately, though not fatally, gunned down. Little eight-year-old Emily Sue Ott was not so fortunate, being hit with a stray bullet and killed instantly. The others present in the store—Emily Sue's grandmother, who represented the Colorado State Historical Society and who had intended to give Emily Sue a "privileged look" at a piece of history; Trenton Lochemont, Sr., owner of the store; his son, Trenton, Jr.; and five store employees—were bound and gagged.

The men got away with a satchelful of gems and a museum-piece necklace rumored to have belonged once to Baby Doe Tabor, second wife of legendary silver king Horace Tabor. The choker consisted of ninety-eight half-carat diamonds supporting a central stone—a forty-six-carat ruby whose color, one reporter wrote, resembled freshly spilled blood.

After the robbery the gang left the city and drove to a shack in the mountains near Idaho Springs, where apparently they planned to divvy up the jewels. But Ed Teague decided to turn his shotgun on Robert Knox and Buddy Meacham, slaughtering them both. He tried for Soames, too, but the store manager got away and ran into the hills.

The next day the police found the bodies of Knox and Meacham—and, in a motel room in Idaho Springs, the body of Ed Teague, shot twice through the head with a small-caliber weapon. In the room with Teague was a twelve-gauge shotgun covered with his prints.

Rueben Archuleta and the satchel of jewels were never seen again.

Four days after the robbery, Charles Soames staggered out of the trees onto the highway about eight miles from Idaho Springs and the murder shack. He was in shock and suffering from exposure and partial amnesia. As he gradually regained his senses, he claimed innocence. He said Teague had forced him to cooperate in the robbery by threatening to kill him and every living member of his family: daughter, granddaughter, and son-in-law.

No one believed him. Because of his participation in the robbery, Soames stood trial for the felony murder of Emily Sue Ott. A jury found him guilty, and Soames got life.

I went through the clippings again and examined the grainy news photos—pictures of Teague and Meacham and Knox in life and in death, police mug shots of Rueben Archuleta, photos of Soames and the jewelry store and the murder shack, and a photo of the Baby Doe necklace behind the heavy glass of a museum display case.

I stuffed it all into Fontaine's manila envelope.

Everyone believed that Rueben Archuleta had gotten away with the jewels. Everyone but Lloyd Fontaine and whoever had shot him twice in the head with a small-caliber weapon—the same method used on Ed Teague. I wondered if that was more than a coincidence. The only person I knew to ask was Charles Soames.

I looked him up in the phone book. No Soames. Well shit, no one said it would be easy.

Then I called the National Insurance Company, Fontaine's

old employer, and asked to speak to whoever was in charge of paying reward money for the return of stolen property. It was possible they'd kept tabs on Soames. The receptionist said the person I wanted was Mr. Carr, but he was in a meeting. She took my name and number, and I took Fontaine's packet home.

Vaz and his wife, Sophia, had the apartment below mine. They'd had it for over twenty years, ever since they'd fled the Soviet Union via Greenland, where Vaz had been playing in an international chess tournament. He'd been in a tough match against another Russian grand master and the game had been adjourned until the following day. While the other Russian and his seconds were hunched over an analysis board seeking a possible checkmate, Vaz and his mate checked into the American embassy, seeking asylum.

I knocked and Vaz answered.

"Jacob, come in, come in."

He was a barrel-chested, heavy-shouldered, large-headed man with legs spindly enough for an end table. He waved me inside. I squeezed into the apartment and stood at the very edge of Sophia's collection. That woman liked furniture.

"I am making coffee," Vaz said. "You want?"

"Sure."

He led me through the maze of bureaus and buffets, chairs and credenzas, davenports and dinettes, and into the kitchen. There was slightly more room to breathe in here, but when Vaz opened the cupboard, I feared an avalanche of saucers and cups, platters and plates. Vaz poured coffee from a heavy silver pot, and I placed the manila envelope on the table between us.

"The man who gave me this was murdered last night," I said, watching Vaz's eyes widen under furry brows. "The killer's identity could be in here."

"Shouldn't you give this to the police?"

"Probably," I said.

Vaz scowled at me.

"The police are conducting their investigation," I said, "and I'm conducting mine. They've got their resources, and I've got that envelope."

"I see. I think. The man who was murdered, then, he was a good friend of yours?"

"No."

Vaz looked at me sideways, then shook his head and dumped out the contents of the envelope. While he pawed through them, I told him all I knew about Lloyd Fontaine, which wasn't much. His eyebrows rose up like startled gerbils when I got to the part about the Lochemont jewels.

"Five million, you say?"

"Give or take a diamond ring."

"Then you are looking for more than a murderer."

Who, me? Why would I look for a fortune in jewels when all it could bring was a life of ease and good times? Who in his right mind would want that?

"Mainly a murderer," I said.

"I see, mainly." He paged through Fontaine's spiral notebook. "A journal of some kind," he said to himself. "These numbers at the tops of the pages appear to be dates. The last one here, nine-fifteen, would be yesterday, September fifteenth." He pushed the notebook aside. "There may be answers in here, Jacob, if anyone could read them."

"So it is a code?"

Vaz nodded. "You can see that each 'word' has five letters, some perhaps four—his scribbling makes it difficult to be certain. This sort of letter grouping is one method used to make code-breaking more difficult. But who can read this—this mess that passes for a man's handwriting?"

"I was hoping you'd give it a shot."

"Bah." He pushed the journal farther away from him, as if it might contain something contagious. "I am not a cryptographer."

"But it's like a puzzle, right? I mean, you're good at chess, so I thought—"

"Chess is not a puzzle, Jacob," he said, offended. "It is an art, a science."

"Sorry. But the mental challenge of—"

"It could take weeks, even months to figure out."

"Even so—"

"And if he used a code wheel or some other device, it could take years, if I could do it at all."

I nodded. Vaz eyed the journal.

"You're probably right," I said with a mock sigh of resignation and began shoving the photos and news clippings back in the envelope. "I was expecting the impossible." Sigh.

"Who said impossible?" He pulled the journal toward him, then scowled at me. He had the eyebrows for it. "You knew I wouldn't be able to resist this."

"I didn't, honest."

"Bah."

"Okay, I hoped."

Later, when I tried again to reach Mr. Carr at National Insurance, he was still in a meeting, so I took the only remaining course of action, namely, spending the afternoon and most of the evening in a sports bar in the shadow of the Colfax viaduct, tossing back draws and watching the Mets take a doubleheader from the Expos.

On the way home, I swung by the office to see if Mr. Carr had left a message on my machine. When I walked past Acme, Inc., I could hear my neighbor still chewing out Murray's ass on the phone.

The moment I unlocked my door, I knew something was wrong.

It might have been an odor or a pressure on my eardrums or a sixth sense; whatever, I could tell someone was in my office. Not that knowing about it did me much good. Before I could react, I got smacked in the head.

I staggered around and swung at shadows and got hit again and managed to fall into the guy and hang on for all I was worth, which at the moment wasn't much. If I'd been spending more of my time in running shoes instead of on barstools, I might have been equal to this guy. As it was, we waltzed around the room with me draped on him like a drunken dance partner. It was too dark to see his face clearly, but I could tell that he was wearing a leather jacket, soft and new-smelling, and that he was a bit smaller than me, but wiry and quick, and that he was trying like hell to hit me with something steel-hard. I took a few blows on the shoulder and tried to run him into the wall, but he twisted out of my grasp and smacked me a good one over the ear, ending the dance and sitting me down on the floor. When he stepped back, pale light from the street fell across his arm and his weapon—a Beretta, probably a nine-millimeter. I wasn't sure whether to beg him not to shoot or just to start praying to my guardian angel. My angel spoke up first.

"Goddammit, Murray!" he shouted. "Don't tell me that!"

The guy looked over his shoulder at the open doorway and showed me his silhouette. Nice features, but troubled. He was thinking that if he shot me, he might also have to shoot Mr. Acme and whoever else might be in there with him. That was too much shooting, so he just reached down and smacked me good-bye with the barrel of his gun. Then he ran out the door. And not a moment too soon for his sake, because I was starting to get pissed off.

4

When I could finally stagger to my feet, I closed the door and locked it. Thank you, Mr. Acme.

I switched on the lights and saw that the office had been rearranged to look like Lloyd Fontaine's. Desk drawers had been yanked out, the fake-leather couch slashed open, and my file cabinets jimmied and their contents dumped on the floor. My only consolation was that the guy in the leather jacket hadn't found what he was looking for. Which meant I might see him again. At least I hoped so, the son of a bitch.

I went home and drank whiskey to soothe my aching skull.

Wednesday morning my head felt like a basketball retired from a slam-dunk contest. I resisted the urge to take more distilled medicine and managed to arrange a meeting with Mr. Carr at National Insurance. Before I left the apartment, though, I put on a gun.

The insurance office was on the ninth floor of the Republic Plaza and offered a tremendous view of the dirty windows of the building across the street.

Mr. Carr was a fifty-five-year-old bachelor struggling to maintain his singles-bar look. It was an uphill battle. However, his haircut nearly managed to hide his bald spot. He had a practiced smile, a fashionable tie, and a few long whiskers on his neck his razor had missed the past few days. There were some plaques on the wall behind him and a small trophy on his desk topped by a striding bronze man with a hat and a briefcase, probably chasing after a hot prospect.

Carr looked me up and down and tried to figure out how much I cleared last year.

"What exactly was stolen, Mr. Lomax?" he asked.

"Several million dollars in gems. Plus a necklace on loan from the state historical museum. All taken from Lochemont Jewelers twenty years ago."

His eyebrows pushed up, wrinkling his brow. "Lochemont Jewelers?"

"Right. I'd like to confirm what reward, if any, is being offered for the return of the jewels." As if I gave a damn about the reward.

"I'll get the file," he said without hesitation. Now that I was talking about money, we could get down to business. He stood, then remembered to suck in his gut. After searching several drawers in his cabinets, he pulled a folder and brought it back to his desk. He sighed when he sat down, glad to relax those tummy muscles.

"I worked on this account," he said, leafing through copies of forms and reports. "I was a sales rep back then, a pretty darn good one, too, and . . ." He stopped and read for a moment. "Yes, I remember now. Just before the robbery Lochemont Jewelers had purchased a special policy to cover the necklace you mentioned. It was all a bit unusual." He flipped the page. "The necklace had once belonged to the Tabors, which, of course, had something to do with it. God, can you imagine the good times *they* must have had? Of course, with all those gold mines, who wouldn't?"

"Silver mines," I said.

"What?"

"Mr. Carr, I understand Lloyd Fontaine was involved in the investigation."

Carr made a face as if he'd just bitten down on a piece of tinfoil.

"Yes, Mr. Fontaine conducted the investigation. With dismal results, I might add."

"You say that as if it were his fault."

"Well, the jewels *were* never recovered," he said.

"Yes, but surely you can't blame Fontaine for—"

"*I* didn't blame him, Mr. Lomax," he said. "Our corporate office in New York held him responsible. They brought pressure to bear upon him and forced him into early retirement."

"I see." And I did. Fontaine had gotten caught in the middle. No wonder he'd felt bitter toward National.

"Mr. Carr, you said the policy on this necklace was unusual. How so?"

"Oh, well, you see the piece was already insured for three hundred thousand, the policy being in effect only while the necklace remained in the museum. Lochemont Jewelers was given the option of paying for a special rider to the museum's policy or of taking out a new policy. Mr. Lochemont chose the latter, a short-term policy to cover the necklace while it remained in his store."

"What's unusual about that?"

"Nothing. But what *was* odd, and what after the robbery became a point of concern for all involved, was that Lochemont reappraised the Baby Doe Tabor necklace for *six* hundred thousand."

"National Insurance went along with this?"

"Of course. It was all quite legal and aboveboard. The controversy began after the robbery. National paid Lochemont six hundred thousand, and Lochemont paid the museum three hundred thousand, claiming that was the value the museum had placed on the piece."

"And Lochemont pocketed the difference?"

Carr nodded, then shook his head. "There was a lot of hollering, I can tell you, but that's the way it ended up. And really it was a small matter compared with the entire settlement—

two million, seven hundred thousand. Of course, the reward for any items returned would be based on today's market, which—"

"Whose idea was it to put the necklace on display at Lochemont Jewelers?"

"Trenton Lochemont, Sr.," he said. "He thought it would be a good way to bring in business. As large as it was, the store was struggling, along with a lot of other downtown interests. Suburban malls and so forth. It took a bit of wrangling with the people at the museum, but Lochemont finally convinced them it would be beneficial for everyone involved."

"Particularly for Lochemont Jewelers, as it turned out."

Carr frowned. "Indeed. Before they paid the claim National investigated all this quite thoroughly and found nothing amiss. But getting back to the reward—"

"First, tell me: Did you work with Fontaine when he was here?"

Carr gave me a brief frown before he answered.

"Not really, no."

"Were you friends?"

"Hardly. In fact, I don't think he had many friends." Carr smirked. "He probably still doesn't."

"You're right about that. He's dead. He was murdered Monday night or—"

"Jesus God." Carr sat back and looked at me as if I were the killer.

"—or early Tuesday morning."

"Murdered . . . why?" Carr's eyes were bouncing back and forth between me and the phone.

"The police are investigating," I said, before he could call in the SWAT team. "Mr. Carr, did Fontaine ever use a code in his work here?"

"What?" Carr was still trying to decide if it was safe to be in the same room with me.

"A code," I said. "Perhaps for security reasons."

"Code? I . . . I'm sure I wouldn't know."

"Is there anyone here who might know?"

He frowned and shook his head slowly. "No, I'm about the only one left from those days. Does this have anything to do with the return of the jewels?"

"It might," I said.

Carr nodded, back in business. "Speaking of which," he said, "National will pay as reward, with no questions asked, ten percent of the appraised value of any and all pieces returned. Employees of the company or Lochemont Jewelers or their relatives are not eligible. You're not a relative, are you?"

"No."

"Good. Then there should be no problem with the reward."

"I'll keep that in mind," I said, "if I stumble over any of the gems."

"If? But I thought—"

"I haven't uncovered the gems yet, but I'm working on it."

Carr's eyes narrowed and his chest swelled. By God, this was his office and he was in charge.

"If you have any information concerning the Lochemont robbery, you'd better tell me now," he demanded in his sternest middle-management voice.

"When I learn anything," I said, trying not to tremble, "I'll be sure to tell you."

He gave me an approving nod. Whew.

"In return," I said, "I wonder if you'd check your file there for any information on Charles Soames?"

"Such as?"

"Where I might find him. I understand he was recently released from prison."

"You don't say?" Carr's interest was definitely piqued. "Then I'd ask Trenton Lochemont, Jr.," he said.

"Junior?"

"Yes, he's been running Lochemont Jewelers for several years, ever since his father passed away."

"And you think he'd know about Soames?"

"He should. He's married to Soames's daughter."

A few years ago Lochemont Jewelers had moved in with the shops at the Tabor Center, a several-block-long, multilevel, steel-and-glass structure laid out along the Sixteenth Street Mall and housing dozens of places for the chic and pseudochic to spend their bucks. Horace Tabor would have been proud. The jewelry store stood between Brooks Brothers and Pappagallo and featured a sparkling fortune under glass. Customers and sales reps spoke in hushed, reverent tones, as if they were in church, which in a way they were. I asked for Trenton Lochemont, Jr., and soon was approached by a tall, skinny character with the clothes of a mortician and the pallor of a corpse. His nose was so long you could hang your hat on it. I introduced myself and asked if we could talk in private.

"Concerning what?" Lochemont looked at me over his beak, like a squid.

"Concerning your father-in-law, Charles Soames."

He breathed in so hard that I hoped my collar buttons weren't loose, lest they get sucked away.

"I have nothing whatever to do with that man," Lochemont said. "And I will ask you to kindly leave the premises."

"This may also concern your father."

"My father is dead."

"But his reputation lives."

"What are you saying?"

"Don't you think we should get off the floor? The customers are being distracted."

Without a word Lochemont turned his back and walked through the store. I followed in his cold wake. He used a key to get behind the counter, then another key to get through a door to the back, and still another to open his office. He sat behind his desk, elbows spread, fingers peaked, nose erect.

"What is this about my father's reputation?"

"I'm conducting an independent investigation for National Insurance," I said, bending the truth until the paint cracked. "We've reopened the case of the Lochemont robbery."

"The robbery? After all these years?"

"Time means little to us at National," I said. "Where can I find Charles Soames?"

"In Canon City, where he belongs."

"I heard he was released weeks ago."

"I wouldn't know." Lochemont's voice was as cold as a diamond.

"He is your father-in-law, isn't he?"

"More's the pity," Lochemont said. "He committed a despicable act for which he is paying heavily and for which Janet and I will never forgive him."

"Janet being his loving daughter?"

Lochemont twitched his beak at me. "What exactly has this to do with *my* father?"

"He worked pretty hard to get Baby Doe Tabor's necklace on display in your old store, didn't he?"

"I suppose he did."

"And the same day it was brought there, the store was robbed."

Lochemont stared icicles at me.

"What are you getting at?" he demanded.

"The fortunate timing. I understand Lochemont Jewelers was struggling before the robbery, but with the help of the insurance settlement, your father was able to—"

"Are you implying that my father was party to the *robbery*?"

"I'm simply speculating."

"You may leave now," he said, but I wasn't ready. My head

was still throbbing from last night's beating and booze, and I wanted to share it with someone.

"Was your father pals with the insurance investigator, Lloyd Fontaine? Or, for that matter, were you?"

"Get out."

"You probably already know this, but Fontaine's been murdered. I think it had something to do with the stolen jewels, which means it probably had something to do with your father *and* your father-in-law, and, therefore, with you."

"Get out!"

I stood. "When I see Soames, I'll tell him you said 'hi.' "

"Out!" he yelled, rustling his nasal hairs.

Out front, the stone-worshipers haggled in whispers.

5

I called the state penitentiary in Canon City, but all they'd tell me over the phone was that Charles Soames had been released six weeks ago.

Which meant if I wanted more, I'd have to drive down there. A minor expense, but still an expense, with more to come and no client to pay the bills. And even if I managed to find Fontaine's killer, I wouldn't earn a dime. Of course, if I found the jewels . . .

Canon City is a quiet, pretty little town about two hours south of Denver. I drove past its frame houses and trimmed lawns and around a gently curving asphalt road, then parked near a fence topped with coils of razor-sharp wire. Beyond the fence were more fences, plus guard towers and a complex of buildings. And hundreds of sociopaths. Watching over it all was Albert Worthy, a beefy, red-faced, middle-aged man with piercing blue eyes and a no-nonsense attitude. He'd been the warden for twelve years.

"Sure, I remember Charles Soames," he said. "A real nice guy."

"Did he get many visitors?"

"Just one," Worthy said. "His granddaughter, Caroline Lochemont. She came here every Sunday for the last two years of his term. Less often before then."

"Was he ever visited by his daughter or her husband?"

"Not since I've been here."

"Do you know where Soames is living now?"

"With his granddaughter, I believe." Worthy checked his file and gave me an address in Lakewood.

"Was Soames violent when he was here?" I asked.

"Not at all," Worthy said.

"Did he ever swear vengeance on anyone responsible for putting him away?" I was thinking about Lloyd Fontaine.

"No, he was a quiet man. Besides, he always claimed he was an innocent victim, not a criminal."

"That's what they all say, right?"

"Most do," Worthy said. "But Soames I believed."

It was late afternoon by the time I got back to Denver. That is, close to Denver. Eight miles south of the city the office parks of Inverness and the Tech Center and Greenwood Village were releasing thousand of cars onto I-25 for the mad rush home. I crawled north with the white-collar work force toward the city suburbs and tightly clustered spires of downtown Denver, small and hazy in the distance, while the September sun baked my brains and cooked exhaust fumes into a more lethal concoction.

Twenty years ago this area had been scrubby, flat land fronting the mountains under clear air and populated only by hawks, jackrabbits, and prairie dogs. Then came high tech and high oil prices—lots of people with lots of money to spend. They covered the perfect, useless, wonderful wilderness with sprawling, ultramodern steel-stone-and-glass structures, chemically treated grass, and absolutely flat black asphalt. So much for wilderness. Although occasionally you can still see a prairie dog—usually in a parking lot and generally with a confused look on his face.

I got off the freeway near the heart of the metro area and took Sixth Avenue toward the mountains, then turned south on Wadsworth Boulevard into the heart of Lakewood, a rambling suburb hugging Denver to the west and featuring a mixture of houses, apartments, shopping centers, and pastures with grazing horses.

Caroline Lochemont's house was a yellow frame trimmed in white. It stood in a row of a dozen others just like it across the street from a small park.

I stopped at the end of the block and watched a brown-skinned, seedy-looking character with dark glasses and a scraggly goatee come out of the Lochemont house and climb into a beat-up green Chevy. He rattled away in a blue-black cloud of smoke. I sat in the Olds with the motor idling and wondered which course of action to take with Soames—tail or talk. Lloyd Fontaine had hung back and shadowed the ex-con and look what it got him.

I went up the walk and rang the bell.

The woman who answered was in her early twenties and could have starred in breakfast commercials. She was five and a half feet tall with an even tan, sparkling blue eyes, and semishort dark blond hair brushed back over her ears. Her jeans were faded and her yellow T-shirt sported a stylized bicycle racer stuck in the valley between her small, firm breasts. Her mother must be pretty, because she sure as hell didn't resemble her father, Trenton, Jr.

"Are you Caroline Lochemont?"

"Who wants to know?" There was tough tomboy in her voice.

"Jacob Lomax." I held out a card and she looked at it through the screen door. "If your grandfather is here, I'd like to talk to him."

"What about?"

"The death of Lloyd Fontaine."

She cocked her head and put her fist on one round, solid hip.

"The police have already been here asking him about that. My grandfather told them he'd never heard of that man."

"That's not what Fontaine told me."

Her eyes narrowed, and she said, "Just a minute," and shut the door in my face.

I stood in the dying sunlight on the tiny, tidy front porch and shuffled my feet like a dumb gumshoe and marveled at how quickly Lieutenant Dalrymple had found Soames. Maybe he was smarter than I was. Or maybe he just had more resources. Yeah, that must be it.

Caroline opened the door and told me to come in.

"It's his idea, not mine," she said.

I followed her through the living room. The furniture was secondhand and the carpet was a bargain-basement shag, but everything was dusted and swept and there were enough plants to give the place life. A faint scent trailed behind Caroline—difficult to identify, but it reminded me of long walks through aspen and pine.

"Here he is, Grandpa."

Charles Soames turned off the black-and-white TV on the kitchen table and looked up at me as if I were another boring rerun. His face was pale and framed with iron-gray hair cropped close at the sides. He wore a blue denim shirt, gray cotton pants, a black belt, white socks, and thick-soled black shoes—prison clothes. Fashion habits are hard to break.

"My name is—"

"She already told me your name," he said. His voice was as low and hard as the floor of a cell. "Just what the hell do you want here?"

"I want to know about you and Lloyd Fontaine."

"There's nothing to know."

"Not according to Fontaine."

"Let me tell you something, Lomax. Before today I never heard of Lloyd Fontaine, and I don't give a damn what you or the cops say."

"He worked for National Insurance, the company that—"

"I know who they are," he said, looking up at me but managing somehow to look down at me.

"Do you mind if I sit?" I asked.

"You won't be staying that long."

I pulled out a chair from the table and sat.

"He don't listen so good," he said to Caroline.

"Fontaine told me he interviewed you after your trial."

"A lot of people interviewed me. Doesn't mean I know them."

"He asked you about the Lochemont jewels."

"*Everybody* asked me about that."

"He also told me he'd been following you since the day you got out of the joint."

" 'The joint,' he says, as if he knows what the fuck he's talking about," Soames said to Caroline.

"Okay, Soames, you've convinced me—you're a hard-ass. And pretty soon you'll be right back with the other hard-asses in Canon City."

"What the hell's that supposed to mean?"

"Look, right now the cops know that Fontaine was tailing you, but they don't know why. I do. The Lochemont jewels."

Soames smiled and shook his head and said, "Shit. There ain't any Lochemont jewels, not like you mean, not anymore."

"That's not what Fontaine thought."

Soames said nothing.

"I have a hunch Fontaine got in your way before you could retrieve those jewels."

"For chrissake, there's nothing to retrieve. Rueben Archuleta got away with them. Everybody knows that."

"Fontaine thought otherwise," I said, watching Soames carefully, "and I figure you got rid of him with the help of your good-looking pal in the leather jacket."

"You're crazy," he said, but there was a tic under his eye.

"Grandpa, maybe that was the man who—" Caroline started to say, but Soames gave her a look and she shut up.

"Who what?" I asked her.

"Nothing," Soames said. "And I've answered enough questions."

The front doorbell rang and Caroline went to see who it was.

"Tell me, Soames, did old man Lochemont put you up to the robbery?"

"What?"

"His profit on that heist was three hundred grand. I've been thinking maybe he arranged it."

Soames laughed. "You *are* crazy."

Caroline came into the kitchen and said, "It's her again," as if she were talking about the plague.

Soames smiled at her, then frowned at me. "Time for you to leave, and I mean *now*."

I stood and said, "I just want you to know that I'm taking up where Fontaine left off."

Soames snorted and got up, and I followed him into the front room. The woman waiting there for Soames was of average height, with auburn hair and hazel eyes. She wore casual clothes, and her looks were somewhere between plain and attractive. I put her age a few years above mine.

"Helen Ester," Soames said, "this is Jacob Lomax. He's a private eye. He was just leaving."

She looked mildy shocked. But I couldn't tell whether it was because of my name, or my profession, or the fact that I was just leaving.

When I got home, I stopped downstairs to see how Vaz was coming with Fontaine's journal. Sophia let me in and gave me an uncharacteristic hard look.

"See what you've started," she said, leading me to her husband, who was seated at the dining room table. It was covered with Fontaine's clippings, photos, and the pages of his journal. "He sits there for hours, mumbling to himself. Last night he was up till midnight."

"Sorry, Sophia," I said.

"*You're* sorry." She walked away in a huff.

"Do not mind her," Vaz said, and made a note on a ruled yellow pad.

"If this is going to cause a problem—"

"It's no problem. Sit down, sit down. What happened to you?" He was looking at the lump bulging out of my hairline.

"I surprised a burglar at my office last night. He was probably after all this."

Vaz's chin dropped a few millimeters.

"Don't worry," I said. "Nobody knows you have this, and we'll keep it that way."

"I would appreciate it."

"Have you learned anything?" I asked him.

"Not much, I'm afraid. Fontaine's handwriting is so bad that I can make out only about half the words, which, of course, aren't words at all, just groups of letters."

"How long before you can break his code?"

Vaz gave me a pained look.

"Sorry," I said.

"Jacob, we must hope that Fontaine used a simple cipher, one that would be quick and easy for him to employ. But easy for him does not mean easy for me, and it would be difficult enough even if I could *read* the infernal thing, but without identifying all the words and letters . . ."

He let it hang to show me the hopelessness of it.

"Well, at least you gave it a shot."

"Did I say I'd given up?"

"No, but—"

"I am going to transcribe Fontaine's notes letter by letter— what I can discern, that is—to give me something more concrete to work with. And why, I wonder, did he use a code at all?"

"Who knows? Paranoia? The man was obsessed."

"That aside for a moment, I did find something."

He pushed the four eight-by-ten photos from Fontaine's envelope in front of me and tapped a blunt finger on the man arguing with the cop.

"That is Ed Teague."

"Are you certain?"

"Look for yourself." Vaz placed a clipping with a news photo beside the big photographs. The news photo featured a man's full face and profile, with the caption "Edward Teague, who was slain shortly after the Lochemont robbery, presumably by another gang member." The mug shot matched the angry man in the four glossy photos.

I flipped over one of the photos.

> The GAZETTE
> —
> H. R. Witherspoon

"We need to locate this guy Witherspoon."

"The photographer, no doubt," Vaz said.

"Probably. The big question is did Fontaine obtain these photos before the robbery? By the looks of that old car they could easily be twenty years old. And if Fontaine knew Ed Teague *before* the robbery—"

"Then he may have been involved more deeply than we thought."

"Could be," I said.

"So we must go to the *Gazette* and ask Mr. Witherspoon."

"Sure, if he's still alive," I said. "And if he still works for whichever of the twenty or so small-town newspapers in this state called the *Gazette*. Assuming it's even in this state."

"I could make some calls," Vaz said. He raised his hand to stop me from protesting. "Please. I want to."

"Well, okay. As long as it doesn't upset Sophia."

"No problem. Sophia likes to kid." But he cast a nervous glance over his shoulder.

6

Thursday morning I found my office just as I'd left it Tuesday night—files dumped on the floor and furniture overturned. I tipped the cabinets back up against the wall, and I was scooping handfuls of papers off the floor and dumping them in drawers when someone knocked. I guess my nerves were still on edge from Tuesday, because I unholstered the Smith & Wesson Chief's Special and held it down at my side before I opened the door.

It was Helen Ester.

"Hello, Mr. Lomax," she said. "Perhaps I should have phoned before coming here."

"Not at all. Please come in."

She wore a high-collared navy blue dress with white accessories. Her reddish-brown hair, loose yesterday, was pulled back in a bun, giving her a business air. She also wore more makeup today. At least I think she did—she'd dropped a few years since I'd seen her in Caroline Lochemont's living room.

She took a step in, then stopped.

"My God."

"Sorry about the mess. I had a burglar."

I put away the gun, then shoved some papers out of the way and set the visitor's chair back on its legs. She looked at it warily. I brushed the seat off with my handkerchief.

"Thank you." She sat with her back straight, knees together, and purse held squarely in the middle of her lap. She wasn't exactly tense, but she was close. "I hope nothing valuable was stolen," she said with polite concern.

"The guy missed what he was after." I sat behind my desk. "What can I do for you?"

She fidgeted with her purse. "This is awkward for me. I, um, I came here for two reasons. . . ." Her voice trailed off.

"Let me guess: Charles Soames and Lloyd Fontaine."

"That's one reason, yes," she said firmly. "Charles is quite upset about you telling the police there's a connection between him and Mr. Fontaine."

"He should be upset."

"Are you planning to harass him further?"

"Look, Miss Ester, if you came here to tell me to lay off, forget it. I think Lloyd Fontaine's death has something to do with the Lochemont jewels, and by association with Charles Soames."

"You have no right to say that."

"Okay, I'll put it this way: Fontaine died while he was following Soames. I intend to find out if that's *why* he died."

"I see," she said.

"Good."

"For what it's worth, I can tell you categorically that Charles is innocent of any crime."

"Including armed robbery and felony murder?"

"Especially that," she said angrily, then looked away, making me feel a bit guilty. Why the hell was I picking on her? Give her a break, for chrissake.

"You said you came here for two reasons," I said, shifting my voice into neutral.

"Yes."

I waited.

"I may know who actually murdered Lloyd Fontaine," she said.

"You *may* know?"

"I have no real proof, but his name is Zack Meacham."

The name sounded familiar. "Have you been to the police?"

"No. As I said, I have no proof."

"Then why do you think he killed Fontaine?"

"Because he is now threatening to kill Charles."

"Then you should definitely go to the cops."

"I would," she said, "but Charles will have nothing whatever to do with the police, regardless of Meacham's threats. In fact, Charles refuses even to take his threats seriously."

I wondered if this little story was intended to draw me away from Charles Soames.

"Why is Zack Meacham threatening Soames?" I asked.

"Zack is the brother of Buddy Meacham, one of the gang that robbed Lochemont Jewelers. After the robbery Buddy was gunned down by another gang member, Ed Teague. But Zack blames Charles, probably because Charles was the only one arrested after the robbery. In fact, at the trial Zack Meacham swore he'd get revenge, he yelled it right out in the courtroom. And now, twenty years later . . ."

Some of this I'd read in Fontaine's clippings.

"What is the nature of his threats, Miss Ester? It is 'Miss,' isn't it?"

She nodded yes. "But please call me Helen," she said. "Thus far, Meacham has confronted Charles only on the telephone. I listened in once on the extension and heard him call Charles one vile name after another. He promised he would shoot Charles to get even for his brother's death. Charles just told him to . . . to buzz off, except he didn't say 'buzz,' and then he hung up."

"So Soames isn't too worried."

"No, unfortunately, or maybe he would go to the police."

"But you are. Worried, I mean."

"Yes I am, and I need your help."

"Miss Es——, I mean Helen, I'm a bit confused about why you'd come to *me*, considering my, uh, harassment of Soames."

She opened her purse and removed a pack of Virginia Slims and a disposable lighter.

"Do you mind?"

With Fontaine, yes; with her, no. She lit up and blew smoke at the ceiling.

"I suppose I was hoping to allay your suspicion of Charles," she said. "Besides, I had been considering hiring a private detective, and you did walk in at the right time. . . ."

"I wondered why you looked surprised yesterday when Soames introduced us."

"I *was* startled. For a moment I thought Charles had hired you, and he's not fond of anyone in law enforcement."

"I'm not in law enforcement."

"What? Oh, no, I suppose not. But you are for hire, aren't you?"

"That depends what exactly you want me to do."

"Find Zack Meacham," she said, "and help me, well, persuade him to leave Charles alone."

"Find him?"

"He's apparently moved out of his house. I've tried to locate him—without Charles knowing, of course—and got no farther than the employees at his business, Meacham's Garage. They told me that he'd left town, but I don't believe them. I know he's still threatening Charles and I think he'd hiding somewhere in the city."

"Hiding from whom?"

She shrugged. "Perhaps no one. Perhaps himself. Obviously he's not behaving rationally. He's been carrying his hatred around for twenty years and it may have finally pushed him over the edge. Will you help me find him, Mr. Lomax?"

"Jacob."

"Jacob. I'll pay you, of course."

"Of course."

"Then you'll find him?"

"I'll try."

She looked relieved. She stubbed out her half-finished cigarette, leaving faint lipstick on the filter, and withdrew a checkbook from her purse.

"Can I ask you a personal question?"

"It depends on how personal," she said, opening her book to a clean green check.

"What exactly is your relationship with Charles Soames?"

"We're old friends." She clicked her pen and filled in the date.

"How can that be? He's been locked up for a generation."

"Is our relationship really that important to you?"

"Let's say it is."

She stopped writing and closed her checkbook. A fool and his money, and so forth.

"Charles and I were lovers before he went to prison."

That surprised me, since Soames was easily in his sixties.

"He must have been a child-molester," I said.

Her face began to turn in anger, then quickly eased into a smile, revealing perfect white teeth.

"Thank you," she said. "I was twenty-two when we met."

"And that was . . ."

"About a year before the Lochemont robbery." She lit another cigarette. "Charles was exactly twice my age," she said and blew smoke toward the window. "Old enough to be my father, as a number of people were quick to point out. But to me he was a sweet, kind man, and the age difference didn't stop me from loving him. We saw each other quite often. We'd even talked of marriage, and who knows? But then, the robbery." She shook her head. "Poor Charles."

"You thought he was innocent."

"I *knew* he was," she said, her voice intense, her eyes flashing. "And I was closer to him than anyone. He was forced to help those men. He was a victim."

She believed in Soames. I still had my doubts.

"What did you do after he went to prison?"

"I stayed in Denver for six months and visited Charles as often as I could. He became bitter, and who could blame him? But when he seemed to grow bitter toward me, I stopped visiting. I moved away."

"When did you move back?"

"I haven't. Not yet. When I learned Charles had been released from prison, I came out here immediately, without even thinking why. I loved him back then. Perhaps I came here to find out if I still do."

"Have you?"

"Found out? I . . . I don't know." She lowered her eyes, then noticed her checkbook and came out of her reverie. "How much will you need?"

"It depends on how long it takes to find Zack Meacham. I'd guess a week or less—that is, if he's in town—so figure . . ."

But she'd already opened her checkbook and was writing. When she'd finished, she ripped it out and handed it across.

"I'll pay you half now and half when you find him. Is it enough?"

It was plenty. She asked me when I could start, and I told her right away. Not only did I need the money, but also it was possible that Meacham could answer a few questions about Fontaine's death. In fact, maybe he *was* the answer. And even if he wasn't, this little exercise would keep me close to Charles Soames.

I got up and walked Helen Ester to the door.

"When you locate Meacham," she said, "please don't approach him until you've talked with me."

"Whatever you say."

"I'm staying at the Westin Hotel, room fourteen-ten. Call anytime. Day or night."

I watched her walk gracefully down the hallway and descend the stairs, out of sight.

She'd made "night" sound like an invitation. Or maybe it was just my libido, suited up and ready to play, begging Coach Lomax to put him in the game.

7

Meacham's house was just off South Sheridan Boulevard in a worn-out section of suburbs. The front lawn was a few weeks tall, weathered newspapers littered the walk, and junk mail was jammed in the mailbox and behind the screen door. I rang the bell anyway.

Nobody home. No kidding.

Drapes covered the front and side windows. At the rear of the house the kitchen curtains were open an inch or so. I could see the end of the table and the sink, which was piled high with dishes.

"He ain't home."

She was skinny, tan, and forty, with bleached-blond hair, pink shorts, and a bright orange halter. She leaned against the chain link fence between the yards and sloshed gin and tonic over the rim of her old-fashioned glass. Behind her on the clothesline a reddish wig had been hung out to dry. It looked like a small, dead animal.

"Where's Zack?" I walked over to her.

"Ain't seen him for two, three weeks." Her breath was heavy with the scent of juniper berries.

"You know where he is?"

She smiled and shook her head. "You a friend of his?" Her eyes had drifted below my belt.

"Zack and me go way back," I said. "How about you?"

"Only known him since he's been living here. About a year. But me and him got acquainted real good, if you know what I mean." She smiled broadly. There was lipstick smeared on her front teeth.

"I can imagine."

"Before that, he rented the place. But then his wife gave him the boot, so he kicked out the renters and moved in."

"I heard he may have left town."

"Who knows?" she said, trying to unbuckle my belt with her eyelashes. Then she turned her head to the sound of a car door in the street. "That'd be my old man home from work. Why'ncha come back tomorrow a little earlier and we can get comfortable inside and talk some more about Zack."

She winked broadly and walked a crooked line to the back door of her cozy home.

Morrison Road begins its trek toward the foothills from within the city limits, where it intersects Alameda at a forty-five-degree angle. This area of the city has a small-town feel, with overwide asphalt lanes fronting one-story commercial buildings, including Meacham's Garage. I parked the Olds in the lot between a pothole the size of a swimming pool and a tow truck plastered with American flag decals, and pushed through the smeared glass door.

A bell jangled over my head.

There was a battered wood counter, dusty at the corners and worn in the middle, supporting a pair of huge parts books, open like Bibles. Behind one end of the counter was a door with a sign overhead declaring "Employees Only." The guy who came through the door was wiping his hands with a greasy red rag. He was about sixty, with short white hair and a face as droopy as a bloodhound's. His name was stitched in white on his blue coveralls. Nolan.

"Help you?"

I gave him a card stating my profession, or maybe it was just a pastime. He smudged it with his thumb.

"I'm looking for Zack Meacham. Is he around?"

"Nope."

"Where is he?"

"Couldn't say."

"Couldn't or wouldn't?"

"I don't want no trouble," he said. "Lou says we don't know nothing about Zack."

"And Lou is who?"

"The manager."

"I'll talk to him, then."

"Lou's pretty busy, plus being in a bad mood. We just dropped the tranny on an old Riviera and we can't get the damn thing to work."

"It won't take long."

"I don't know," Nolan said. He glanced sideways toward the door. He didn't want to get Lou pissed off.

"I'll just be a minute," I said and walked around the counter and through the door. Nolan didn't try to stop me.

The work area was lit with a mixture of blue-white fluorescence from above, and yellow sun filtered through fly-specked windows high up on the walls. There were three cars and five employees. One guy was changing the tires on a blue Chevy, two were hoisting the engine out of a Ford, and two others were arguing by a decade-and-half-old Buick Riviera.

"Christ, Lou, I already tried that." The guy was on his back on a wheeled skid, his legs under the Buick. Lou was standing over him, fists on hips. One fist was stuffed with an oversized crescent wrench.

"Then try it again, goddammit, only this time do it right."

"But the bracket's bent."

"It's not bent, you dumb jackass, it's made that way."

Lou was as broad and thick as an engine block, with shiny black hair greased back in a duck tail and sleeves rolled up over hefty pale arms. He spoke in a deep, hoarse voice. But not as deep as it should have been. When he turned around, he turned into a she.

"Get over here, Nolan, and show—hey, employees only, pal," said Lou, as in Louise.

"My name is Jacob Lomax. I'd like to ask you a few questions about Zack Meacham."

"You got a car needs working on?"

"No, I—"

"Then beat it."

"When was the last time you saw your boss?"

Lou walked toward me.

"Didn't you hear what I said? Out."

Everyone in the garage stopped working to watch.

"Where is Meacham staying these days? It's important that I talk to him. A phone number would do."

Lou got right up close to me. She wasn't a guy, but she was close—shorter than me but stockier, with muscles from the soles of her work boots right up to the fringes of her fine, thin little mustache.

"Hit the road," she said, and waved her crescent wrench to show me the way.

"Tell me where your boss is and I'm history."

"You're history now."

She tapped me on the chest with her wrench. It left grease on my shirt.

"You got grease on my shirt," I said.

"There's gonna be blood on it in about three seconds unless you get your faggot ass out of here."

I turned sideways but kept her in my peripheral vision.

"Nolan, will you please tell me where your boss is? Lou here seems to be on the rag."

Nolan said, "Uh."

Lou swung her wrench.

I ducked, and the wrench barely brushed my head, but it touched a bruise left over from Tuesday night and it hurt like hell. I grabbed Lou's wrist, and she yanked away, strong as a bear from bench-pressing trannies and kicking the crap out of truck drivers down at the local bar. She faced me in a crouch, waggling the wrench at her side. Her face was flushed but her lips were wax-white. She was between me and the door, or I might have just left. On the other hand, there were five guys watching and I had my male pride to think about. Lou swung the wrench at my face and I backed out of the way, feeling its faint breeze. When she swung again, I came in fast and hit her with a brisk left to the chops, knocking her spread-eagled into a pyramid of Pennzoil cans. She crashed with the cans to the floor.

A couple of the guys rushed over to help her up. One of them said to me, "You gotta lot of goddamn nerve, hitting a woman like that."

"Let go," Lou said, getting to her feet.

She picked up her wrench and I thought we were going into round two, but instead she turned and went back to the Riviera.

"Can we talk about Meacham now?" I asked Nolan.

"Uh, sure, I guess."

We walked out to the front counter and I apologized for knocking over his oil cans.

Nolan rubbed his chin. "Lou can be one mean sumbitch when Zack ain't around."

"Where is he?"

"I really don't know. He took off a couple weeks ago. Said he was leaving town. Said he had something important to do. Hell, he said a lot of things." Nolan shook his head.

"What?"

"Zack's been acting goofy for months—hell, a year. The middle-age crazies or some damn thing. First he leaves his wife and kids, then he takes up with a topless dancer half his age. Then he starts talking about how he can finally even the score with some guy who's back in town."

Charles Soames. "Do you know the guy?"

"Zack wouldn't say. He just kept mumbling to himself half the day, being real absentminded, like he couldn't think of nothing else. And Art back there told me Zack told him he bought a gun because of this guy." Nolan shook his head. "But if you ask me, Zack's all talk. Hell, he wouldn't hurt a fly."

"Maybe so, but I want to find him before he does anything stupid."

"How can you find him if he's out of town?"

"He may not be out of town. Who's his girlfriend?"

Nolan gave me her name and where I could find her, and then he gave me the phone number for Meacham's ex-wife.

"I sorta doubt she'll be much help, though," Nolan said. "And look here, if you do find Zack, you be kinda careful. Especially since maybe he really did buy a gun."

"I thought you said he wouldn't hurt a fly."

"He wouldn't. But Zack Meacham never did think much of cops. Private or otherwise."

8

That evening, I phoned Meacham's ex-wife. She was not a happy woman. She did not want to chat with any of Zack's buddies, nor did she know where Zack was, nor did she care.

"He can roast in hell," she said. "Him and his underage stripper girlfriend."

It was about ten when I got to Fancy Dan's. It's on Federal Boulevard and there's nothing fancy about it. Nothing Dan, either—the owner's name is Freddy. The sign out front said "30 Gorgeous Women 30," but inside all I found were dim lights and smoke and maybe eight women eight. There was a bar, a score of tables, and a semicircular runway with low stools for impresarios desiring a close-up view of the artiste, currently a busty, chunky blonde, naked expect for high-heeled slippers and a sequined G-string. She was more or less dancing to a slow rock tune.

I sat at the bar and ordered a beer in a bottle from a young guy with long hair and a long face. When he brought my change I told him I was looking for Wendy Apple.

"Why?"

"She's a friend of a friend."

"You a cop?"

"Nope."

"You ever met her?"

"Nope."

"She's onstage," he said.

Wendy finished her routine of slow, rolling humps and bumps and hustled off the ramp and through a curtain. Five minutes later a young black woman had taken her place and Wendy was out on the floor hustling drinks. She'd put on a skater's skirt and a bikini top. I left my beer at the bar and sat at an empty table in the area she was working. She walked over with an exaggerated wiggle.

"Looks like you need a drink," she said brightly.

She was not quite pretty, but neither was she hard to look at—smooth complexion, clear blue eyes, and an easy, open smile. An Iowa farmgirl lost in the city, waiting to be found by Mr. Right. What's a nice girl like you, and so on. Except I'd recently been staring at her bare butt.

"I'll have whatever you're drinking," I said, "if you'll sit with me."

"I can't."

"Am I that ugly?"

She gave me a playful punch in the shoulder. "Heck no, I mean I have to keep working."

"How about on your break? What do you like, champagne?"

"Yes! But how did you know?"

"A wild guess. Okay? You can bring a bottle."

"Well . . . sure, why not," she said and bounced away.

She worked the floor for the next hour while I and the two dozen other slobs in there drank our drinks and watched the naked ladies dance. When she finally returned to my table, she brought a cheap green bottle and two glasses.

"Sixty bucks," she said, "and I'm on in fifteen minutes."

I gave her five twenties. "The rest is for you."

She folded her arms on the table—a safety net for her breasts, which threatened at any second to jump over the edge of her skimpy top. "Forty dollars for me? For what?" Her pale brows were bunched in a tiny frown. She really was a sweet kid.

"For talking with me, that's all." I popped the plastic cork and we sipped our candy-flavored sparkling wine. Ah, the good life.

"I'm looking for Zack Meacham," I said.

She put down her glass and gave me a troubled look.

"Are you a policeman?"

"Private investigator." I gave her my card. "I'm just trying to find Zack."

"Did he . . . has he done something wrong?"

"Not yet. But he's making nasty threats to my client."

"Oh, Zack," she scolded, as if he were sitting with us.

"He's apparently hiding out," I said. "Do you know where?"

She shook her head. "He's been acting weird for weeks. I mean, I didn't see him for almost two weeks and then a few nights ago he came to my apartment real late and made me promise not to—well jeez, I guess I blew it, huh?—not to tell anybody he'd been there. He wants everyone to think he's out of town."

"Why?"

"It's too weird."

"Tell me."

"It's just too weird," she said, rolling her big blue eyes. "He said he was thinking about killing a man, and when he did it, his alibi would be he wasn't in town. He's got some friend in Kansas City or someplace who'll swear Zack was with him."

"When is Zack planning to kill this man?"

"Jeez, never, I'm sure. It's just talk."

"It might be more than that, Wendy. Did he say when?"

"No, he just said he was thinking about it."

"Why did he risk his alibi by going to your apartment?"

"He said he missed me."

I knew what he missed.

"I tried to get him to stay," she said, "but he left early next morning. I was just so glad to see him, so glad he wasn't hurt or anything."

She poured more champagne.

"What do you mean, glad he wasn't hurt?"

"What? Oh. Glad, I guess, that he hadn't run into my boyfriend. Ex-boyfriend, I mean. Vince and I broke up six months ago, and then I started dating Zack, only Vince doesn't always think we're broken up."

"You were afraid he might have done something to Zack?"

"Sort of. I mean, they're both pretty tough guys, but Vince is maybe in better shape, a few years younger, too, I guess. But not *too* young, though. I guess I like older men." She looked at me and blushed. "Anyway, Vince told me a few months ago he was going to get rid of Zack so I'd come back to him. I knew he was just talking, just the way Zack is talking now, but even so, when Zack disappeared all of a sudden and I didn't hear from him for a week or two, I started wondering if maybe Vince had done something. Then Zack showed up, and I knew everything was okay. I got to get back to work."

She stood and so did I.

"Do you have a key to Zack's house?"

"What?"

"I'm going to search the place and it'll be easier to use a key."

"Easier than what?"

"Kicking in the door."

"You'd do that?"

"Or pick the lock, but the neighbors might holler. Look, Wendy, you want me to find Zack, don't you? I mean before he does something he might regret."

"Yes, but breaking into his house . . ."

I waited.

"Well. Okay. I guess."

I followed her through the bar to the dressing room in back. There were mirrors and chairs and some clothes on hangers. Wendy was digging through her purse when another dancer pushed in through a heavy curtain. She was nude and her ebony skin glistened with sweat.

"Stay away from that dude in the Hawaiian shirt, honey. He pinches like a goddamn lobster. Hey, good-lookin'."

Wendy gave me a key and I told her I'd return it.

" 'Fi was you, honey, I'd tell good-lookin' to *keep* the damn key."

It was midnight when I parked down the block from Zack Meacham's house. The neighborhood was quiet and dark. I took a flashlight from my glove box, walked down the street and up the walk, and let myself in with Wendy's key.

The air was close and musty and the house was dead still. After a few minutes I could make out shapes in the dark— mounded furniture, oval doorways. I pointed the flashlight at my feet, switched it on, and moved through the house.

The walls in the front room were bare and the furniture was sparse and new and cheap and hadn't been dusted or moved for months, maybe a year, maybe since Meacham had it delivered to this, his new vacant home.

Off the front room was an empty room that could have been used as a den or a guest bedroom. Meacham hadn't used it for anything.

I went though the kitchen. Dirty cups and pots and silverware were piled on the counter and there was a heap of empty frozen dinner trays under the sink. The refrigerator held only two bottles of Coors, a half-empty jar of mustard, and a Baggie with some green-and-white stuff that used to be cheese. Next to the kitchen table was an RCA color TV on a metal stand. The table itself was bare except for a couple of ashtrays overflowing with butts and a handful of matchbooks. Their covers advertised Meacham's Garage, King Soopers, Fancy Dan's, and The Ace Cafe.

In the bathroom there was a pile of dirty clothes in the corner, a disintegrated cigarette butt in the toilet bowl, and a ring around the bathtub you could stub your toe on.

The last room in the house was the bedroom.

The bed was unmade. Socks and underwear hung out of dresser drawers. Lined up on the floor were cardboard boxes of clothes Meacham hadn't bothered to unpack. One box had a framed picture of a man and woman and two little girls. I found more photos on the dresser. A strip from a vending machine—5 Pix for a Buck—the family man and Wendy mugging it up for the camera. I put the photo strip in my pocket and searched the closet. There were a bunch of shoes kicked into the corner and clothes on hangers. I went through the pockets of everything and found nothing except another book of matches from The Ace Cafe. I kept it.

At the rear of the closet shelf was a weighty paper sack and inside was a box labeled ".38 Special Silvertip Hollow Point Super-X." Half a dozen shells were missing from the box. I found a cash register slip at the bottom of the sack listing one Colt .38 revolver with a six-inch barrel and one box of fifty shells. The slip was dated four weeks ago.

When I got out to the Olds, I rechecked the matchbook for the address of The Ace Cafe. It was in a sleazy district on the lower edge of downtown, exactly two blocks away from the office of the late private eye Lloyd Fontaine.

9

Friday morning I skipped my shower and shave, put on my downtown clothes—soiled black denim pants with ragged cuffs and a cracked leather belt; two pairs of gray socks that used to be white; leather work boots with worn-down heels and broken laces; a moth-eaten T-shirt under a faded plaid flannel shirt; a frayed and colorless cardigan sweater, shiny with age and ripe with old sweat; and a crumpled old coat with one elbow ripped out and half the buttons missing—and went out for a walk.

It was a blue-sky morning, with a hint of fall in the air. I walked west on Seventh Avenue to Broadway, then north to Sixteenth Street. The downtown shoppers and office types gave me a wide berth all the way to Larimer Square. So I smelled bad. So what? They were slaves and I was free and they knew it. I could sleep late, drink my breakfast, and hang out all day on the streets if I felt like it. They, on the other hand, had to wear certain clothes, be in certain places at certain times, and do what certain people told them to do. Slaves. Of course, they had credit cards and double garages and tickets to the play and I had twelve bucks.

By the time I turned northeast on Larimer my feet hurt, my armpits itched, and my T-shirt was plastered to my back.

I crossed Twentieth Street, the present shoreline in the ever-shifting ebb and flow of urban decay and redevelopment. Behind me were high-rises, good restaurants, and clever shops in carefully restored old buildings. Ahead lay depression. Gin mills, pawnshops, and cheap hotels stood side by grimy side, their windows either boarded up or covered with heavy wire mesh. Men slumped together in small groups or sat alone in doorways. Some of them watched me pass. Most watched nothing at all.

The Ace Cafe was conveniently located between a liquor store and a pawnshop, in case you wanted to hock your shoes for a meal and an after-dinner drink. Inside it was all red linoleum, brown vinyl, and greasy food.

I sat at the counter elbow to elbow with a big drunken white guy using his hair for a napkin and eating chili for breakfast, managing occasionally to get some of it in his mouth. I opted for the burned hash browns, slimy eggs, and coal-tar coffee.

There were six men and one woman in the cafe. None of them looked like the photos I'd seen of Zack Meacham. In fact, it was a thousand to one against finding him in here, since all I had to go on was a couple of matchbooks. But Meacham was hiding someplace, and if you wanted to hide out, this was the perfect neighborhood, because it was doubtful that you'd bump into anyone you knew.

I sauntered around the neighborhood for the next few hours, digesting my meal and searching faces and thanking the Great Spirit for the hundred thousandth time that I hadn't been raised by depraved or deprived parents or born with a brain defect or predisposed toward masochism or afflicted with dumb blind rotten luck or whatever the hell it was that dumped people in this hopeless dead-end corner of life.

Lunch was a sack-wrapped bottle of port shared in a vacant lot with some of the guys—"Dutch" and "Benny" and "Jonesy" and "Red." I was "Jake from up north."

I spent that afternoon on the streets, that evening in the bars, and that night on a buck-and-a-half cot in a two-story, two-room hotel with about forty other lucky gents. The unlucky ones had to sleep outside in thirty-degree weather.

The next day was Saturday, but down here it could have been any day of the week. They were all the same—stay warm, get a little food, a little booze, stay alive.

All morning and afternoon I walked the streets between Twentieth and Twenty-fourth, Larimer and Champa. There were scores of down-and-outers roaming the area, but no Meacham. Maybe it was time to check in with my client. Or maybe I just wanted to have a conversation with someone who used soap. I dialed Helen Ester's hotel room from a pay phone near the Sixteenth Street Mall.

"Have you found him?" she asked.

"Not yet. What say we talk about it over dinner."

At eight o'clock I was scrubbed and suited and waiting in the foyer of the Augusta Restaurant in the Westin Hotel across from the Tabor Center. It was the type of place Horace and Augusta Tabor would have approved of. Baby Doe would've loved it.

Helen Ester was right on time. She seemed to look better each time I saw her. Maybe it was the clothes. This time she wore a shimmering pale melon-colored silk dress, which did something to my throat, or else I'd tied my tie too tight. The maître d' led us to a table near the center of the room, and soon we had linen napkins in our laps, polite waiters at our elbows, and murmured conversations in our ears. There was crystal overhead and crystal on the table and I didn't see one drunk eating chili. I ordered a scotch and soda for Helen and Glenlivet on the rocks for me.

"The waiter was staring at your whiskers," she said with a smile.

"He envies us rugged types."

"I assume your not shaving has something to do with your search for Zack Meacham."

I filled her in on the past few days—discussions with Nolan and Lou at Meacham's Garage, my talk with Wendy Apple, the search of Meacham's house, the matchbook, the skids.

"It seems like a long shot, looking for him down there."

"Right now it's all we've got," I said. "Has Meacham phoned Soames in the past few days?"

"Yes, and Charles merely laughed at him and hung up. I don't know, perhaps he's right after all, perhaps Meacham truly isn't a threat."

"I'm afraid he is," I said. "He bought a gun a few weeks ago."

"Oh, no."

"Something else. It could be just a coincidence, but The Ace Cafe is only two blocks from Fontaine's office."

"Oh, my God, then maybe he *did* kill poor Lloyd."

"Maybe. And you say 'poor Lloyd' as if you knew him."

"I did."

"What?"

"Shouldn't we order?" she said.

I signaled our waiter and he listened to us and nodded politely and averted his eyes from my unkempt face. When he left, I asked Helen how she knew Lloyd Fontaine.

"It was twenty years ago," she said. "Lloyd showed up just before Charles's trial. I think he talked to everyone involved—me, Charles, the police, Charles's daughter, and her husband. Now that I think about it, he probably questioned Zack Meacham. Lloyd didn't seem to care about innocence or guilt or punishment, he just wanted the jewels back."

"You haven't seen him since then?"

"No. I'd forgotten all about him until I heard of his death."

After our appetizer of shrimp consommé with red pepper and black mushrooms, Helen asked me if the police had any leads on Fontaine's murderer.

"The police rarely confide in me," I said.

"No, I suppose not. I was wondering, though, when I came

to your office Thursday and it was all upside down and you said you'd been burglarized . . ."

"Yes?"

"Did that have something to do with Lloyd?"

"No doubt. Fontaine had left an envelope with me, and I think that's what the guy was after."

"An envelope?"

"It contained mostly old newspaper clippings of the Lochemont robbery, plus a journal of some sort, but it's in code and so far I haven't made any sense of it. And some photographs."

"Photographs of what?"

"Ed Teague and a pal being stopped by a traffic cop."

"Teague? From the Lochemont robbery?"

I nodded yes.

"Did you give it all to the police?"

"No."

Dinner arrived—spit-roasted Long Island duckling with raspberry mint butter sauce for her, grilled Hawaiian swordfish with preserved oranges and a Moroccan sauce for me, and a bottle of Pouilly Fuissé.

Later, after our waiter retrieved the bottle from the ice bucket and poured the last of the wine, Helen asked me why I hadn't given Fontaine's envelope to the police.

"Good question," I said. "Maybe the answer is the Lochemont jewels."

"What do you mean?"

"It could be a treasure map. Fontaine said he knew approximately where the jewels were hidden."

"Lloyd said that?"

I nodded yes. "He also said Charles Soames knew *exactly* where they were hidden."

She put down her wineglass. "That is simply not true."

"Is that what Soames told you?"

"Jacob, I was very close to Charles back then, and I'm close to him now, and believe me, if he knew where to find a fortune in gems, I would most certainly know about it."

"I see."

"I'm sorry to disappoint you," she said.

"I can see that."

"I suppose, then, that the material Lloyd gave you is worthless."

"Not necessarily," I said. "It could still lead me to his murderer."

When the bill came, Helen insisted on paying. I like that in a woman. I liked it even better when she invited me up to her room for an after-dinner drink.

The windows faced northwest and were filled mostly with the towering Tabor Center across the street, but I could still see beyond the buildings of lower downtown and over the railroad yards and past the strung-out lights of the suburbs all the way to the mountains, black against a clear, starry sky. Helen Ester poured Cordon Bleu into a pair of snifters and handed me one. She looked different than she had in the restaurant and I suddenly realized it was her eyes—they seemed to change color with the ambient light. Now they were more green than brown. We sat on a large divan and looked out on the night lights and she asked me how in the world I'd ever become a private eye.

"I sort of fell into it after I left the cops," I said.

"You were a policeman?"

"For a while."

"You don't seem like a policeman."

"How do they seem?"

"I don't know," she said. "Insensitive, I suppose. What made you join?"

"Guilt."

She laughed. "You've *got* to be kidding."

"Well, maybe."

"What did you feel guilty about?" she asked, still smiling.

"Would you believe not going to Vietnam?"

"Now you *are* kidding."

"Maybe I felt guilty about not fighting over there, so I decided to fight the bad guys over here. Anyway, I didn't have the correct genes to make it as a physician or a politician or a priest or a plumber."

"So you picked policeman."

"It seemed like a good idea at the time."

"Then why did you quit?"

"That's another story," I said. "Let's talk about you. For instance, I don't even know where you live."

"San Francisco," she said, turning toward me, crossing her legs, making her silk dress whisper. "I've lived there off and on for years. I love the city and so did my husband."

"Your husband?"

"Yes. He died there four years ago."

"Oh, I'm sorry."

"It's all right. He'd suffered through a long illness and it was . . . it was a blessing when he passed away." She sipped her brandy and looked away.

"I didn't mean to pry."

"You're not prying."

"We can talk about something else."

She put her snifter aside.

"We don't have to talk," she said, her voice soft and low.

I was close enough to her to smell her faint perfume and see the light glistening on her lips. I found myself thinking that Charles Soames was a lucky man to have a woman like this. No, that wasn't quite it. He didn't *deserve* a woman like this. And I wanted nothing more than to take her away from him, to have her right then, right there on the couch. But something held me back. Guilt? Because she was, as they used to say, spoken for. Or fear? Because of the possible commitment. Or maybe I was just heeding that simple rule laid down by an early private detective, perhaps the earliest: Don't sleep with your clients.

I held her shoulders, gave her a brief kiss on the lips, and stood up.

"I'd better leave," I said.

She looked surprised, then angry. Then embarrassed.

"I . . . I'm sorry. Perhaps inviting you up here was wrong. Perhaps I, I mean we—"

"There's nothing to be sorry about," I said. "I'll call you in a day or two."

That night, alone by choice, I struggled with sleep and tried to decide if I was fucking stupid or what.

The next morning, Sunday, found me at The Ace Cafe, wearing smelly clothes and choking down greasy food. I roamed the streets and low-life bars, searching faces. I slept that night on a cot under a buggy blanket and dreamed of island women and rare rum and silk sheets.

Monday morning I was back on the streets wondering just how much more cheap chow and bad booze my stomach could handle. By nine that night I was cold and tired and nearly ready to give it up. I walked into some nameless dive to get a drink.

Zack Meacham was sitting at the end of the bar.

10

Meacham had grown a beard, but otherwise he looked the same as his pictures—stocky body, coarse features, and one bushy eyebrow that ran nearly from temple to temple and dipped down to the bridge of his nose. He was leaning forward with his elbows on the bar and his hands wrapped around a glass of flat beer. There was an empty stool beside him. I took it.

"What's yours?" the bartender said when he was finished blowing his nose.

"Beer."

He slapped a foamy one down in front of me and only charged me six bits, but then I didn't get a cocktail napkin.

Meacham nursed his beer for twenty minutes and I kept pace with him. Neither of us spoke. I listened to the rise and fall of background voices and waited for Meacham to drain his glass.

"Gimme another one," he said.

"Me, too. I'm buying."

He looked at me from under his bushy brow, eyes like an animal's peering out of a cave. "I buy my own goddamn beer."

"Just being neighborly."

"Fuck off," he said and moved to the other end of the bar where he could drink without being hassled by creeps like me. He had a few more and so did I, and then he climbed off his stool, zipped up his ski parka, and walked out. I followed.

Meacham walked in a semistraight line down Larimer, leaving the tall city lights farther behind us, then turned right on Twenty-third. He crossed Lawrence, then the wide intersection where Broadway angled through, then Arapahoe. Near the corner of Twenty-third and Curtis he went into a three-story sagging brick building that threatened to collapse at any minute. The neon sign hadn't worked for a decade, but the flaky painted letters declared the place to be the Frontier Hotel. I gave Meacham a few minutes, then went in.

The night clerk looked like a vampire. He was skinny and pale with slicked-back black hair, red lips, and buck teeth. His black shirt was buttoned at the throat, no doubt to hide the fang marks from his pals.

"I'm supposed to meet my friend in his room and I forgot the number," I said.

He stared at my jugular vein. "What's his name?"

"Stocky guy with a beard. He just walked in."

"You mean Cliff."

"Yeah, Cliff."

"Room twelve, third floor rear."

The stairs creaked and sagged and the banister threatened to come off in my hand, but I made it to the top floor. The hallway smelled as sour as despair, as stale as death.

Light seeped out from under Meacham's door. Through the keyhole I could see the bottom of a window, the corner of a battered dresser, and the end of a bed. Meacham crossed my view, then the bedsprings creaked and his stockinged feet moved to the end of the bed, toes pointed at the ceiling. After a few minutes he was snoring.

I was tempted to kick in the door and ask him a few pointed questions about Lloyd Fontaine, perhaps expediting his replies by breaking a finger or cracking a rib. He might even give me a hint about where to find a pile of jewels. But patience. Helen Ester deserved first try at him, and Meacham didn't look like he was going anywhere soon.

I walked out past the night creature downstairs, took the bus home, and phoned Helen.

"I found him."

"Where?"

I told her, then asked her how she wanted to proceed.

"I want to offer him money to leave Charles alone."

"I'm not sure this guy will listen to money."

"A lot of money, Jacob, and in cash."

"It might be more effective if I just beat the hell out of him, then turn him over to the cops."

"Let's try it my way first, okay? I'll meet you at your office tomorrow night—say, around eight. I'll have the money with me and we'll go talk to him together."

Dumb idea. "Fine," I said.

Tuesday morning I shaved for the first time in days, ate a steak-and-eggs breakfast, and drove to the office. There were three messages on my machine. A guy selling storm doors; another guy selling Jesus; and Abner Greenspan, attorney-at-law, the man who four years ago had introduced me to Lloyd Fontaine.

I'd worked with Greenspan a number of times in the past—enough times so that we gave each other discount rates on services provided. Of course, his base rate was a hell of a lot higher than mine. On the other hand, I'd saved his life once, so I suppose that counted double.

Actually, it wasn't *his* life I'd saved, it was his client's. But Greenspan was egotistical enough to believe that when the husband in a big alimony suit brought a gun to the courtroom and pointed it at the plaintiff's table, he was pointing it not at his wife, but at his wife's attorney. In any case, I'd jumped on the guy and knocked him to the floor before any shots were fired, and Greenspan had wept with gratitude.

All that aside, I knew Greenspan wasn't calling just to be sociable. He socialized only with people who had money, power, or political influence—in short, anyone who had something he wanted.

I phoned him, and he answered on the first ring.

"Jake, how goes it?" he said.

"Okay."

"I heard you were the one who found Fontaine. Rough stuff."

"Yeah. Rough."

"I'm the executor of his will."

"Oh?"

"You're in it," he said.

"You're kidding."

"No. I'm in it, too. Apparently Fontaine had few friends and no relatives. Of course, a few may pop out of the woodwork before the will gets through probate, but I doubt it. So you and I get to split the meager pickings."

"What pickings?"

"As executor, I am to liquidate all his assets, of which there are few, and pay off all his bills, of which there are fewer, and keep the rest. Except for the contents of his office. You get that—desk, files, and so on."

"I don't want it."

"How do you know?"

"Abner, please. I was there, remember? The place is a dump. If he had cases pending, I don't want them. And I don't want his desk—I think it's got blood on it."

"He had a safe, too, Jake. A man from the safe company is meeting me there today to open it up."

"Let me know what you find."

"I need two witnesses."

"You and the safe guy."

"I don't count."

"Christ, Abner."

"Maybe it's full of money. Come on, I'll buy lunch."

"All right, all right."

The van parked in front of Fontaine's building had a sign on it: "Security Lock and Safe, Inc." Parked beside it was a new shiny silver Mercedes. It didn't have any signs. It *was* a sign.

Greenspan and the safe guy were waiting inside Fontaine's office.

The safe guy was down on his knees before Greenspan, who stood over him like a medieval prince receiving a peasant. The prince was thin as a long-distance runner and a few years younger than I was. His face was smooth and tan. So was his suit. He wore a diamond ring and a thirty-dollar haircut and shoes that cost more than everything I had on. Also, he was in debt up to his eyeballs. He wasn't exactly crooked, but if he didn't make big bucks honestly and soon, he was the type who could and would circumvent the law.

"Is that the right combination?" he asked. Then, "Hello, Jake."

Greenspan's voice was a well-modulated baritone trained to impress clients, charm judges, and intimidate opponents. He was an effective attorney. I tried not to hold that against him.

"Hi, Abner."

The safe guy stood, rubbing his knees. "I hate these goddamned floor safes," he said.

"Well?" Greenspan asked.

"The original number's been changed. I gotta get my tools." He left.

"I understand Lloyd was sitting here when he got it."

"Yeah, about there," I said.

Greenspan went to the desk and ran his hand across it. Then he checked his fingers for dust, or maybe blood. "A friend of mine in the department says it looked like a professional job. Two shots to the head, bam bam, one almost on top of the other. Twenty-two-caliber magnum."

"Are you saying the cops think it was a mob hit?"

Greenspan shrugged. "Nobody's sure. In any case, they'll never get the guy who did it. They don't have squat."

The safe guy came back with a heavy box of tools.

"How long will this take?" Greenspan was checking his gold watch.

"As long as it takes," the guy said and went to work.

"I've got phone calls to make." Greenspan went out to his car to make them.

I looked over my inheritance—empty file cabinets with their contents scattered all over the floor, two broken-down chairs, and a big rolltop desk. And now a safe in the floor with a ruined lock. I kicked through the papers on the floor, some typed, some decorated with Fontaine's illegible scrawl. Two pages clipped together caught my eye, and I picked them up just as the safe guy stopped drilling.

"I can open it now," he said and went out to get Greenspan.

When they came back, the guy opened the safe door, then stepped aside. Greenspan grimaced at the dirty floor.

"Do you mind? These are expensive slacks."

The safe guy looked at me, then got down on his knees and reached into the safe.

"Empty," he said.

"Great."

"Are you certain?" Greenspan said.

"See for yourself."

"That safe's been in here forever," I said. "Fontaine probably never even had the combination."

Greenspan muttered to himself, filled out a form, then gave it to me and the safe guy to sign. The guy packed up his tools and left.

"Well, Jake, it's all yours," Greenspan said. "I've spoken with the landlord and you've got three days to cough up six months' rent."

"What?"

"Or else move everything out of here, which will cost right around five hundred bucks. I checked."

"Jesuschrist, Abner."

"It's mostly the desk. They really built these babies in the old days." He drew his hand lovingly across its blemished surface. "You know, this would look pretty nice in my office. I mean, after it was reconditioned, stripped, and stained. I could take it off your hands."

"I wondered why you wanted me down here."

Greenspan smiled.

"Okay, okay. You pay to have everything moved out, and you can keep the desk and burn the rest."

"Deal," Greenspan said.

He took out another form and I signed the desk over to him. Then he checked his watch, said, "Got to run," and was gone. I guess he forgot about buying my lunch.

11

The two sheets of paper I'd picked off the floor of Fontaine's office were held together with a paper clip. The top sheet was a typed letter, possibly copied from the second sheet, which was filled with Fontaine's illegible scrawl. Together they might give Vaz a clue about Fontaine's journal.

But what had originally caught my eye were the contents of the letter:

Mrs. Gloria Archuleta
P.O. Box 3929
Santa Fe, NM 87502

Dear Mrs. Archuleta:

Good news. I am close to recovering the missing property. The cooperation you have given me throughout this entire affair will soon be rewarded. Of course, money alone cannot make up for those many years without Rueben, but it may make life a little easier for you and your children.

Yours truly,

Lloyd Fontaine
Private Investigator

Fontaine had been corresponding with the wife of one of the Lochemont robbers—*the* robber, in fact, who nearly everyone believed had escaped with the jewels, everyone but me and Fontaine and Fontaine's murderer and apparently Rueben Archuleta's wife, Gloria. I wondered about the phrase "those many years without Rueben." Did that mean he'd died, or that he'd run off after the robbery and never come home?

I drove to my apartment and gave the pages to Vaz.

"Archuleta? From the robbery?"

"The same," I said.

He looked from one page to the other.

"Let us pray that these help me with Fontaine's journal," he said. "Otherwise it is hopeless, because this is as far as I can go."

He showed me a pile of ruled yellow sheets, each covered with his heavy block writing in soft-leaded pencil. The first line of the first sheet looked like all the rest:

?GXU? R??EG S?DNI ??LF? M?PHD

"Are these question marks yours?"

He nodded yes slowly. "He scribbled, Jacob. The man didn't even *need* a code."

"I appreciate your efforts, Vaz."

"Speaking of which," he said, "I've located our Mr. Witherspoon from the *Gazette*."

"All right."

"I made a few dozen phone calls and finally found the correct newspaper in Idaho Springs."

"Idaho Springs," I said. "That fits."

"Yes, the site of the murder shack and so on. In any case, Mr. Witherspoon is the editor, and he's been with the paper for years. I described the photos to him, but he can't recall them."

"Did he know Fontaine?"

"He said the name sounded familiar, but that's all."

"He didn't remember giving Fontaine the photos?"

"No."

"Okay, Vaz, good work. I'll take the photos up there tomorrow and talk to Witherspoon in person."

I got to the office at seven-thirty and waited for Helen Ester to show up with the money for Meacham. Whether Meacham accepted it or not, I intended to question him about Lloyd Fontaine and the Lochemont jewels.

Helen showed up just after eight, wearing a high collar, too much makeup, and oversized dark glasses. She walked past me into the room and sat stiffly in the visitor's chair.

"Do you have the money?" I asked.

"I . . . yes."

"What's wrong? And why the shades?"

"I . . . I've just come from talking with Zack Meacham."

"You what? Dammit, we agreed to go down there together. That neighborhood is—"

"I know. Jacob, I—"

"What happened? And take off those glasses."

"I wanted to talk to Meacham alone, to reason with him. I thought he'd . . . listen to reason."

"Goddammit, take off the glasses."

"He was surprised that anyone knew where he was. Surprised and angered. I asked him to please leave Charles alone. I told him if he would, I was prepared to give him ten thousand dollars. He wouldn't listen. He just became more angry."

I was getting angry myself. I reached out for her glasses and she pushed my hand away. Her collar opened slightly, revealing a large red mark on her neck.

"He . . . he hit me, Jacob."

She took off the glasses. An ugly purple bruise showed through the makeup high on her cheekbone, and her left eye was nearly swollen shut.

"Jesuschrist." I touched her face and she winced and drew back. "I'd better take you to a doctor."

"No, it's okay, really."

"Then I'm sending you home in a cab." I put on my jacket over my gun.

"Jacob, please." She held my arm.

"I'll just talk to him. More or less."

"No."

"It's not your decision to make," I said.

"Please, I want to give him another chance to accept the money."

"You can't be serious."

"He'll listen to me now, with you there."

"Forget it. You're going home now in a cab."

"I'm going with you, Jacob."

"Like hell you are."

"Like hell I'm not."

By the time we got to the Frontier Hotel, I had cooled down a bit. I was almost ready to let Meacham live.

"I . . . I'm afraid to go back in there," Helen said. "Can you bring him down here? We can talk in the car."

"All right, just stay put and keep the doors locked."

I started to get out, but she held my arm. Her bruises were invisible in this dim light, and I could almost forget what Meacham had done to her. Almost, but not quite.

"Be careful," she said. "He's like an animal at bay. And I saw a gun when I was up there."

I crossed the street. It was empty and dark, lit only by the city glow from a cold, overcast sky. Traffic noise was continuous but distant, faint, and blocks away the office towers stood watch over the city with tiny, unblinking lights.

Dracula the night clerk sat behind the front desk, waiting. He watched me cross the filthy lobby and climb the stairs. The third-floor hallway was silent and lit only by a weak light at my back. As I started down the hall, I heard a horn honking from the street outside. Was it Helen? Maybe she'd seen Meacham down in the street.

I turned to go back, and suddenly two gunshots rang out from the end of the hallway, Meacham's end.

I ran down the hall to number twelve. No one on the floor had opened a door. Either they hadn't heard the shots, or they were trying hard not to get involved. Meacham's door was ajar, so I pushed it open, keeping out of the doorway.

"Meacham?"

No answer.

I took a quick peek inside. Then I went in, gun first.

Meacham lay on his back on the bed, staring at the ceiling. There were cuts and lumps on his face, and his lip had been split open, but his main problems were the two bullet holes in his chest. His shirt was soaked with blood.

I felt the side of his neck. Nothing.

Then I stepped to the open window, where a chilly breeze moved the curtains. There was a fire escape, which zigzagged down three stories to the alley. A guy was jumping off the last few steps.

"Hold it right there!" I yelled and pointed the snubbed-nose .38 at him—a fairly useless gesture at this distance.

He looked up and I saw his face in the faint light from the street. He was a good-looking dude in his midthirties, possibly Latino, with shiny black hair and a shiny leather jacket. He raised his arm, and flame came out the end. The bullet hit the metal railing and ricocheted into the night. He fired again, and when I fired back a couple of times, he took off down the alley.

I clambered down the fire escape, dropped to the cement, and ran after him.

He was already across Twenty-third and into the darkness of the next alley—too far away for me to try a shot. My best chance was to stay with him and wear him down. By the time I'd reached the street, he was a block ahead of me, dodging cars on Broadway, heading for the center of town and still going strong. Meanwhile, I was struggling in my street shoes and stumbling through dark things underfoot. He gradually increased his lead, and when he turned the corner onto Twentieth by the bus depot, I was a block and a half back. By the time I got there, he was nowhere in sight. There were a few cars and no pedestrians. I stood there sweating and huffing and trying to remember when I'd been in better shape. I searched a few streets and alleys on my way back to the Frontier Hotel, but the guy was probably already home, cleaning his gun and having a beer.

When I stepped around the corner of the Frontier Hotel, the street was busy with cops and citizens. Nothing like a gunfight to get everybody's attention. Helen Ester was standing by my car, talking to a uniform. I started to holster my gun when somebody behind me yelled, "Freeze!"

I turned, slowly, my arms at my sides. The young cop was in a crouch, and he held his .38 Police Special in both hands, arms extended, muzzle pointed at the middle of my chest, just like they'd taught us in the police academy.

"Drop it, motherfucker," he said.

They'd never taught us to use words like that, but I dropped it anyway.

Another cop hustled over.

The first one said, "This dude came out of the alley carrying that piece."

I told them who I was and what I did for a living. "I was chasing the man who probably killed Zack Meacham. He's the stiff upstairs in twelve."

The cops glanced at each other. A few citizens had drifted over to check out the new development in the evening's entertainment. In their midst was one old hag with more hair curlers than hair and a pink bathrobe that looked like something she'd found in the street.

"That's him, Officer," she said, her voice graveled by a lifetime of booze, her gnarly finger aimed at me. "That's the man I seen run down the fire escape right after the shooting started."

"You're under arrest," the first cop said.

"Look, I just told—"

"Lean against the wall and spread 'em."

"But I'm a private—"

"You have the right to remain silent."

"Shit."

12

They took me to the main police building on Thirteenth and Cherokee, where I was allowed to use the phone. I called Helen Ester. No answer. For all I knew she was in another part of this building. I called Abner Greenspan at home and got him out of bed.

"I've been arrested."

"For what?"

"Suspicion of murder."

"I'll be there in twenty minutes. Don't say anything to anybody."

I was pictured and printed, then turned over to a pair of homicide detectives, Healey and O'Roarke. Healey had a sad face, and O'Roarke was Oriental. They looked like the same two who'd been with Dalrymple when he'd questioned me about Fontaine's murder. Small world.

"You want to talk to us now, or wait for your attorney?" Healey asked.

"I'll talk now if you can bring in Lieutenant MacArthur."

"He's on vacation."

"Terrific."

"Lieutenant Dalrymple will handle this."

"Oh, great."

"So, you want to talk?"

"I'll wait."

"We'll have to lock you up," Healey said, raising his eyebrows to see if maybe I'd change my mind. So far, he'd been the only one talking. O'Roarke just watched me and said nothing.

I sat in an empty holding cell downstairs, waiting for Greenspan and thinking about my Latino friend in the leather jacket. He was definitely the same guy who'd waltzed me in my office and probably the one who'd killed Lloyd Fontaine. Busy little bastard. I wondered if Soames had hired him to do Meacham or if the guy had done it on his own.

When Greenspan arrived, they let him talk to me alone upstairs in an interrogation room.

"What happened?"

I told him.

"And that's all?" he asked when I'd finished. "I mean, all that happened between you and Meacham."

"That's all."

"Do you want to talk to the police now? You don't have to, you know."

"I'll talk to them. Why wouldn't I?"

"And you'll tell them what you told me?"

"Yes."

"And you're sure that's all?"

"Yes."

"All that happened, I mean."

"Yes, goddammit."

Dalrymple and Healey asked the questions and I gave the answers and Greenspan piped in now and then with, "I would advise you not to answer that." O'Roarke just looked and listened. He was beginning to get on my nerves. Maybe that was the point.

I went through it all without once mentioning Meacham's threats to Charles Soames. I wasn't certain whether it was because I felt an obligation toward Helen Ester, or because I wanted first crack at Soames myself. When it was over, Dalrymple wasn't convinced I was telling the truth, but since Greenspan swore he'd surrender me to him upon request, he let me go. At least, he said, until after ballistics compared the bullets in my gun with the slugs the coroner would soon dig out of Meacham.

When we left the room, Greenspan told me there was nothing to worry about. But he sounded worried when he said it.

We saw Helen Ester sitting on a bench just inside the front entrance, and she stood as we approached.

"Jacob, thank God. They told me you were being released."

"Are you all right?" I asked.

"Yes," she said, but her face looked drawn. "They asked me a lot of questions and I told them everything except . . ." She glanced at Greenspan.

"He's on our side," I said.

Greenspan sighed audibly and looked up at the ceiling.

"I didn't tell them about Charles," she said. "I told them Meacham had been threatening me instead. Was that wrong?"

"It was just right," I said.

Greenspan cleared his throat.

"Oh. Abner Greenspan, Helen Ester."

"How do you do," she said.

"I'm tired and it's late and I have to be in court tomorrow at nine," he replied.

Greenspan dropped us at my car, and I drove Helen to her hotel. On the way, I told her about finding Meacham and chasing his murderer. The more I talked, the more frightened she looked.

"Jacob, I . . . I don't want to be alone tonight."

"Neither do I."

We huddled together in her big hotel bed. She was scared about there being a killer on the loose and still hurting and upset by her treatment at the hands of Meacham and I was right on the edge of being in big trouble with the cops. So there was no romance, or even sex, for that matter. We just lay there in each other's arms and held on for dear life.

In the morning we made love without hesitation, without thinking why or why not, as if it was the most natural thing in the world, which, of course, it was.

Afterward, though, she seemed embarrassed and hurried off to her shower, taking her clothes with her.

It made me remember a time in high school, having sex with a red-haired girl named Judy in the backseat of my parents' old Buick and thinking this is what Heaven must be like, and I'd no sooner shot my wad when Judy pulled up her panties, straightened her hair and bra and lipstick, and acted as if nothing had happened, making me wonder if I'd been fantasizing and maybe nothing *had* happened, or if maybe *two* things had happened, two completely different things—one to her and one to me.

I dressed slowly and met Helen in the next room. The bruise under her eye looked worse than it had last night when she'd come to my office, and I was almost glad that Meacham had died the way he had. Almost.

I reached out for Helen and touched her hair, but when I tried to kiss her, she turned her head and moved away. She sat at the small table by the window, wrote out a check, and handed it to me, averting her eyes.

"The other half of your fee," she said, her voice barely audible.

"And what was that stuff in bed this morning, a bonus?"

She drew back as if I'd slapped her. Her mouth was open and she shook her head as if she couldn't believe I could say such a thing.

"Sorry," I said. "I didn't mean that. I'll just be leaving."

"Jacob, wait." She stood and put her hand on my arm. "I . . . I don't know what to think. I mean, about this morning, about us."

I said nothing.

"It would be easy for me to fall in love with you, Jacob, and I'm not certain that's such a good thing."

"Thanks."

"You know what I mean."

"No, I don't," I said.

"I mean, I . . . I think I'm still in love with Charles."

"I see."

"I feel something for both of you and it's . . . confusing."

"Life's full of little decisions."

"There's no need for sarcasm." Her voice was brittle.

"No, I suppose not." Sex had definitely changed our attitudes toward each other. "Look, I have to ask you something and I don't want you to get upset about it."

"What is it?"

"Did Soames know Meacham was staying in the Frontier Hotel?"

"No. How could he?" She looked puzzled.

"You didn't tell him?"

"Of course not. He doesn't even know I hired you."

"You're certain?"

"Yes," she said, irritation creeping into her voice. "Why are you asking me this?"

"Because it's possible Soames hired someone to kill Meacham, assuming—"

"What?"

"—assuming he took Meacham's threats more seriously than you thought."

"You're accusing *Charles*?" Her face had gone white, giving stark contrast to the bruise around her eye.

"I'm only speculating."

"No," she said, shaking her head. "How can you think . . . my God." She turned her back and stepped to the window.

I stood behind her and put my hands on her shoulders. She

tensed but didn't move away. Her hair shone more reddish than brown in the reflected sunlight, and the sweet scent of it stirred memories of this morning.

"I have to go," I said. "I'll see you."

She nodded, ever so slightly.

I left.

When I got to Caroline Lochemont's house, there was a beat-up green Chevy parked in front. I'd seen it before, pulling away from the curb the last time I was here. I knocked, and Caroline opened the door. She frowned, which was too bad, because she had a face meant for smiling.

"Am I the only one around here with a job?" she said. "You might as well come in."

I followed her inside.

Charles Soames was sitting in the living room with the seedy-looking character who belonged to the green Chevy. There was a small pile of empty beer cans on the coffee table between them.

"Hey, if it ain't that legendary private eye Lomax," Soames said, overly cheerful from his breakfast cereals—barley and hops. "Grab a seat and have a beer. We've been talking over old times down in Canon."

"Disgusting," Caroline said and went in the kitchen. I heard water running and the clink of dishes.

"This here's Willy Two Hawks, my next-door neighbor for about the last eight years."

"Pleased to meetcha," Willy said, his voice raspy from years of talking tough. Or maybe in his spunkier days he'd been kicked in the throat. He was a small man in his fifties, with the mahogany skin and high cheekbones of a Native American. He wore blue jeans, cowboy boots, a plaid shirt, and a faded Levi's jacket. His eyes were hidden behind glasses dark enough for a blind man, and his goatee was made up of exactly twenty-seven hairs.

I pulled a Bud out of the broken six-pack, popped the top, and sat in a Windsor chair. It jabbed me from every angle.

"Zack Meacham is dead," I said, "but I guess you already knew that."

Soames glanced at Willy, and Willy's eyebrows rose above his pitch-black shades.

"Is that a fact," Soames said flatly.

"Somebody shot him last night in his hotel room."

"Serves the asshole right," Soames said. His grin was tight and his lips were moist from morning brew. I tried to picture this man as once having managed the largest jewelry store in the city. I couldn't. Prison had changed him too much.

"I thought you could tell me something about it," I said. "Like the name of the man who pulled the trigger."

"Hey, it wasn't me. Caroline can vouch for that."

Caroline came out of the kitchen. "Vouch for what?"

"Nothing," Soames said.

She shrugged. "I'm going to work now, Grandpa." No one paid her any attention.

"I saw the killer, Soames. Your Latino friend in the leather jacket."

Caroline stopped by the front door and faced us. Soames sensed her there and turned in his seat.

"You go on to work, Caroline," he said.

"But, Grandpa, that—"

"I said, go on!" he yelled.

Caroline recoiled as if struck, a look of surprise on her face. She wasn't used to being yelled at. She glared at us all and slammed the door on her way out.

"What about it, Soames?"

"What about what?"

"Who shot Meacham?"

"How the fuck should I know?"

"If you want me to call my sons," Willy said, "say the word and they'll toss this joker out on his ass."

"You know who shot Meacham," I said, ignoring Willy, "and so does your granddaughter."

"You leave her out of this."

"She's already in it. Now, you can talk to me or talk to the police. So far I haven't told them about you and Meacham."

Soames sat back in his chair and crossed his legs, ankle on knee. The skin showing beneath his trouser cuff was as white as his socks and lined with blue veins.

"You don't know nothing about me and him," he said.

"I know enough. He was threatening to kill you to avenge his brother's death."

"Who told you that?"

"Who do you think?" I said, keeping my voice neutral and my eyes on his. The woman I slept with last night, that's who. "Your girlfriend."

"Helen . . ." He looked surprised.

"She hired me to find Meacham so she could pay him to leave you alone."

Willy snorted, facing Soames. "This is how you handle things now?"

"I told her to forget about Meacham," Soames said to us both. "This guy was nothing but mouth."

"Helen didn't think so," I said.

"Helen didn't think so," Willy said, mimicking me. "Jesus, Charley, you're letting a woman take care of business."

"I never told her to—"

Willy snorted again and stood. "I got to take a leak." He bumped my leg on his way out to show me how tough he was.

"You and your granddaughter know this Latino dude," I said to Soames. "Now, cut the crap and give me his name."

"We don't know his name," Soames said, avoiding my eyes.

"I've never even seen him, but it sounds like the guy Caroline thinks has been following her."

"Following? Since when?"

"I don't know, a few weeks, a month. She's spotted him a couple of times."

"And neither of you know who he is?"

He shook his head no.

I think I believed him.

"Look," he said, leaning forward and lowering his voice so Willy couldn't hear him from the bathroom, "Caroline's a sweet kid and I never meant for her to get involved with these people."

"Which people?"

"Willy and his sons and Meacham and whoever this grease-ball is."

"And Helen Ester?"

"Helen's different," he said, challenging me. "The others, they just want one thing."

"What?" As if I didn't know.

"Hell, man, they think I can lead them to the Lochemont jewels."

Soames finished his beer and crushed the aluminum can.

"I'll tell you something else," he said. "It's the same thing I told all the others and not one of them believes me and I'm telling you now it's the goddamn truth. Rueben Archuleta got away with the jewels."

"You're sure about that?" I asked, not believing him for a minute.

"You bet I am."

"I suppose you even know where he is."

Soames smiled broadly.

"Oh, he's hiding out, Lomax, he's hiding out *real* good."

13

I left Soames with his pal Willy and headed home. Along the way, I was speculating why the Latino dude had been following Caroline Lochemont, when I noticed a tan Ford following me.

I sped up and changed lanes a few times, and the Ford maintained its distance. The guy kept several cars between us, so I couldn't get a good look at his face. If it was my Latin friend, I doubted he'd try anything in the bright light of day or on a busy street. On the other hand, I wished I had a gun—the cops had the .38, and my other piece was at home.

I continued east on Alameda, and when I slowed to turn left on Lincoln, the Ford got close enough for me to see the driver's face.

He was somebody new—definitely blond, apparently skinny, and probably tall. Maybe a friend of the Latino. Or maybe a friend of Dalrymple. Whether cop or enemy or both, he tagged along behind me on Lincoln and then on Seventh until I got a block from home, and then he was gone.

When I opened the door to my apartment, I got another little surprise: The place had been ransacked.

It had probably happened last night when I'd been with Helen. The furniture was slashed and the stuffing was pulled out, like the entrails of butchered animals. My visitor had emptied the kitchen cabinets and piled the contents on the counter and table. Piled, not dumped, so he'd been quiet about it. Everything I kept in the medicine cabinet was now in the bathroom sink, the mirror had been taped and broken and peeled off, and the tank top and toilet float lay on the tile floor. The clothes in my closet were pulled off the hangers, the dresser drawers were upended on the carpet, and the mattress and box springs were ripped apart.

But the safe was still locked.

It was a hundred-pound steel cube, two feet on a side, wedged in the corner of the closet. The only things now in it were a few thousand bucks in emergency cash and my other gun, a .357 magnum with a four-inch barrel. I strapped on the shoulder holster and locked the safe.

Then I heard someone. I unholstered the magnum and peeked around the corner.

Detectives Healey and O'Roarke stood in the middle of the mess that had once been my living room.

"Knock knock," Healey said when he saw me.

I came out of hiding.

"Nice place," the Asian O'Roarke said, moving a clump of chair stuffing with the toe of his shiny loafer. I believed those were the first words I'd heard him utter.

"It's the cleaning lady's day off," I explained.

"Take off your gun and put on your coat," Healey told me. "Lieutenant Dalrymple wants you downtown."

"What for?"

"Let's go," O'Roarke said. I think I liked him better mute.

Dalrymple was waiting for us in his office. He closed a folder, put his beefy freckled hands on the desk, and leaned back in his chair. He wore a dark blue suit, a limp white shirt, and a tie with a tiny badge for a stickpin. He looked as solid as a building and as patient as a bureaucracy. The scar on his face stood out like a flag.

"Sit down," he said, and I did, in the straight wooden chair facing his desk.

Healey closed the door and he and O'Roarke stood close behind me. It all reminded me of a movie I'd seen starring John Garfield. Or was it Garfield the cat?

"Do you own a nine-millimeter automatic pistol?"

"No. Why?"

"That's what the lab people say you used on Zack Meacham."

"I didn't kill Meacham. You've read my statement."

"We'd like to search your office and apartment for the gun, in case you were stupid enough to keep it."

"There's no gun. And if you want to search, get a warrant."

"No problem," Dalrymple said and nodded at O'Roarke, who left without a word.

"Somebody's already been through his apartment, Lieutenant," Healey said. He described my place to him.

Dalrymple raised his thin pale eyebrows, furrowing his forehead with thick ridges.

"Sounds like Lloyd Fontaine's office, doesn't it?" he asked me.

"Does it?"

"What do you suppose they were after, Lomax?"

"My baseball cards?"

Healey must have smiled behind me, because Dalrymple glared at him. He looked back at me and worked the muscles in his jaw.

"There's some connection between you and Zack Meacham and Lloyd Fontaine and I want to know what it is."

"I don't know what you're talking about, Lieutenant," I said.

"I'm talking about you cooperating and me giving you a chance to cop a plea."

"What?"

"Your arraignment's tomorrow, Lomax. We've already notified your attorney. The D.A. feels we've got a good case for second-degree murder, but if you confess now, he'll knock it down to manslaughter."

"What case? You can't be serious."

"I'm deadly serious." He looked it, too, but then he usually did.

"You've got nothing, Dalrymple. You've got no hard evidence, you've got no witnesses, you've—"

"We've got witnesses who saw you enter the hotel before any shots were fired and witnesses who saw you run down the fire escape after the shots were fired. We've got your own admission that you went up there angry at Meacham and that you were alone with him in his room with a loaded gun."

"He was already dead, for chrissake, and I was shooting it out with the guy on the fire escape. There are windows all along that side of the building. *Somebody* must have seen it."

"We've talked to everyone in that hotel," Dalrymple said. "Some of them saw nothing and some of them saw one man running down the fire escape, but nobody, and I mean *nobody*, saw *two* men on the fire escape."

He smiled suddenly, savagely, as if he'd just seen some weakness in my face.

"You've got no weapon," I said. "Meacham was killed with a nine-millimeter and we both know that without that gun you may as well forget going to trial."

"Ah, yes, as for the gun . . ." Dalrymple's thick fingers kicked around the papers on his desk. "We had your girlfriend, Helen Ester, up here first thing this morning and she told us all about it. Here," he said, reading from a paper, or maybe just pretending to. " 'He had two guns, one tucked in his belt. It was a flat black gun.' Those are her words, 'flat black gun.' Sounds like an automatic, doesn't it?"

"Let me see that."

"Sorry, Lomax, official police document. But believe me, it's signed and witnessed."

I didn't believe him, because he would have shown it to me. He was lying to make me squirm.

"I know why you shot Meacham," he said, "and I can't say I blame you."

"I didn't shoot him."

"He beat up your girlfriend and then he, let's see, how did she put it?" Dalrymple shuffled through more papers on his desk. "Oh, yeah, 'He hit me several times and then forced me to have sex with him.' "

"She never told you that."

"She sure did, and in detail, too. Fucked and sodomized."

He raised his eyebrows, waiting for me to comment. I clamped my jaws and said nothing.

"I suppose Meacham just couldn't resist the temptation," he went on. "You know, the man was probably horny as hell and he's up in his hotel room with a fine-looking broad and she won't put out. I mean, I saw her up close, Lomax, and she's got it all, nice set of tits, fine-looking ass, good, strong legs. Who knows, maybe she even went down on him first and then changed her mind when he wanted more. What do you think?"

I stood up and Healey put a hand on my shoulder. I shrugged him off. Dalrymple just sat there, smiling.

"Temper, temper," he said. "Is this how you felt when you went up after Meacham?"

"Are we through here?"

"Only if you're stupid," Dalrymple said. "We can say it like this: You struggled with Meacham and the gun went off. Manslaughter. Simple. In two or three years, you'll be out on parole. Of course, you might have a tough time finding clients."

"Shove it."

"Have it your way," he said. "See you in court."

Healey and I went out the door just as O'Roarke was approaching with the search warrant.

"You can ride with us if you want," Healey said, his tone as sad as his face.

"Thanks."

"The lieutenant has it in for you personally, doesn't he?"

"You noticed."

We drove first to my office, and I stood around and watched them do a thorough job of searching for a gun that wasn't there. Then we drove to my ruined apartment, where they carefully sifted through the mess in each room. They asked me to open the safe.

Healey showed O'Roarke the envelope with my cash.

"You should put that in a savings account," O'Roarke said.

"Hey, thanks for the tip."

14

When Healey and O'Roarke left, I phoned Helen Ester. I wanted to know exactly what she'd told Dalrymple. No answer. And there was also no answer at Caroline Lochemont's house.

Downstairs, Vaz was busy transcribing Fontaine's coded journal—with the help of the dead man's letter to Gloria Archuleta. I told him about my apartment and asked if he'd seen anybody suspicious hanging around or if he'd noticed a tan Ford in the neighborhood.

"I heard some noises upstairs last night, Jacob, but I thought it was you." He shrugged. "Sorry."

"Forget it," I said. Then I gave him a full account of my recent adventures at the Frontier Hotel. Vaz was most interested in my description of the shooter.

"How old was he?" he asked.

"Hard to tell exactly. Midthirties."

"Could he have been older?"

"I suppose. If he's been keeping himself in shape. Why?"

"It is possible, then."

He shuffled through the old newspaper clippings, then pulled one out—a faded photograph of a young Chicano male with black, wavy hair.

"Rueben Archuleta," Vaz said. "He was twenty-one years old

when he disappeared after the Lochemont robbery, which would make him forty-one today."

I looked closer at the picture. There was a vague resemblance to my Latino friend, but it was mostly the black hair and dark complexion.

"I don't know, Vaz."

"But it's *possible*, yes?"

"It's possible," I said.

"Jacob, I believe the man who killed Meacham and Fontaine is none other than Rueben Archuleta. Everything fits, if you accept the fact that Archuleta got away *without* the jewels."

"How so?" I asked, but I was beginning to see his point.

"Let's say when he got away, he left Soames behind to stash the jewels."

"Let's say."

"Then Archuleta would have to hide out, maybe even from his wife and children, as Fontaine's letter implies, and wait for twenty years while Soames sat in prison. When Soames was released, Archuleta followed. Maybe he approached him, maybe not. In any case, Archuleta soon bumped into the nosy and perhaps greedy private eye Lloyd Fontaine. Fontaine was a nuisance, or more, a threat if he recognized Archuleta. So he had to be killed."

"And Meacham?" I asked, already knowing and beginning to agree. Or maybe I just wanted to believe in buried treasure.

"When Meacham began threatening Soames, he was threatening Archuleta's chance for the gems. Too bad for Mr. Meacham."

"I suppose. But you know, Soames swore to me that Archuleta made off with the satchel."

"Then he's lying."

I didn't argue.

* * *

Idaho Springs is less than an hour's drive from Denver along Interstate 70. The trip took considerably more time in 1859, when gold was discovered near the present townsite, at the confluence of Chicago Creek and Clear Creek. The rush was on, and folks didn't mind bouncing over ruts or stubbing their frostbitten toes as long as they had a chance to strike it rich. Even Horace and Augusta Tabor stopped there briefly seeking fortune, but they moved on because by then the pickings were already slim. It was some years later when Tabor hit silver near Leadville, and a few years more before he divorced the stern and stern-faced Augusta in favor of the lovely and fun-loving Baby Doe. Sometime in there he bought her a nice necklace.

My ears popped from the altitude just before I turned into town. I cruised down Miner Street past some old houses and saloons and storefronts, then turned left on Fifteenth Street and parked at the curb.

The *Gazette* was housed in a dull red brick building that had been built when Grover Cleveland was president—the first time. The woman behind the counter may have voted for him. Her hair was as white and crusty as old snow, and the rhinestones in the frames of her glasses sparkled like ice. According to the nameplate, she was Gladys Hicks.

"I'd like to speak to Mr. Witherspoon," I said, handing her my card.

She sighed, rose with some effort, then shuffled through the room toward the back. That left me alone with a young woman buzzing away on an IBM Selectric and a young guy polishing the lens of his Nikon. Lois and Jimmy.

Gladys returned and told me to go on back to the editor's office, which happened to be the only office back there.

H. R. Witherspoon was middle-aged and wiry, with dark brown hair, short on the sides and curly on top. The sleeves of his white shirt were rolled up past lean forearms corded with tendon and muscle. He had a number-two pencil wedged behind his ear and small lump of snuff stuffed inside his bottom lip. He sat in the aftermath of a paper blizzard. His desk—in fact, the entire office—was inundated with piles of newsprint, drifts of typed sheets, and a packed base of bound books. He held up my card like a rare square snowflake.

"Private eye, huh? Pleased to meet you, Mr. Lomax."

We shook. He had a grip like a pair of pliers.

"Call me Jacob," I said.

"And you can call me Harry. Sit down, sit down."

I did, after moving a stack of folders from the chair to the floor.

"What can I do for you?" he asked, and spit in a metal wastebasket at his side.

"I'm a friend of Vassily Botvinnov. He phoned—"

"Sure, the gentleman who called about the photographs."

There were green sparks in Witherspoon's brown eyes and laugh lines etched deep in his face. They gave the impression that he knew more than he'd ever reveal.

I handed him the contact sheet and the four eight-by-tens. Witherspoon put on a pair of glasses with round lenses and steel frames and examined the photos, front and back. He shook his head and smiled.

"I'll be damned," he said and spit in the basket.

"Did you take those pictures?" I asked.

"I sure did."

"Do you remember when?"

"I do now. That call from your friend got me thinking, so I dug around until I found the file." He slapped his hand down on a fat folder amid the debris on his desk. "The Lochemont jewelry heist."

"You're familiar with the robbery?"

"Hell, yes. I covered it for the *Gazette*. I was a reporter back then. *The* reporter, actually. Also photographer, printer's devil, and janitor. It was just me and Stan Downey then. He was publisher and editor, and his wife handled the advertising, and his daughter—well, I *married* her."

"Do you remember giving those photos to Lloyd Fontaine?"

"Sure do," he said. "It was right after the Lochemont robbery. But say, how did you come by them?"

"Fontaine gave them to me a week and a half ago, along with a journal and some old news clippings. Later that night he was murdered."

"You don't say," Witherspoon said, his eyes flashing green sparks.

"He'd been tortured and his office had been ransacked. The next night I got a taste of the same." I described my first encounter with the Latino—and then my second, at Meacham's hotel.

"Zack Meacham murdered. I'll be damned."

Witherspoon opened his Lochemont folder and flipped through the pages. A lot of them were pasted with news clippings.

"You know," he said, "I was in the courtroom the day Meacham swore he'd kill Charles Soames when Soames got out of prison. And what do you know? Soames gets out and it's Meacham who gets knocked off. That's quite a coincidence, if I believed in them, which I don't."

"Neither do I," I said.

"Can I ask you something? How did you get mixed up with Zack Meacham?"

"I was hired to find him by a friend of Soames."

Witherspoon spit in the basket. "Another coincidence?"

"The only coincidence is that Lloyd Fontaine knew us all."

"I see."

"Tell me about these photos, Harry."

"Well, of course I didn't know it at the time, but it was about a week before the Lochemont robbery. I was driving back to the paper after covering a house fire and I saw a cop pull over some guy who'd drifted through a stop sign, and pretty soon the two of them are yelling at each other. That's news in this town, and I had a few frames left in the camera, so I started snapping away. Anyway, the driver turned out to be Ed Teague. Like I say, I didn't know it at the time."

"When did you find out?"

"When Lloyd Fontaine came up here after the robbery. He was an investigator for the insurance company . . . but you already knew that. Anyhow, he had police photos of all the people involved in the heist—Soames, Buddy Meacham, Ed Teague, Robert Knox, and Rueben Archuleta. He must have questioned half the people in town. Teague had been seen by a few people before the heist, since he'd been staying down the road at the Six-and-Forty Motel. I recognized his mug shot when Fontaine showed it to me. That's when I realized what I had, and I gave the photos to Fontaine."

"You've got a good memory, Harry. That was a long time ago."

"You'd remember, too, if you'd been up here then," he said. "It was a regular carnival after Soames wandered out of the trees. Before, during, and after his trial, people came from all over, swarming through these mountains looking for the lost Lochemont jewels. Of course, it wasn't just the gems that caused the treasure fever, it was the Baby Doe necklace. History, you know. That piece was rumored to have been the last luxury Tabor sprang for before the bottom fell out of the silver market in 1893, and it was the first thing he supposedly sold off to start paying his creditors. But I digress. As I was saying, this town was a circus." He grinned. "The hardware store sold every pick and shovel they had, and the locals were peddling treasure maps on the street corners."

"You're kidding."

He winked and said, "Nope. I sold a few myself. The hottest item was a U.S.G.S. quad map with a dashed line showing Soames's probable route through the mountains and big X's marking the most likely spots to dig. We still get a few folks up here looking around for those jewels."

"After all these years?"

"I'll tell you something," he said. He raised his head so that the light glared off his glasses and hid his eyes. "If the robbers hid that satchel of gems in the hills like some people think, there's a damn good chance it's still up here."

"But you said the area was swarming with treasure hunters."

"Hell, you can lose *people* up there, much less a small black satchel. And if the robbers didn't bury it, they had about a hundred mine shafts and tunnels to hide it in."

"You may be right."

"Maybe, hell." A faint flush had risen to his face. He liked the idea of buried treasure, too. "I'll tell you something else: If those gems *had* been found, we'd have heard about it. No treasure hunter can strike it rich and keep quiet. At least none that I've bumped into."

"I guess," I said. "Tell me, Harry, do you have the negatives of these photos?"

"I might still have them. Why?"

"I'd like to blow up these two frames, the ones I think Fontaine had with him when he died."

Witherspoon checked the contact sheet with an eight-power magnifier. "If this wasn't in such bad shape," he said, "I could make blowups from it. I'll look around for the negatives."

"Thanks. I appreciate all your help."

"Anytime," he said. "And if you want a guided tour, let me know. I can show you the motel room where Teague bought it and the site of the infamous murder shack. The shack's long gone, but some people say the house they built there is haunted. How's that for local color?"

"Maybe next time."

We shook hands and I walked out through the open front room. Lois and Jimmy and Gladys Hicks were still poised, waiting for news to break.

15

When I got down from the mountains, I stopped by my office to check the answering machine. Just one message: Abner Greenspan telling me to meet him in court tomorrow morning. If Helen Ester were there, too, we could probably get this thing cleared up before it went any further. But there was still no answer at her hotel number. I tried the Lochemont house and Caroline answered.

"She was here, but she left with my grandfather." Caroline didn't like the idea. Maybe I didn't either.

"Where did they go?"

"How should I know?" she snapped. "Out on a date. He thinks . . ."

"What."

"He thinks he's in love," she said and hung up.

Caroline sounded jealous. And why shouldn't she? She'd been the only one displaying love for Soames all the years he was in prison, and as soon as he gets out, his old flame shows up and turns his head.

I locked up and drove to the disaster area I called home. It took me all day to clean up the mess and put everything back where it belonged. The chairs, couch, mattress, and box springs looked like a total loss, so I dragged them all into the middle of the living room, like a huge pile of kindling. That night I slept on the floor on blankets and dreamed that Charles Soames and

Helen Ester were dancing naked around a large bonfire in the next room.

In the morning I called the agent for my renter's insurance, and then a guy at a rubbish removal company who said he'd have a truck and a couple of boys out there this morning. I told him to get the key from Mr. Botvinnov.

I went downstairs and explained things to Vaz, then headed out for my day in court.

Greenspan met me inside the main entrance of the City and County Building.

"You're late," he said.

"So sue me."

We walked through the high, wide, echoing, block-long hallway toward our designated courtroom.

"Have you talked to anybody?" I asked.

"Dalrymple and the assistant D.A."

"What'd they say?"

"Not much, but they seem fairly confident. Also, I get the impression Dalrymple hates your guts."

"He does."

"Why?"

"It's a long story."

The big room was three-quarters full of people waiting to have their lives altered or waiting to make money on the alterations. Presiding over it all was a middle-aged black man, who banged his gavel and kept the flow of people moving before him as efficiently as an auctioneer at a stock show. Greenspan and I sat in a wooden pew and waited our turn. I saw Dalrymple in the front row. He didn't need to be here, but this was too entertaining for him to miss. Helen Ester was not in sight.

"The court calls Jacob Lomax," the bailiff said.

Greenspan and I stood before the bench. Standing to our right was Bert Krenshaw, district attorney. I'd met him once before, and he seemed like a nice guy.

Krenshaw spoke. "We charge Jacob Lomax with second-degree murder in the death of Zachary Meacham, and we recommend bail be set at two hundred thousand dollars." So much for Mr. Nice Guy.

Krenshaw outlined his evidence against me. It didn't seem like much to me, but it did to the judge, and he was ready to send me to trial. Greenspan requested, and was granted, a preliminary hearing. The judge set the date on October second, one week from today. Then Greenspan requested bail reduction, explaining to the judge that I had been a trusted member of the community for many years, that I had served with honor on the Denver police department, and that I was now in service as a private detective. He could have left off the PI part. However, the judge did drop the bail to fifty grand, which was still a hell of a lot, on the condition that I swore not to leave his jurisdiction—namely, the state of Colorado—before my hearing. I so swore. Then Greenspan asked me offhandedly if I had fifty thousand dollars in property to put up.

"What, are you kidding?"

He gave me a withering look. "Then a friend who does?"

"You?"

Greenspan frowned. He didn't think that was funny.

"We'll call a bondsman," Greenspan told the judge.

I made the call. Bondsmen generally charge a client 10 percent of the bail, which in this case would mean a cash outlay on my part of five thousand dollars. But this guy owed me a favor and I talked him down to a thousand, which was still a thousand more than I was counting on, since he knew damn well I wasn't going to run. He said he'd be right over.

I looked for Greenspan and found him in an anteroom talking and joking with Krenshaw. This was great fun. Krenshaw nodded at me and walked out.

Greenspan gestured toward the retreating prosecutor. "He says Lieutenant Dalrymple is really pushing him on this."

" 'This' meaning me."

"Correct," he said. "What is it between you two?"

"It's a long story."

Greenspan checked his poker-chip-thin black-and-gold watch.

"How about the condensed version?" he said. "Seriously, Jake, I want to know about this. Maybe I can use it."

"I doubt it."

"Regardless."

"It happened about nine, ten years ago," I said. "Dalrymple and I were in uniform together and—"

"Seriously? I didn't know that."

I nodded. "Dalrymple had been a cop for about four years— and he was one gung-ho mother—when I was a rookie. MacArthur started when I did, too."

"That I knew," Greenspan said. "And I have a feeling if he were handling this, we'd be home free."

"No doubt."

"But anyway," he said.

"But anyway, Dalrymple and I were working the Five Points area and we took a call on a possible gang rape. Some guy had seen three men pull a woman into an abandoned building. Just as we hit the front door, these three black dudes, teenagers, came busting out, knocking us on our butts. One guy had a razor, and when they ran over us, he slashed Dalrymple across the face."

"Jesus. That's how he got the scar."

'That's how. The slasher and one kid took off down the street with Dalrymple chasing them, blood pumping out of his face. I chased the other kid into a dead-end alley. When he turned around he was pointing a gun. I was about to put a slug in his chest, when he dropped the gun and raised his hands. By the time I'd cuffed him and got him back to the car, smoke was sifting through the boarded windows and pouring out the door-way of the building, which the three dudes had torched to destroy the evidence. I called for fire trucks and backup for Dalrymple, who still wasn't back, then went inside, looking for the rape victim. She was just a kid, maybe thirteen, gagged and tied to the radiator pipes. It was a good thing I found her right away, because the building was going up fast."

"What about Dalrymple?"

"He caught up to the other two guys about six blocks later in the backyard of a house and shot them both dead."

"Jesus. They both had guns?"

I shook my head no. "The only weapons found were a razor on one guy and a pocketknife on the other. They'd been trying to break in the back door of the house—their house, it turns out. When Dalrymple ordered them to stop, he says they turned and attacked him."

"Is that what happened?"

"There were no witnesses," I said. "But I believed Dalrymple. He may be hard, but he's not a killer. Trouble was, he wanted me to lie for him."

"About what?"

"He and a couple of his buddies wanted me to back him up on something he'd told the internal affairs guys—namely, that when those black kids ran over us, at least two of them had been carrying guns. One of Dalrymple's pals went so far as to hint that if I said I'd seen another gun, they'd *find* a gun. But the only gun I'd seen was the one pointing at me in the alley, and I stuck to the truth. It didn't help Dalrymple any. I guess I was too honest, or maybe just too new."

"You did the right thing, Jake."

"I suppose," I said. "In any case, there was a lot of flak from the black community—a white cop killing two black kids in their own backyard. To keep a lid on things, the department suspended Dalrymple for six months without pay and gave him an official reprimand. And to make things worse, at least from his point of view, I got a citation for bravery for saving the girl and capturing an armed rapist."

Greenspan shook his head. "Considering his suspension and all, I'm surprised he made lieutenant."

"Don't be," I said. "When he got back in uniform, he worked twice as hard as before, which was about eight times harder than anybody else. Kept his record as clean as a nun's bib. In fact, if it hadn't been for that one incident, he'd probably be a captain by now."

"And he blames you for that?"

"I guess I'm convenient."

The bondsman arrived—a squirrely-looking dude named Hensey. He was prepared to put up my bond, but he wanted his thousand bucks.

"It's at home," I said.

"Hey, Jake, come on."

"You come on."

"Look," Hensey said, lowering his voice, darting his watery blue eyes here and there as if we were surrounded by Gestapo, making Greenspan sigh in irritation, "I shouldn't even be taking less than five grand."

"Yeah, yeah." I looked at Greenspan. "Uh, Abner?"

"Christ almighty," Greenspan said.

"Hey, I'm good for it. Besides, didn't I give you a nice rolltop desk just the other day?"

"Having that desk restored is costing me three thousand dollars."

"Oh."

"Christ."

He wrote Hensey a check, and ten minutes later we were outside.

"You can mail me a check for the thousand," Greenspan said as we descended the long concrete steps. "I'll see you in a week at the hearing. Try to stay out of trouble."

"I'm not just going to sit still."

Greenspan stopped and grabbed my arm. "Meaning what?"

"Obviously, Dalrymple and Krenshaw aren't looking past me to find Meacham's killer."

"So what? That has nothing to do with how we'll proceed with your defense."

"Whatever. I intend to question the residents of the Frontier Hotel."

"I'll get someone to do that," he said.

"*I'll* do it."

"You can't conduct your own investigation."

"Why not?"

"Because you can't possibly be objective."

"Objectivity is overrated."

"Look, Jake, if you go kicking around over there, you'll just get frustrated and probably intimidate a witness or maybe step on a cop's toes and Dalrymple will bust you for obstructing justice and the judge will raise your bail and—"

"I'm only going to talk to them, Abner."

"As your attorney I would advise against it."

"I'll call you in a few days," I said.

16

I finally reached Helen Ester at Caroline's house. I realized I was starting to get defensive, because there was nothing gentle about my mood or my tone of voice.

"Jacob, I've been trying to reach you," she said.

"What a coincidence."

"The police have been hounding me day and night. I think they're trying to pin Zack Meacham's murder on *you*."

"Funny you should mention that. I'm coming over there now to talk to you."

"Ah, well, can we get together later tonight instead? Charles and I were—"

"Now."

She put her hand over the mouthpiece and I heard her muffled voice. Then she said to me, "All right, if you insist."

Twenty minutes later I was parked in front of Caroline Lochemont's house, right behind the beat-up green Chevy of Willy Two Hawks. There was a rusty brown pickup across the street by the small park. Two guys, both about Caroline's age, sat in the truck and nipped wine from a bottle in a paper sack. The driver looked enough like Willy Two Hawks to be his son. The passenger had similar features—brown skin, flat nose, high cheekbones—but he was as big as a bear, with long, black braids that fell forward across his shoulders. They watched me get out of the car and go up the walk.

They were still watching when Caroline Lochemont opened the door. She glanced nervously past me toward the truck, then led me into the living room.

"Hello, Jacob," Helen said. She sat on the couch with Soames—too close to him, I thought. Willy Two Hawks slouched in the Windsor chair. He nodded at me and smiled from behind his coal-dark shades.

"Have a seat," Soames said, "but make it snappy. We were on our way out the door when you called."

"What've you been telling the police?" I said, standing in front of Helen.

"What do you mean, Jacob? I told them what happened that night."

"Plus a few extra lies."

"What do you mean?"

"You know damn well."

"Don't be talking to her like that."

"Shut up, Soames."

"Why, you son of a bitch . . ."

He started off the couch, and Helen grabbed his arm. "It's all right, Charles," she said.

"Get out of my house," he told me.

I ignored him. "What about it, Helen?"

"Get the fuck out or I'm calling the cops," Soames said.

"Jacob, I swear to you, I only told the police what I know. You went into the hotel to talk to Meacham and then I heard shots. That's all."

"Did you hear what I said?" Soames asked.

"Go ahead and call the cops," I told him. "I'm sure they'll be interested to know that before Meacham died he was making threats to a convicted murderer."

Soames started to speak, then clamped his jaws shut. The veins in his neck stood out like small, purple vipers. I turned to Helen.

"You told Dalrymple I had an automatic with me that night."

"Automatic? I don't understand."

"Don't play dumb. 'A flat black gun,' you called it. An automatic pistol."

"Jacob, no, I . . . I never said anything like that."

She looked frightened. Lomax the meanie, picking on a little girl. Soames sensed it and held her hand.

"What's he talking about, babe?"

I didn't like him calling her babe.

"Meacham was shot with a nine-millimeter automatic," I said, "and the cops haven't found the gun. Without it, they have practically nothing to make a case against me—nothing, that is, unless an eyewitness swears she saw me carry such a gun up to Meacham's room."

"But I never—"

"They've *charged* me, goddammit. The D.A. wouldn't file unless he had something, and you're it."

"No." She shook her head. There were tears in her eyes.

"Dalrymple told me."

"No . . . no, why would he *say* that?"

I'd been coming on strong to make sure she wouldn't hold anything back. She wasn't lying; it was Dalrymple. Even though he had no case against me, he wasn't going to drop things, not yet, not until he'd made me squirm, or worse, took me to court with falsified evidence. His hatred went deeper than I'd imagined.

"Jacob, I . . . I swear." Tears ran down Helen's cheeks, leaving thin streaks of mascara.

"You satisfied now?" Soames said, disgust in his voice.

"Want me to call in my boys?" Willy said. He sat comfortably, looking amused. "They can take care of this joker."

Soames shook his head. "No. We're leaving now for the mountains, like we should've in the first place."

He stood and so did Helen. She wouldn't look at me. Soames

gave me a small shove as they stepped past. Willy slapped me on the arm, grinning like a thief.

"See you in the funny papers."

I watched through the front window as they walked away from the house. Soames and Helen climbed in the backseat of Willy's Chevy. Willy spoke to the two guys in the rusty pickup, then got in his car and drove off.

Caroline came into the living room.

"Oh. Where's my grandfather?"

"He left. They all left."

Outside, the bear with the braids got out of the pickup and crossed the street. He stood next to my Olds.

"You can leave, too," Caroline said.

"Your grandfather said they were going to the mountains. Where in the mountains?"

"As if you don't know."

"I don't, honest."

The big Indian was squatting down near the hood of the Olds. I could just see the top of his head.

"Please leave," she said.

"At least tell me where they went."

She cocked her head to the side, letting her short hair fall away from her face.

"You're not with them?" She nodded toward the front window. The big Indian was back in his pickup.

"Who, those guys?"

"Yes, those guys. Tom and Mathew Two Hawks. Willy's sons."

"The big one's his son, too?"

"That's Tom," she said, a trace of fear in her voice. "Now please leave."

"You know what I think?"

"I could care less," she said.

"I think you need a friend."

Her face softened for a brief moment, then she put on her little-tough-guy look. At least she tried to.

"Go away," she said. "Please."

When I got to my car, the two Two Hawks were still sitting across the street in their pickup. They looked pleased. And why not? My left front tire was flat—the valve stem had been cut off. I opened the trunk and got out the spare. It was dirty and mushy. I hoped there was enough air in it to drive on.

"Whatsa matter, pard, got a flat?" big Tom asked.

"Hey, you're not as dumb as you look."

I wrestled out the jack and hauled it around to the front of the car. Apparently Tom hadn't appreciated my remark, because he climbed out of the truck and crossed the street. The magnum was beginning to feel comfortable under my arm. I crouched down and shoved the jack beneath the front bumper.

Tom came up and stood over me. Loomed, actually. He wore cowboy boots, blue jeans with a silver-and-turquoise belt buckle, and a faded red chamois-cloth shirt. The shirt had enough cloth in it to cover the backseat of my Olds. It pinched Tom at his biceps and shoulders. He looked as strong as a grizzly. When he spoke, he sounded like one, too.

"How'd you like to change that tire with a broken arm?"

"Is that a rhetorical question?"

Tom blinked, then decided to stick with his original train of thought. "A lot of guys around here get flat tires, pard, plus broken arms and busted heads."

"Pop said take it easy, Tom," brother Mathew said from the truck.

I hoped Tom was listening, because I knew what was on his mind—my people had stolen the land from his people and shoved them around for a few hundred years and sooner or later his people were going to rise up and pay us all back and now was as good a time as any to get started.

"If I was you, I wouldn't come back here no more," Tom told me. "Stay away from Charles Soames."

I started loosening the lug nuts with the four-way wrench.

"Understand?"

"Do me a favor," I said. "Start jacking up the front end. That's it over there on your left."

I spun the wrench on the last few nuts while big Tom formulated his reply.

"Get up, asshole," he said.

I put down the wrench and reached under my jacket for the magnum. In no way did I want to tangle with this hombre. But Tom had other ideas, or else he'd seen my move, because before I knew it he'd grabbed my arm and collar, picked me off my feet, and slammed me into the car. I swung with my free left arm and nearly broke some knuckles on his chin, then stomped on his instep with my heel, but that just made him madder. He shifted his grip and got me in a bear hug, arms locked around my chest, the top of his head shoved into my face. If he didn't crack my ribs and squeeze all the air out of me, he'd surely break my spine. I hit him a few times in the side of the head, but he didn't seem to mind, and I would have shot him if I'd been able to get at my gun. The blood was rushing to my head and I wondered exactly which part of me would give out first and I made one last effort and jammed my thumbs deep into the nerves under his ears. Tom let out a war whoop and backed off. I gave him four stiff fingers in the larynx to shut him up. He squawked and gurgled and I fumbled with the shoulder holster and came face to face with brother Mathew, holding the four-way wrench like a stubby crucifix above his head.

He hit me with it.

17

I woke up in the street with Caroline kneeling beside me. She looked worried.

"Are you okay?"

"Are there any more Indians around?"

She helped me to my feet and walked me to her house. The inside of my head felt like the aftermath of a buffalo stampede.

"Shall I call the police?"

"No."

She led me to the bathroom and sat me on the toilet lid, then soaked a washcloth in cold water, wrung it out, and dabbed at a very tender spot on my head. When she rinsed out the washcloth in the sink, the water turned pink.

"Maybe you should see a doctor."

"I'm all right." I stood. "See? Besides, I get hit on the head every week or so."

She gave me a wry smile. "You act tough, but you're not."

"Don't tell anyone, okay? It would be bad for business."

I followed her out of the bathroom, then realized how seldom I get the chance to play on anyone's sympathies. It's a tough business, but somebody's got to do it.

"Gee, I do feel kind of dizzy," I said, holding my head. "Could I rest for just a minute?"

We sat in the kitchen.

"The warriors out there told me to stay away from your grandfather," I said.

She looked at me carefully.

"So you're really not with them, are you?"

"I'm not with anybody."

"Oh, yeah? What about Helen Ester?"

"Okay, maybe her. A little."

"You like her, don't you."

"A little."

"I think she's a sneaky, conniving bitch," Caroline said.

"Hey, don't sugarcoat it on my account."

"I mean it."

"I believe you," I said. "Where did she and Willy take your grandfather?"

Caroline stared out the kitchen window and gritted her teeth, showing me a small bunched muscle under her little gold hoop earring.

"They're looking for the jewels, aren't they?"

"All these . . . *people,*" she said to the window. "They're clinging to my grandfather like leeches because they think he knows where the jewels are."

"Does he?"

"Of *course* not." She looked at me, then quickly looked away. "I've told them and he's told them, but still they hang around. Why won't all of you just leave us alone?" There was a note of pleading in her voice.

"I'm not with them, remember? Look, Caroline, I don't give a damn about the jewels." Not much. "What I want is the man who killed Fontaine and Meacham, and it's in your best interest to help me find him."

"Why?"

"Because he's probably the man you saw following you. I'm pretty sure it's Rueben Archuleta."

"What?"

"That's right. He thinks your grandfather can lead him to the jewels, and he'll kill anyone who gets in his way. If your grandfather knows where they are, he could help me trap Archuleta by—"

"He doesn't know!" she shouted at me, then turned away, embarrassed at her outburst. When she spoke again, it was with restrained calm.

"Why does everyone refuse to believe that my grandfather was a victim?" she said. "He was *forced* to take part in that robbery, and he was lucky to escape with his life. But everyone's against him. They are now, and they were back then. I was too young to know then, but he's told me all about it. The police, the insurance company, even my other grandfather, Trenton, Sr.—they all wanted him to go to prison. It was like a conspiracy. And it's the same today. I feel like it's him and me against the world."

"What about your parents?"

"My parents," she said in disgust. "They want nothing to do with us, and that's fine with me. Do you know they didn't once visit him while he was locked away? Not once. They can both go to hell."

"I see."

"I wonder if you do," she said. "Don't you think if my grandfather knew where the jewels were, we'd have done something about it by now?"

"What *would* you do?"

She nearly smiled.

"Use them to take my grandfather far away from here and . . . but it doesn't matter. The Lochemont jewels will never be found."

She didn't much like the idea. Neither did I.

Outside, the front tire on the Olds was still flat. By the time I got it changed, my head was booming and I was dizzy. Maybe Caroline was right—I wasn't so tough after all.

* * *

When I left Caroline's house, I drove toward the office. I soon found I wasn't alone. Following me a dozen car lengths back was the blond guy in the tan Ford.

He tailed me all the way down Alameda, just like the first time I'd seen him. There was one difference, though: This time I had a gun. I crossed the South Platte River and turned north on Santa Fe. Two blocks later I swung into a warehouse parking lot and whipped the Olds around in a U-turn, ready to take the guy head-on.

No guy.

When I nosed out onto Santa Fe, the Ford was nowhere to be seen. I checked my mirror all the way to the office. The cute bastard stayed out of sight.

There was one message waiting on my machine: Wendy Apple said it was urgent that I call her right away. I let her phone ring a few dozen times before I called Fancy Dan's. She wasn't there, either. Then I remembered I hadn't returned Zack Meacham's house key. Maybe Wendy just wanted it back.

I locked up and drove to the Frontier Hotel. Nosferatu was still working the desk. He didn't act like he recognized me, but then he didn't lift his eyes above my neck. I flashed him something with my picture on it.

"Investigator Lomax," I said. "I want to ask you some questions about Zack Meacham."

"Who?"

"The guy who bled all over room twelve."

"Oh, him. I thought his name was Cliff." His eyes stayed glued to my neck.

"How many visitors did he have the night he died?"

"I already told you guys all I know."

"Tell me again. Unless you'd rather talk downtown."

His lips drooped over his canines.

"I don't want no trouble. Like I told you before, I don't remember."

"You don't remember if he had *any* visitors? Male or female?"

"No."

"Did anyone other than a guest enter the hotel that night?"

"I don't remember."

Some witness. Helen Ester, Rueben Archuleta, and I had all gone up to Meacham's room.

"I'm going upstairs to question a few people. Don't phone to warn them. If you do, I'll bust you for obstructing justice."

"I resent that," he said. "Besides, there's no phones."

In addition to Meacham's room, there were five rooms in the hotel that overlooked the fire escape and the alley.

At room number ten I met a snaggletoothed old geezer who was practically deaf and legally blind. See no evil, hear no evil.

Behind door number eight came the blast of a TV turned up full volume. "Come on, wheel! Come on, big money!" I pounded on the door. "Four hundred dollars!" I pounded again. "I'd like an ess, please!" I pounded some more. "Come on, big money!"

I moved on to door number six, which was answered by a short, fat Hispanic dude wearing an Army-green T-shirt that didn't quite cover his stomach. He was barefoot and holding a tall can of Miller Lite.

"¿Qué?"

I asked him about the shooting in twelve.

"Jew a cop, or wha'?"

"What do you think? Were you home that night?"

"Jew got a bahdge, or wha'?"

Bahdges? We don't need no stinking bahdges. "I asked you if you were home."

"Chure, man, I was here. An' I din' see nothin'."

He slammed the door in my face.

So did the black dude staying in four, when I couldn't produce a stinking badge.

Behind door number two I found the old hag who'd pointed me out on the street Tuesday night. She was still wearing her scummy hot pink bathrobe and carrying twenty pounds of steel curlers in her hair.

"Who are you?" she demanded.

So much for the witnesses for the prosecution.

"Investigator Lomax. I'd like to ask you some questions about the shooting the other night."

She smiled. Or it could have been a gas pain.

"Investigator, eh?" Her voice sounded like a chicken chewing sandpaper. "Where does the police department find all you big hunks?"

"Talent scouts."

She cackled. "Step right in, honey."

She held the door for me, then looked hopefully up and down the hall. Bad luck; no one saw a man enter her room.

"You wanna creamy?" she asked.

"I beg your pardon?"

"Candy," she said. There was an open box of chocolates by the bed. She'd been lying on top of the covers, watching TV. The sound was off. The people on the screen were spinning a large painted wheel. It made them all very excited.

"No, thanks."

"The other cops already asked me about that night."

"I'd like you to tell me again, miss."

"Why? And call me Winetta."

"Winetta. Just routine. And call me Jacob."

"Okay, Jacob," she said, and sat seductively on the edge of the bed. The springs groaned for me. She patted the colorless blanket next to her. "Take the load off."

"I would, but I might get ideas." Plus body lice.

"You men," she said and clucked her tongue and crossed her legs, exposing her calves, as white and veined as cave fish.

"What were you doing Tuesday night?"

"Oh, this and that. Watching the TV."

"Tell me what happened."

"I heard a bunch of shooting and then I heard somebody banging down the fire escape."

"Are you saying that all the shots came at once?"

"I guess."

"You didn't hear shots and *then* someone on the fire escape and *then* more shots?"

"No. I mean, I don't know." She squinted one eye at me.

"Did you look out the window?"

"What do you think? Sure I looked out the window."

"What did you see?"

"A man with a gun." She was still looking at me squinty-eyed.

"Just one man?"

"Yes. And he looked . . . he looked like . . ."

Oh, shit. "Like what?"

"Y-you."

She scooted across the bed.

"It *was* you! Y-you're no cop!" She bounced off the mattress and stumbled to the window, screaming, "Help! Police!"

I got the hell out.

Okay, so maybe Dalrymple had *one* witness.

18

The next morning, the fresh head lump created by Mathew Two Hawks had roused the old head bumps from ten days ago and was leading them in a war dance on my scalp. It was distracting enough that I hardly noticed being stiff and sore from sleeping on the floor. Somehow I forced myself out of the apartment to shop for furniture.

A couple of times I thought my rearview mirror picked up a tan Ford with a blond guy driving. But if he was my shadow from the other day, he was being careful and staying too buried in traffic for me to be certain.

It took me half the day to find some pieces that felt comfortable and looked like they wouldn't fall apart the first time I put my feet on them. After I beat the guy down on the price as much as I could, and still paid him what seemed like a hell of a lot, I stopped by Greenspan's to pay back the thousand bucks I owed him for the bondsman. My remaining bank account could now hide under a rat's ass.

When I got home, I dialed Wendy Apple. She answered on the second ring.

"I need to see you right away," she said.

"If it's about the key to Meacham's house, I can—"

"It's not about the key," she said. "It's . . . it's about Zack's murder."

Ten minutes later I was parked in front of Wendy's place on

Pearl Street, a few tree-lined blocks south of Speer Boulevard. The area featured old, solid brick houses and newer but not-so-solid apartments, the latter thanks in part to the designer of Wendy's building, who'd believed in straight lines, weak steel, and sandy concrete. When I climbed the stairs to the second floor and walked along the outside landing, the entire structure vibrated. It vibrated again when I knocked on Wendy's door.

"Thanks for coming," she said and let me in.

She wore a tight pink sweater and tight white pants and apparently nothing underneath. Her blond hair wasn't the only thing that bobbed when she walked into the living room.

The place had rental furniture and cheap carpeting. There was heavy dust in the corners. A fish tank gasped and gurgled beneath the window, and goldfish moved lethargically through suspended scum. I sat on a thin-cushioned couch with fake wooden arms, and Wendy curled up in a chair beneath a painting on black velvet—a matador performing a *veronica*.

"I'm sorry about your loss," I said. "I should have called you right after Zack died."

"That's okay." She smiled weakly. "The funeral was this morning. It was nice—I mean, lots of people and flowers and all. I stayed way in the back, though, because Zack's wife and kids were there. Ex-wife, I mean. I guess I didn't want to, well, embarrass Zack. Isn't that silly?"

She folded her hands in her lap and stared down at them, as if she were praying. When she spoke, it was so softly I barely heard her.

"I think my ex-boyfriend Vince Pesce killed Zack. I think he did it out of jealousy for . . . me."

Before I could explain to her that Rueben Archuleta had killed Meacham, I was suddenly overcome by that vague feeling I often get soon after I believe I have all the answers, that vague feeling called stupidity.

"Wendy, what does Vince look like?"

"What? Oh, he's cute—I mean, *I* think he is. And he's kind of tall, about like you. He's about your age, too."

"What color hair?"

"Black."

"Do you have a picture of him?"

"I'm pretty sure."

Wendy went to the bedroom and returned with a photo album. There were so few pictures in it that I found myself feeling sorry for her. She had only one of Vince. He was sporting a beard, black streaked with gray, and wearing dark glasses and a shit-eating grin. He stood dripping by a swimming pool, cradling Wendy in his arms. All I could tell for certain was that he had black hair, an olive complexion, and good muscle tone. He might or might not have been the Latino I chased from Meacham's hotel. The picture was months old, Wendy told me, and Vince had since shaved off his beard.

"How long have you known Vince?" I asked.

"Almost two years."

"Is he from Denver?"

"No. When I met him he said he'd just moved to town."

"Moved from where?"

Wendy chewed her plump lower lip.

"You know, I don't think he ever said. Is it important?"

"Maybe." Maybe he was from Santa Fe and had a wife named Gloria. "Where is Vince now?"

"I don't know," Wendy said.

"What makes you think he killed Meacham?"

"I . . . I'm not certain that he did."

"But there's a good chance, right?"

"Yes," she said and lovingly touched his photo. "Vince came over here last Saturday, the day after you'd been in Fancy Dan's talking to me about Zack. He was on edge about something, and when I asked him about it, he told me not to worry. He said in a few days everything would be just like it was before. Those were his words, 'just like it was before.' "

"Before what?"

"He didn't say, but I knew. Before I started seeing Zack."

"I see. Why did Vince come here?"

She frowned. "What do you mean?"

"Didn't you tell me you'd broken up with him?"

"Oh, well, broken up. I mean, I still went out with him sometimes, just mostly I went out with Zack. There's nothing wrong with seeing two guys, you know."

"Right." Maybe there was from the guy's point of view. "Have you seen Vince since then?"

"No, but he phoned here two nights ago, the night after Zack had been murdered. I was already in pretty bad shape—I mean, I'd just learned about Zack's death from the newspaper. It was all so . . . I don't know. I couldn't think straight, I couldn't even cry." Her eyes were wet now.

"Why did Vince call?"

"He said he was in trouble and he needed money, a lot of money. He knew I had almost four thousand dollars saved up, and he wanted me to send it to him. He sounded scared. I'd never heard him like that."

"Where did he want you to send the money?"

"He didn't say. He gave me a phone number and told me to get a cashier's check and then call him."

"And?"

"I said I would."

"Have you?"

"Sent the money? No, I . . . the more I thought about it, the more I thought Vince must have shot Zack and wants the money to run away. Then I thought, what if he wants the money to hire a good lawyer? Then I didn't know what to do. So I called you."

She looked at me with her eyebrows arched and her mouth partly open and waited for me to solve her problem. I probably would have in any case, even if it hadn't been my problem, too.

"What's the number Vince gave you?"

"I'll get it."

When she left the room, I looked closely at the photo of her and Vince and tried to picture him without the beard and sunglasses. He was the same size and apparent age as Rueben Archuleta, same color hair, same general features. But I couldn't tell for sure if he *was* Archuleta. I'd have to see him in person.

Wendy came back and handed me a cashier's check for thirty-nine hundred dollars and a scrap of paper with a string of numbers beginning with "(702)" and ending with "rm 309."

"How long will Vince be here?" I asked.

"I don't know. but I told him I'd call him in a few days, and that was two days ago. I'm afraid he's going to be mad. And he'll be even madder because he made me promise not to tell anyone."

"Don't worry, Wendy, he's not going to hurt you."

"I'm not worried about *that*. I just don't want to hurt *him*."

"Oh, yeah, right," I said. "Don't call him yet, okay, not till I've had a chance to find him."

"What are you going to do?"

"Talk to him." I held out her check. "And put this back in the bank."

Wendy shook her head no.

"Please give it to Vince."

"Wendy, how long has it taken you to save up this much?"

She gave a tiny shrug. "It doesn't matter. Vince needs it now more than I do."

"If Vince gets this, you'll probably never see it again."

She put her hands on her almost-but-not-quite heavy hips and smiled smugly.

"You don't know Vince like I do," she said. "He'll pay me back. You can count on that."

"Sure I can," I said. I could also count on the Cubs winning the pennant. The question was when.

When I got home, I dialed Vince's number. Area code 702 was Nevada.

A man answered. "Desert Mirage Hotel and Casino."

"Where exactly are you located?"

"Right at the end of the Strip, sir."

"In Las Vegas?"

"Yes, sir, Las Vegas. It's in the state of Nevada. Ask around, you can't miss it."

"Smart ass."

The next available flight to Vegas was at 5:00 P.M. At five-thirty I was looking down on the Rocky Mountains from thirty thousand feet—they looked pretty damned rocky, even from up here. At seven o'clock—six, local time—I was driving a rented Nova out of McCarran International Airport onto Las Vegas Boulevard.

19

The sun was still high enough above the desert to hold the temperature at an even ninety degrees. My jacket was draped over the passenger's seat next to my red-tagged bag. I'd checked the bag through rather than carry it on the plane, and the tag was to announce the presence of the .357. I'd also brought a leather sap, twenty feet of clothesline, and a pair of handcuffs. If Vince Pesce was Rueben Archuleta, he was going to have a long, uncomfortable ride back to Denver in the backseat of the Nova.

I cruised along the Strip, lined with grand and glitzy hotel-casinos, standing like proud but aging ladies of the evening. In this hot sunlight you could see their wrinkles and the edges of their makeup. But tonight, in the soft, dark desert air, when they draped themselves in a million jeweled lights, they'd be irresistible.

The Aladdin and the MGM Grand slid by on my right, the Dunes and Caesars Palace on my left. Out near the Sahara lay the Desert Mirage—gaudy, sure, but not as large or pretentious as the others. A working-class retreat.

I turned into the lot.

A mousy-looking woman wearing a string bikini lay on a lawn chair and watched her three children splash in the small hotel pool. Hubby was probably in the casino getting free drinks at the blackjack table and losing his vacation money. Hit me again. Ah, damn.

I wondered if Vince was killing time in the casino. Maybe he was just hanging around his room, waiting for Wendy's call.

I carried my bag up to room three-oh-nine, which was in the economy section—a row of outside entrances facing a brick wall. If Vince questioned me through the locked door, I'd be from Federal Express, his dream fulfilled. If he opened up, I'd be his worst nightmare.

He didn't answer. I opened the door with my picks, then closed it behind me.

The room was cool, almost chilly. Weak light sifted through heavy drapes and fell across twin beds, a nightstand, and a dresser with a big, ugly TV bolted on top. A stuffed vinyl chair sat in the far corner, in case you wanted to sit and admire the room.

The drawer in the nightstand contained only Desert Mirage stationery, a Gideon Bible, and color brochures of half-naked showgirls. I searched the dresser and found socks, underwear, and the bottom page of an airline ticket: Denver to Las Vegas, coach, nonsmoking, seat 21C, Vincent Pesce. Hanging in the closet next a to couple of polo shirts and a pair of cotton blend slacks was a nice leather jacket. It was too heavy to wear in this heat, but it would be perfect attire for clambering down hotel fire escapes and shooting at people in alleys.

The bathroom hadn't been used since the maid's last visit—razor, toothpaste tube, and toothbrush were all in a row, and the water glasses were sealed in paper envelopes.

I turned down the air conditioner, sat in the vinyl chair, and waited for Vince.

Gradually the room got dark. I left the lights and the TV off and tried not to fall asleep. By eight I was hungry and by ten I was starved. I drank water to fool my stomach. It was not amused.

At eleven-oh-five I woke up to the sound of a key scratching a lock. I hustled across the semidark room and stood against the wall, sap in hand.

The door opened. A shadow figure stepped in and reached for the light, and I laid the sap behind his ear. He collapsed like a tent. I closed the door and got out the cuffs.

"Wha——?" he asked, coming to. I guess I'd been too gentle.

I grabbed a handful of his curly hair, remembered how Meacham had looked shot to death in his hotel bed, and slammed his forehead into the floor. Then I remembered Lloyd Fontaine, so I slammed it a few more times.

He lay still.

Working in the dark, I pulled his arms behind him and cuffed them together. Then I took a few turns around his ankles with the clothesline, looped it through the handcuffs, and cinched it up. I dragged him across the floor and lifted him into the chair.

He moaned.

I turned on the light and got my first good look at him. He wore a navy blue silk shirt with the collar open, pearl gray slacks, and pearl gray patent leather shoes. He had a gold chain around his neck and a gold ring on his pinky, plus a red bruise on his forehead and drool in the corner of his mouth.

He groaned.

So did I. He was Vince Pesce, all right, but he wasn't the guy I'd chased from Meacham's hotel. On the other hand, he'd had a reason to want Meacham dead, and he'd fled the state right after the murder.

"Don't kill me, man, please."

He was fully awake now, and he looked scared. Who wouldn't, for chrissake?

"Shut up," I said, and yanked the wallet from his hip pocket. It contained a few hundred bucks, plus a Colorado driver's license and a few other cards with his name on them.

"That's all the money I've got," he said with a whine, "but I can get the rest, I swear to God, just please don't kill me."

"Nobody's going to kill you," I assured him.

He did not look convinced.

"Tell Fat Paulie I'll have four grand for him in a day or two," he said. "I'm waiting for the call right now, just please don't hurt me, okay?"

Fat Paulie? I sat on the corner of the bed. The .357 was poking me in the side, so I pulled it from my belt and set it beside me. Vince stared at it as if it were a ticking bomb.

"Okay, Vince, tell me about you and Rueben Archuleta and Zack Meacham."

"Huh?" He blinked a few times and looked up from the gun, fear giving way to confusion. "What the hell are you talking about?"

"Archuleta killed Meacham and you're involved."

"Zack Meacham? He's dead?"

"Don't play games, Vince, I'm not in the mood."

"Who the fuck are you, anyway?" Vince was no longer afraid—he was pissed off. I liked him the other way, so I picked up the gun and let it dangle over my knee. Vince stared at it and swallowed hard. That was better.

"Talk to me about Meacham's murder," I said.

"Hey, I swear, I don't know anything about it."

"You wanted Meacham out of the way because he was sleeping with Wendy."

"*Wendy.* You got to be kidding. Wendy sleeps with everybody. Shit, man, *I* introduced Meacham to her."

That made me blink.

"What is this, anyway?" Vince asked, perplexed. He wasn't the only one. "I thought you were from Fat Paulie DaNucci."

That explained a few things. DaNucci ran perhaps the largest book in North Denver. He employed a pair of notorious bone-busters to collect money owed, and they were enthusiastic about their work.

"Think of me as being from Fat Paulie, Vince, and tell me why you left Colorado in such a hurry."

"Because I'm trying to raise the eighteen grand I owe your boss. Jesus, man, the word is out on me in Denver and I can't even get a bet down. All I need is a chance to win back the money I owe Fat Paulie and, you know, make things like they were before."

Like they were before. That's what Vince had told Wendy.

"I'm getting four grand tomorrow or the next day," he said, the whine creeping back in his voice. "I can hand it right over. Just please don't hurt me."

"How well did you know Meacham?" I asked him.

"What's that got to do with anything?"

"Answer the question, Vince."

"Jesus, I don't know. I knew him, that's all. I'd see him in Fancy Dan's sometimes and we'd buy each other drinks. That's it."

"Did he ever talk about a guy named Charles Soames?"

"Soames, Jesus, that's about *all* he talked about the last few times I saw him."

"What did he say?"

Vince squirmed in his chair, trying to find comfort.

"Do you think you could take off these cuffs?"

"Maybe later."

Vince winced, then looked at the plaster on the ceiling.

"Okay, let's see. Meacham told me this guy Soames had killed his brother Buddy after a big jewel heist some years back and now Soames was out of prison and Meacham was going to square things."

"By killing Soames?"

"So he said. But for my money, Meacham was fullashit. No guts. Fact is, he even told me he wasn't sure he could do it and that he was trying to work up the nerve. He threatened Soames on the phone and even went to his house once, but he said Soames had some bodyguards. Indians, he said. I mean, seriously, Indians? The guy's gotta be fullashit, right? Also, he said Soames had hired some guy to follow *him*."

"Soames hired someone? How did Meacham know that?"

"Well, he didn't actually *know* it, he just figured it out. A week or so after he started bugging Soames, Meacham spots this guy hanging around his garage. He's afraid the guy's going to murder him in his sleep or something, so he tells me he's going to hide out until he gets Soames. But I guess the guy must've found him, right?"

"Get up."

Vince swallowed hard. "What for?"

"So I can uncuff your hands."

He stood unsteadily, feet together. I took off the cuffs. He rubbed his wrists, then sat down and untied his ankles.

"I'll pay Fat Paulie back in a few days," he said, "I swear to God. I came out here with fifteen hundred and this afternoon I had it up to almost seven grand, so I know I can do it."

"Where's the money? I only saw three hundred bucks."

"I . . . I lost it, but look, with the four grand I'm getting tomorrow . . ."

I took out Wendy's check and showed it to him.

"Here's your four grand, Vince. Wendy wanted you to have it, but I told her to keep it." I ripped it into a dozen pieces, figuring Wendy still had the receipt. "She's keeping it. Don't ask her for money again, unless you want *me* to deliver it."

Vince stared at me with his mouth hanging open.

"You're not one of Fat Paulie's guys?"

"That's the good news," I said. "The bad news is if I found you, so can they."

I left Vince sitting there—confused, scared, beat up, and broke. Another Vegas success story.

20

I caught a late flight back to Denver, and since they hadn't yet delivered my furniture, I slept again on the floor. The phone woke me up Saturday morning. It was Abner Greenspan.

"You're in deep shit, Lomax," he said.

"Good morning to you, too, Abner."

"I tried to get hold of you yesterday. Where were you?"

"It's a long story. What's wrong?"

"Plenty," he said. "The D.A. is considering changing the charge against you from second- to first-degree murder."

"What?"

"That's right. Lieutenant Dalrymple handed Krenshaw a statement signed by Helen Ester saying that you went up to Meacham's room with the intent of murder."

"That's bullshit, Abner."

"Krenshaw showed me the statement. It's got her signature on it and—"

"You mean, *somebody's* signature," I said.

"Yeah, somebody named Helen Ester. She states that before you left your office to drive to the Frontier Hotel, you said, and I quote, 'I'm going to kill that son of a bitch, and I've got just the gun to do it with, one the cops won't find,' unquote."

"That's bullshit."

"You said that already."

"Look, Abner, Dalrymple is playing with the facts. He's got no real evidence."

"He has Helen Ester's testimony."

"No, he doesn't."

"Are you saying he falsified evidence?"

"It looks that way, doesn't it?"

Greenspan was silent for a moment.

"I can't believe he'd do that," he said.

"Believe it, Abner. When Helen shows up at the preliminary hearing and—"

"Is she going to be there?" he asked.

"She has to, doesn't she? I mean, if the D.A. is going to use her statement."

"Not necessarily. Her signed statement and Dalrymple's testimony plus whatever else the D.A.'s got will probably be enough to satisfy the judge to have you bound over for trial."

"No way. I'll have Helen Ester at the hearing to dispute Dalrymple's phony statements."

Greenspan was silent again.

"Well?"

"Are you sure about her, Jake?"

"You're goddamn right I'm sure," I said, louder than I'd intended.

"Okay, okay, take it easy."

"Sorry."

"I just want you to be sure, that's all. Because if she turns on you in front of the judge, then—"

"She won't," I said.

"Okay, fine."

"When she disputes Dalrymple's faked evidence, *he'll* be the one in trouble, and the D.A. will have nothing on me."

"I wouldn't say 'nothing.' You're the only one who saw the guy on the fire escape. Krenshaw's got the night clerk, who saw you go in, and one of the residents, who saw you on the fire escape."

"Winetta somebody," I said, "and her testimony could be shaky. She didn't even recognize me when I first talked to her."

"*You* talked to her." Greenspan was mad. "I thought I told you to stay away from those people. If Dalrymple can prove you intimidated a witness, he—"

"I didn't intimidate her. She offered me candy."

"What else have you done that I should know about?"

"Nothing," I said. "Much."

Greenspan sighed into the phone. "Let's hear it."

"I went to Las Vegas."

"After Judge Sanchez told you not to leave the state?"

"Right, Las Vegas is in another state."

"Don't be a smart ass. If Sanchez finds out—"

"He won't," I said.

He might, I thought. If the airline ran a check on me and my gun, some cop somewhere knows about it, and most cops belong to the same computerized gossip club.

"If he does find out, Jake, he can raise your bail so high you can't possibly pay it."

"Just like that?"

"Hell yes, he's the judge, he can do what he wants. Why do you think they call it the judicial system? You might have to sit in jail until your hearing."

"Great."

"And if things go badly at the hearing, they might lock you up until your trial."

"What trial, for chrissake? Come on, Abner."

"Hey, I'm doing all I can, Jake," he said. "Your hearing's Thursday at one o'clock. Try to relax until then."

"Relax? You just said if this goes to trial, I could rot behind bars for months."

"Maybe not."

"Look, Abner, I'm not going to risk being put away while Meacham's killer roams free."

"Meaning what?"

"Just for the sake of argument, what if I don't show up for the hearing?"

"Then you'd be fucked. As your attorney I would advise you to be there no matter what."

He hung up.

I phoned Helen Ester at her hotel. When I got no answer, I tried Caroline Lochemont.

"She was here not five minutes ago," Caroline said, "and I sent her away in the same cab that brought her. My grandfather is sick in bed. He's exhausted."

"Where was Helen going?"

"Back to her hotel, I think. Uh, Mr. Lomax, I—"

"Call me Jacob, okay?"

"Jacob. I—that is, my grandfather and I—want to talk to you about, well, about helping us."

"Helping you?"

"Well, yes."

"I could be there—" my watch said almost nine, and I was thinking I first needed to catch Helen at her hotel for a long, serious discussion—"say, around noon."

"Could we make it tomorrow?" Caroline said. "By then I hope my grandfather will be feeling better."

"Tomorrow, then, at noon."

I got dressed in a hurry, had a glass of water and an old doughnut for breakfast, and drove to the Westin Hotel. I parked the Olds in the second underground level and walked toward the elevator.

Then I saw someone familiar, not fifty feet away. Black hair; dark, handsome features; murderous black heart. Rueben Archuleta. He was standing beside a new maroon Chrysler New Yorker with Colorado plates, and he was wearing the same leather jacket he'd worn on the fire escape outside Meacham's hotel. He was talking to a woman—angrily, it seemed, although

I couldn't hear his words. The woman's back was to me, but she looked familiar, too.

Just as I unholstered the magnum, Archuleta spotted me. In one fluid movement he jerked the woman around in front of him, curled his left arm around her neck, and pulled out a sleek automatic pistol, a Beretta.

The woman was Helen Ester. Archuleta pressed the gun to her head.

"Don't do it," I said to him, straining to keep my voice calm and the gun down at my side. "Just let her go."

He didn't let her go, but he did move his gun. He pointed it at me.

I dove behind a Volkswagen bus as he popped a few rounds in my direction, punching holes in the metal. When I edged around the back of the bus, Archuleta again had the gun to Helen's head. He pulled open the door of the Chrysler, reached in, and started the engine. Then he shoved Helen away, sending her sprawling to the concrete. In an instant Archuleta was behind the wheel and smoking the tires, first in reverse, then in low, steering toward Helen. She barely managed to roll out of the way as he squealed past her. He fired twice more into my guardian bus, then sped toward the ramp at the end of the building.

I came out in the open and took careful aim at Archuleta's profile, firing as he slid the Chrysler into a tight left turn. But I'd led him too far—the slug ricocheted off the concrete wall, and the car disappeared up the ramp.

I went to Helen Ester and helped her to her feet. She clung to me, shaking uncontrollably.

"Oh, my God, Jacob, that man . . . who . . ."

"He's Rueben Archuleta, back from the past."

"Jacob, he said . . . he said if I didn't stay away from Charles, he'd kill me."

21

We found a phone and called the cops. By the time we got back underground, a patrol car with two uniforms was cruising through the parking structure, looking for us. The Volkswagen bus, though, was gone. Apparently its owner had returned and driven away, oblivious to the bullet holes in the side panels. The cops took our statement, then drove us to headquarters, where we were led to none other than the sad-faced Detective Healey. We repeated our story to him.

"I'm still not clear about why this man threatened you, Miss Ester," Healey said.

"Because he wants me to stay away from my friend Charles Soames."

"Yes, but why?"

"Because—"

"Because he's crazy," I said. "What difference does it make? I'm the one he shot at."

Healey looked at me. "And he's the same man you allegedly saw the night of Zack Meacham's murder?"

"There's no allegedly about it."

Healey nodded sadly. "Are you certain his name is Rueben Archuleta?"

"I'm certain," I said. Ninety-nine percent.

"Do you know where he lives?"

"I wish I did."

Healey said he'd check it out and call us if anything turned up. By the time Helen and I got back to the hotel, it was after noon. I suggested lunch, but she had no appetite.

"I just want to take a Valium and lie down," she said.

We rode the elevator up to her room. She disappeared into the bathroom, and I heard water running. When she came out, she looked a bit more relaxed. And older, I thought—she'd washed off her lipstick and mascara. She sat with me on the couch.

"How do you feel?" I asked.

"Okay, I guess. Considering." From a pack on the end table she shook loose a cigarette and lit it with a silver lighter.

"I don't want to upset you further, but we need to talk about something."

"Oh?" She arched one eyebrow.

"Abner Greenspan told me Dalrymple said you signed another statement implicating me in Meacham's death."

She blew smoke and shook her head and gave me a wry smile.

"That is complete and utter nonsense."

"You're saying Dalrymple's lying."

"Of *course* he's lying. Jacob, I would have told you this sooner, but I didn't have the chance: Lieutenant Dalrymple brought me into his office yesterday and accused *me* of helping you murder Meacham. He said if I confessed, I could avoid prosecution as a state's witness. A witness against you. He already had a statement typed and ready for me to sign. I tore it up and walked out."

I said nothing.

"You don't believe me, do you?" she asked.

"I believe you. It's just that . . . ."

She started to get up and I grabbed her arm.

"I feel like Dalrymple's got a noose around my neck."

She tried to pull away.

"He's fabricating evidence against me and I don't know how far he'll take it."

"You're hurting my arm."

I let her go. She didn't get up, only turned away from me to tap ashes from her cigarette.

"Was there anyone else in Dalrymple's office when you talked to him?" I asked.

"No. And what difference does *that* make?"

"Look, Helen, Dalrymple can be a very dangerous man. We've got to be careful about all this and we've got to stick together, because judges and juries tend to believe homicide lieutenants, not accused murderers and their character witnesses."

"Are you saying he could bring us both to trial?"

"He could. But don't worry too much. It's me he's after."

"Of *course* I'm worried," she said and put her hand on mine. "I would be in any case, but especially so because I . . ."

"You what?"

She let go of my hand and put out her cigarette in the ashtray, slowly, carefully tapping and turning the butt until the fire was dead. She brushed invisible ashes from her fingertips.

"I almost said, 'because I think I'm in love with you.' "

"Are you?"

"There's no need to get *angry* about it," she said softly, a smile touching her lips.

"Well?"

"Maybe I am. And why are you getting so upset?"

Because of what had happened to the last woman I loved, I thought. I knew that those things would never happen again, not in my life. I knew it. Logically. But I didn't *feel* it. Because those things *had* happened, and part of me saw them occurring in orderly progression: love, then marriage, then . . . death. A horrible, violent death.

"I need you with me Thursday at the preliminary hearing."

"What is it, Jacob?" she asked. "Are you afraid to love me

back? Is that it? Or are you simply afraid of love? Some men are, you know."

"And you should stay away from Soames."

She leaned forward and kissed me, and I kissed her back.

"At least while Archuleta is still around," I said.

"Anything you want, Jacob."

Later, when I went down to the lobby, Helen was asleep in her bed, I suppose from the Valium.

I phoned my friend Monroe at the motor vehicle department. I'd caught a piece of Archuleta's license number and I'd forgotten to give it to Detective Healey. I think I'd forgotten. Or maybe I was simply maintaining that time-honored ritual known as taking the law into your own hands.

"Jacob, my man."

"I've got a partial license I'd like you to run down, if you would, please."

"What's this 'please' shit?"

"It's G-H-something something-nine-two."

"Those somethin's you mentioned comprise 'bout two hundred and sixty ve-hicles."

"The plate was on a new Chrysler New Yorker."

"Wait a sec." I heard clickety-click and pictured his brown fingers doing a dance on his keyboard. "Got two New Yorkers, one black, one maroon. I want the black one."

"It was maroon."

"Rental car, Jacob. Avis." He gave me the entire license number.

"Who rented it?" I asked.

"Hey, man, this ain't goddamn *Star Trek*. My computer got limitations."

"Sorry. Which rental office?"

"Don't say. Just give the main address downtown."

"Thanks, buddy. I owe you."

"What's this 'owe' shit?"

* * *

Mr. Fyfe was the assistant manager at the Avis office. He wore a friendly smile and a cheap toupee. My card turned over and over in his pudgy pink hands.

"A private detective. My, my. It must be an exciting profession."

"It has its moments."

"I'll bet it does," he said with a sigh and pictured himself tracking down public enemy number one and solving the crime of the century. Fyfe, PI. It had a nice ring to it.

"About the car," I said.

"What? The car, of course." He picked up the phone. "Dolores, would you print out the current status of a Chrysler New Yorker, this year's model." He gave her the license number. A few minutes later, Dolores wiggled in and dropped a sheet of paper on Fyfe's desk. She smiled at me and snapped her gum.

"The car was rented on June fifteenth to a Mr. Anthony Villanueva," Fyfe said. "It was done through our office in Vail."

"Does Villanueva still have the car?" I asked.

"According to our records, yes."

"What's his address?"

"He had a California driver's license."

"I mean, where's he staying locally?"

"Oh. He has a condo in Vail." Fyfe gave me the address and unit number. "Will this help us track him down?"

Us. Fyfe and Lomax always get their man.

"It might," I said. Unless we get our ass shot off first.

I steered the Olds onto I-70 heading west and hoped the old girl wouldn't fall down and break a hip on Vail Pass. By four o'clock I was cruising past Idaho Springs, and an hour later I was in

Vail, an Old World village built in the 1960s by a few folks who thought skiing was fun. Apparently others agreed. This time of year, though, the ski runs were just ugly gashes in the mountainsides. However, the aspens were putting on quite a show, boasting brief golden leaves against a dark background of firs. Also appearing briefly were the fair-weather tourists, hitting the shops and exposing roll after roll of Kodachrome, while the locals and the evergreens waited patiently for snow.

I stopped at a gas station for directions to the Sky View Condominiums, and fifteen minutes later I was parked in the lot. The maroon Chrysler was not in sight.

The building was three stories high with balconies all around. Number thirty-seven, Fyfe had said. I went up the stairs to the third floor, drew out the magnum, and listened at the door. Faint radio music—country. I knocked, but I stayed to the side, out of range of the peephole. This time I'd make certain it was Archuleta/Villanueva before I smacked him in the face with the gun.

The door opened and there was no one there.

"Hi."

"Huh?" I looked down. A little girl, about five.

"Is that a real gun?"

I held it behind me. "Is your daddy home?"

"I betcha it ain't real," she said.

A woman appeared behind the girl. She had a bobbed nose, designer jeans, and hair sprayed rigidly in place. "Yes?"

"Mrs. Villanueva?"

"Why, no, it's not," she said with a soft Texas drawl. "Ah mean, ah'm not."

"Is Anthony here?"

"He's got a gun, Momma, but it ain't real."

"Hush, hon. Ah'm afraid you have the wrong apartment."

"Who is it, Martha?" a man asked.

He stood in the middle of the room behind her. He was a skinny character with short hair and long sideburns.

"Sorry to trouble you," I said.

"Ask him if it's a real gun, Momma."

"Kids," I said.

22

I made the long drive back to Denver.

Archuleta, alias Villanueva, had given Mr. Fyfe a phony address in Vail. I wondered, though, if there were some reason why he'd picked Vail. Of course, it could have been the same reason he'd picked "Villanueva"—no reason at all. And his California driver's license might or might not mean he'd been living out there. One fine deduction after another.

When I got home, it was well after dark, and I felt tired and ready for bed, and then irritated when I remembered I didn't have one. But I woke up in a hurry when I saw my apartment door standing wide open. I moved toward it, gun in hand, hoping whoever had trashed my place four nights ago was in there now having some more fun.

Then I relaxed. From inside I could hear Mrs. Finch, my batty old landlady.

"I *told* you he wasn't here," she squawked from the center of my furnitureless living room. "If you want to wait for him, you can do it outside. Now, git. I won't have strangers loitering in my house."

Her powdered cheeks were flushed and her tiny fists were on her hips. She glared up at Detectives Healey and O'Roarke. The men looked besieged.

"You heard her," I said. "No loitering."

"And as for you"—she aimed a gnarled finger at my nose—"I

haven't decided whether you can stay in this house or not. You're on probation, mister, remember that."

"Yes, ma'am." I'd only lived there for three years.

She bustled out, ruffled but righteous. The detectives seemed relieved.

"Dalrymple wants to see you," Healey said.

"Tell him I'm busy."

"Now," the Asian O'Roarke said.

"Am I under arrest?" I was in no mood to trade quips with cops, particularly Dalrymple.

"Not unless you won't come with us," Healey said. "And we'll take the piece."

They stood there, unmoving as only cops can, as if getting their way was a foregone conclusion. I gave Healey the magnum.

"Careful," I said, "it's loaded."

We drove downtown. Lieutenant Dalrymple was waiting, heavy and solid, behind his desk. His mouth was pressed in a tight line and his eyes were cold and without emotion. Shark's eyes. He told me to sit. Healey and O'Roarke stayed in the background.

Dalrymple held up a piece of paper. "I've got a complaint here signed by a Cosmo Runderman, night manager of the Frontier Hotel, and a—"

"His name is Cosmo? You're kidding, right?"

"—and a Winetta Essex, one of the residents. They both state that you impersonated a police officer and harassed them."

"I did neither."

"You passed yourself off as a cop, Lomax. That's against the law."

"I never said I was a cop and I never showed them any stinking badges. Can I go now?"

"Also, you've been carrying a gun without a permit."

Healey stepped up and put my magnum on the desk, grip toward Dalrymple, muzzle toward me.

"I've got a permit for that," I said.

"It was revoked when you were charged with Zack Meacham's murder."

"No one told me."

"Doesn't matter. Carrying a concealed weapon is a felony. It wouldn't look too good if you were busted a few days before your preliminary hearing."

"Then arrest me, and see how it looks when my attorney charges some fat pig cop with harassment."

Dalrymple's expression turned ugly and for a moment I thought he was going to climb right over his desk to get me.

"Wait outside," he ordered Healey and O'Roarke.

They closed the door on their way out. Dalrymple picked up my gun, thumbed back the hammer until it clicked, then pointed it at my sternum.

"Watch it, that's about a four-ounce pull," I told him.

"I could say you attacked me."

"With what, my shoe?"

"You went berserk. I didn't want to shoot you, but I had no choice."

"Fuck you, Lieutenant. If you've got something to say, say it. Otherwise, I'm out of here."

He raised the gun and looked down the barrel at my eye. "Bang," he said, then put it down. I relaxed. Not that I'd thought he'd shoot. Not much.

"How are you and the Ester woman getting along these days?" he said pleasantly.

"Why?"

"Just curious. I read that little story you two cooked up about Meacham's phantom killer attacking you in the parking garage."

"You think we made that up?"

Dalrymple lifted one corner of his mouth in what passed for a grin.

"All we have is your word that it happened," he said. "The

mystery Volkswagen took all the phantom's slugs and disappeared into thin air."

"The owner of that bus is going to notice those bullet holes sooner or later, if he hasn't already, and call the cops, if he hasn't already. You can match those slugs with the ones taken from Meacham's body."

Dalrymple was smiling and shaking his head and tapping his thick fingers on the desk.

"Why would we invent something like that?" I said.

"You, to convince people, especially me, that this guy exists."

"He does exist."

"Her, I don't know. Maybe she's changed her mind and wants you between her legs instead of behind bars."

I let that pass. "You're working extra hard to pin Meacham's murder on me, Lieutenant, and we both know why."

"Because you're guilty."

"Because you hate my guts."

He waved his hand. "That's beside the point. You killed Meacham, and Helen Ester is prepared to testify against you."

"You're wrong on both counts."

"I've got *two* statements signed by her, Lomax."

"You're a fucking liar."

Dalrymple's face went hard.

"Be careful," he said, his voice low.

"Careful, my ass. You've been manufacturing evidence against me. And—"

"What?" he roared, not quite restraining his anger.

"—and at the preliminary hearing it's all going to blow up in your ugly face."

He forced himself to stay in his seat. His pale eyebrows went up and his big face slowly rearranged itself into a smile. It looked like a painful process.

"I'll tell you what will come out at the hearing. Ester wanted Meacham dead, one, because he was threatening her old loverboy Soames, and two, because he'd fucked her socks off up in his hotel room, presumably, against her will. So she gets you to go up there and take care of business. Tell you the truth, nobody, including me, is shedding any tears over Meacham. We've talked to his ex-wife, his employees, and his stripper girlfriend, and they all say the same thing: The man was selfish, arrogant, loud, obnoxious, and a bully."

"It's easy to see your faults in other people," I said.

"What?"

"Nothing."

Dalrymple gave me a sour look before going on.

"So on that fateful night, you go up there with blood in your eye. Maybe she paid you to kill him, maybe not. She probably wouldn't have had to, though, not after telling you the naughty things he'd just done to her."

"That's all a load of bullshit."

"So now you're steamed, the old rage is burning. Maybe you're remembering how you quit the force after your wife's murder, how you didn't have the stomach to be a cop anymore because her killers got away, and how they left her, cut up and raped and—"

I came out of the chair. "You're just about to cross the line, Dalrymple."

"Sit down, Lomax, you're proving my point. Maybe you weren't thinking about that, it doesn't matter. I said sit down. In any case, you went up there pissed off and—goddammit, sit down!" He yelled so loud that papers rustled on his desk.

"Don't ever talk to me about my wife's death."

"Yeah, all right, forget I said it. The point is I think Helen Ester sent you up there to kill Meacham, and you did it. Out of anger. But she planned it in cold blood."

"You're too obvious, Dalrymple. You're not going to scare either one of us into confessing."

"Believe it or not," he said, "I'm trying to help you."

"Help me into prison."

"Wake up, Lomax. I want the main person responsible for Meacham's death, not just the dummy who pulled the trigger. If you testify against her, I can get you off easy."

"That's the same line you used on her."

"I'm giving you one last chance."

I said nothing.

"Okay, smart guy," She said, "have it your way. This discussion is over. Get out of my sight."

"I'll take my gun," I said. "And the thirty-eight, I want that back now, too."

"I told you to get out."

"You can yank my carry permit, Dalrymple, but you can't keep my property without cause."

"We'll keep it until the paperwork's done, which could be a long time if it happens to get lost."

"What paperwork?"

"*The* paperwork."

"You don't have the right to—"

He slammed his fist on the desk hard enough to make the .357 jiggle.

"Don't tell me about rights, Lomax!" he roared, his face red, his scar yellow-white. He glared at me for a few heartbeats, and when he spoke, his voice was strained, barely under rein. "We both learned about rights ten years ago," he said. "We both acted properly in the line of duty, the way we saw fit, the way we'd been trained. And then you left me hanging out there alone. And for that"—he touched the puckered line on his face—"I got this and a suspension and a permanent obstacle to my career and you got a goddamn medal. That's all I need to know about rights. Now get the fuck out."

I walked to the door.

"Enjoy your freedom while you can," Dalrymple said. "It won't last long."

23

     Sunday morning I went downstairs to see how Vaz was coming with Fontaine's journal.

"I've finished copying it into something legible," he said. "But so far I've had no luck with the code."

I picked up a ruled yellow sheet from the dining table. Vaz's careful printing filled the lower half of the sheet:

9–15

```
HGXUO RTOEG SGDNI HTLFI MIPHD
EECNL LIBEK AJNEE SLNLI TSARI
FSWEM AOQST UOBTU CELWF ILNLA
RODFY TNUEL PMXEH THOTI WNQIE
MEDKA TOJTE VADHL LYCEH TAGVE
UNPAL LISVD NAQRE TSPEO TSDOT
OHNPE HTBWO HSELL ITSHG INSOT
```

"That's an exact copy of the last page of his diary," Vaz said. "If 'nine-fifteen' is the date, then he made this entry the same day he came to your office."

"Christ, Vaz, it looks impossible."

"It may be, Jacob. If Fontaine wrote this using a chart or

code wheel, there's no way I can decipher it. You'd need an expert. Our only hope is that he used a quick and easy-method, and then perhaps I can hit it by trial and error. And it's entirely possible that this code is so childishly simple that we'll kick ourselves for not seeing it at once."

"How are you proceeding?"

"First I tried a straight substitution of letters—A equals B, B equals C, then A equals C, B equals D, and so on. I got nowhere. Then I counted the letters to find those most frequently used. In normal writing, E appears most often, followed by T, A, O, and N. But in Fontaine's journal—"

Sophia bustled out of the next room, talking as she came.

"Vassily, get that mess cleaned up before—oh, hello, Jacob, how are you?—before my friends arrive, which is in exactly ten minutes. We have *important* work to do, do you hear me, Vassily?"

"Yes, yes, Sophia," he said, picking up his papers. "As I was saying, in Fontaine's journal the order of frequency is E, T, L, O, and I. So he may have substituted for some letters, but not for others. I am working under that assumption. Of course, he may have used a different method entirely."

"If it weren't so important, Vaz, I'd say forget it."

"I know. Don't worry, I'm not ready to quit. Now tell me what's been going—"

"I *mean* it, Vassily," Sophia called from the kitchen.

"Yes, yes." He smiled sheepishly at me and shook his head. "Some women friends or other for some church group or other. Let's go outside. I want to know what's been going on with you."

Before we left, Vaz tucked his battered chessboard and box of pieces under his arm. They were his security blanket and prayer beads, and he never went far without them.

We walked out to the backyard—Mrs. Finch's pride and once joy. An era ago she'd played back here with her older sisters, rolling hoops, playing tag, pushing each other in the tree swing.

Her father had been a wealthy merchant when he'd built this house—the finest mansion on the block. Life had been simple and good and would, it seemed, last forever. But now the fortune was gone and Mrs. Finch was alone and the great house was split up into eight apartments.

Vaz and I sat near the huge elm. He set up the board on the rickety folding table and began arranging the pieces for a game, the white men on his side. The late September sun was warm, and the air was still and dry.

"I've got a lot on my mind, Vaz, I don't know if I'd be much competition." Not that I would anyway. Vaz had been to the chess world what Mickey Mantle had been to baseball—maybe not the best who ever played, but definitely Hall of Fame material.

"Come, Jacob, it will help you relax. I will give you rook odds."

"At least make it queen odds."

"As you wish," he said, removing his queen from her square with great reluctance, as if he'd already lost the game. This from a man who'd once played blindfolded against twelve lesser opponents, beating ten, drawing with two. He moved his pawn to king four.

"I haven't seen you since Wednesday," he said. "Any new developments since then?"

I answered with pawn to king four. "A few. For openers, I've been formally charged with the murder of Zack Meacham."

He looked up from the board. "What? That is insane."

"Nevertheless." While I filled him in on the tireless efforts of Lieutenant Dalrymple, including the forged statements against me, we both played pawns to our queen three and king bishop four squares. "Dalrymple says I can save myself if I give him Helen Ester."

"Then he suspects her?" Vaz's heavy eyebrows did a few push-ups. "And he's willing to trade you for her?"

I nodded and so did Vaz.

"What, you're agreeing?"

"No, no, Jacob. Not exactly."

"Okay, let's hear it."

"There's no reason to get angry."

"Who's angry?" I took a breath and gestured with open hands. "Okay, okay, I'm not. Really. Tell me what you're thinking."

He played his queen knight to bishop three.

"These statements by Miss Ester, you're certain they are forgeries?"

"Absolutely certain," I said and snapped up his king pawn.

Vaz took back with his queen pawn. "You see, Jacob, I was just wondering, what if Miss Ester is working in concert with Archuleta?"

"Christ, Vaz, where the hell'd you get that idea? Never mind, there's no way. Archuleta tried to kill her." I told him about yesterday morning in the parking garage, when Archuleta had shot at me and attempted to run over Helen. I moved pawn to queen rook three, a purely defensive move, perhaps wasted. Vaz remained silent.

"Well?"

"Well, okay," he said. "My suspicions about her were false."

"Thank you."

"You're welcome."

I told him how I'd learned that Archuleta had rented the car using the name "Villanueva" and how I'd made a wasted trip to Vail. We exchanged pawns in the center, relieving the tension. Then I backtracked a bit and described my talk with Wendy Apple, my trip to Las Vegas, and my conversation with Vince Pesce.

Vaz slowly shook his massive head and attacked my pawn with his king's knight.

"You attacked an innocent man, Jacob?" His tone of voice was meant to inspire feelings of guilt. It worked.

"He didn't *look* innocent," I said lamely, then changed the subject to Harry Witherspoon. I told Vaz about the *Gazette*'s editor explaining how and why Lloyd Fontaine acquired the photos of Ed Teague.

Vaz nodded. "So Fontaine had no prior knowledge of the Lochemont robbery."

"Apparently not."

I played bishop to queen knight five, pinning his knight to his king. Vaz seemed unperturbed.

"Could Fontaine have teamed up with Archuleta since the robbery?"

"It's possible, I suppose. Why?"

"If not, then perhaps Soames and Archuleta are working together."

"Somehow I doubt that," I said. "What are you getting at?"

"We've been assuming that Archuleta killed Meacham because Meacham was threatening Soames, right? If so, how did Archuleta learn of these threats?"

"I'm not sure. He may have one or more accomplices." I told Vaz about Willy Two Hawks and sons and the blond guy I'd seen tailing me in the tan Ford. "Those Indians probably know everything that's going on in Caroline Lochemont's house."

"I see. And now Archuleta wants Ester out of Caroline's house and out of the picture."

"It would appear."

Vaz attacked my queen with his bishop. I pushed her ahead two squares, out of the line of fire. Vaz attacked her again, this time with his rook.

"Then he certainly wants you out, too," he said.

"No doubt. But I intend to stick close to Soames until Archuleta shows himself again." I moved my queen to safety on king knight three.

"That is most dangerous," Vaz said.

He brought his rook all the way to my edge of the board, giving check. I had only one move—king to bishop two.

"I don't have much choice, Vaz. One thing, though: I think I have an ally in Caroline Lochemont. I'm meeting her today at noon. She wants me to help her and Soames with something."

"Perhaps to dig up the jewels?" Vaz said, a gleam in his eye.

"Fat chance."

"But if so, what would be your share?"

He checked me with his white-squared bishop. I was running out of moves.

"My main interest in Soames is Archuleta," I said. "That little killer is sticking close to the old man, and when he shows up again, I intend to drop on him like a safe."

"Are you saying you're not at all interested in buried treasure?"

"I suppose a bit." I blocked his bishop with mine.

Vaz snorted. "A bit. Hah!" He dropped his knight on my king pawn. "Checkmate."

"Shit."

"Your game needs work, Jacob."

"No shit."

"You're not thinking far enough ahead. Let me show you something." Vaz usually didn't preach, but now he moved his rook back to queen one and tapped it with his forefinger. "When I moved my rook here," he said, "you should have taken it with your queen, even though it meant losing her. True, it can be most unpleasant, giving up your lady, but in this case it is forced, essential to your survival." He picked up my black queen. "If you try too hard to protect her, it can cost you everything."

"Are you talking about Helen Ester?"

"Why, no, Jacob," he said with exaggerated innocence. "I'm talking about chess."

24

On the way to Caroline Lochemont's house, I thought I spotted the blond guy in the tan Ford. But if it was him, he was keeping his distance. I parked in front of the house, right behind the beat-up Chevy of Willy Two Hawks. Caroline answered the front door, and I followed her inside. She limped.

"What's wrong?" I asked.

"I twisted my ankle on a rock."

"She stumbled around up there like a drunken squaw," Willy said from the couch. He sipped beer from a can and smiled at me from behind his dark glasses.

"What's he talking about?" I asked Caroline.

"Willy made Grandpa show them where he'd run."

"Run?"

"After the Lochemont robbery," Willy said with a belch. "When he ran away from Teague and Archuleta and hid the satchel of jewels."

"He never *had* the jewels."

"He never *had* the jewels," Willy mocked.

Caroline turned to me. "Willy and his sons forced my grandfather and me to—"

"We never forced nobody," Willy said, getting off the couch. "What's taking Charley so long out there, anyhow? I need another beer." He walked bowlegged to the kitchen.

"He didn't actually hold a gun to our heads," Caroline said when he'd gone, "but the threat was plain enough—show them or else. My grandfather's not well, but we went along to avoid violence. The more we tried to tell them there are no jewels, the harder they pushed us on—especially that big ape, Tom. So I ended it by twisting my ankle."

"On purpose?"

She nodded yes with a smile.

"How is it now?"

"I'll live," she said.

Willy came back.

"Charley's making lunch out there," he told Caroline. "He wants your help."

Caroline went to the kitchen. Willy popped the top on a fresh can of Coors and sprawled on the couch.

"I'm surprised you came back here," he said, "after that little run-in with my boys the other day. Mathew told me he used a tire iron to get his point across."

"I hardly noticed."

"That ain't what I heard," he said and smiled wide enough to let me admire his gold molar.

"Willy, why don't you take your beer and hit the road. You've worn out your welcome."

His eyebrows raised above his blacked-out eyes. "What makes you think I ain't welcome here?"

"Just an educated guess. As in education. You've probably heard of it."

Willy's mouth turned down. I'd hurt his feelings. Then he grinned. "I get it, Lomax. You want some of that action out there." He raised his whiskery chin toward the kitchen. "Don't worry, though, she's a frisky enough bitch to take care of us all, maybe even two at a time. But my boys get first crack at her, you remember that."

I stepped over to Willy and grabbed him one-handed by the

neck and yanked him off the couch. He dropped his beer on the floor and pried at my fingers. His toes barely touched the carpet.

"I don't want to see you around here again," I told him, trying hard not to choke the little bastard to death.

He swung feeble fists at my head, but his arms weren't long enough to reach past my shoulder. His mouth was round and turning blue.

"If you bother these people again, you'll wake up in intensive care." I slapped off his glasses with my other hand, revealing bloodshot eyes. "Blink twice if you follow my meaning," I said.

He did.

I let him go, then gave him a shove toward the front door. He gasped for air and rubbed his throat.

"What's going on?" Caroline asked, entering the room.

"Willy was just leaving."

Willy picked up his glasses with one hand, still rubbing his neck with the other. He tried to speak but could only sputter.

"You'll be . . . sorry . . ."

I stepped toward him. He scrambled out the door and down the walk, then got in his truck and drove away.

"Whatever you said to him, thanks," Caroline said.

"My pleasure."

"There's lunch, if you're hungry. The weather's so nice, we set up outside."

I followed her through the kitchen and out the back door to the cement-slab patio covered by a green-and-white-striped plastic awning. Warm green sun washed over the redwood picnic table, which was set with a platter of sandwiches, a bag of potato chips, and a six-pack of Coors. Suburban cuisine.

"Where's Willy?" Soames said. The greenish light on his gray face reminded me of a fish underwater.

"Jacob told him to leave." Caroline put her hand on my arm. "Sit down. Grandpa and I have a proposition for you."

I figured it had to do with protecting them from Willy and his sons.

"I rarely work as a bodyguard," I said.

Caroline glanced at Soames. He popped the tab on a beer and shoved it at me. "We don't need you to guard any bodies, Lomax. Have a sandwich."

"We want you to help us find the jewels," Caroline said.

I looked at Soames. He grinned and guzzled beer. I think my palms started to sweat. Five million dollars.

"You're, uh, are you saying you know where they are?"

"If I knew, I wouldn't need you," he said.

"Grandpa knows approximately."

"I dropped the satchel down a mine shaft," he said. "The problem now is finding the right shaft."

My palms *were* sweating. I rubbed them on my pants.

"Then you were in on the robbery after all."

"Hell no, I wasn't," Soames said. "Teague *forced* me to help." His eyes challenged me to disagree. I took a bite from my sandwich—bologna and American cheese on Wonder bread. Mmm.

"You told me Archuleta got away with the jewels."

"So I lied." But Soames looked away when he said it. "While Teague was in that shack, blowing the others to bits, I grabbed the satchel of gems and ran for my life. Then Teague came after me with his scattergun."

"What about Archuleta?"

His eyes narrowed. "What about him?"

"Was he chasing you, too?"

"Yeah, sure."

Soames wasn't telling all he knew about Archuleta, but now wasn't the time to press him about it. And there was something else that bothered me: Why would armed robbers leave an unattended hostage alone with their swag?

"Anyway," Soames said, "I hid the satchel in case he, I mean they, caught up with me. I planned to lead the cops back to the mine if I made it to safety."

"Why didn't you?"

"Because by the time they found me, I'd been wandering around for four days. I'd damn near frozen to death each night, and I'd taken a bad fall and cracked open my head. I don't even remember being found. They told me later that I'd been about one day away from dying."

"But eventually you remembered," I said. "I mean about hiding the satchel."

Soames took a long pull on his beer.

"Sure, eventually. But by then I realized my situation."

"Meaning what?"

"Meaning they were out to pin everything on me."

" 'They' being the cops?"

"The cops, the insurance company, my boss, even my own daughter and her goddamn husband. Everyone wanted the jewels back, all right, but they also wanted to hang me for the little girl who got it during the robbery. I was the patsy. It wouldn't have helped me one damn bit to lead them to the jewels. My only consolation was that *nobody* would get them."

That made sense, but something else didn't.

"Why do you want me?" I asked.

"Before Willy and the others showed up," Caroline said, "we searched a few mines ourselves. But there are scores of mines in that area, and it's just too much for me to carry all the equipment and help Grandpa up and down the slopes."

Soames squirmed, embarrassed.

"But why me specifically?"

"We trust you," Caroline said.

"Sure you do."

"Let's put it this way," Soames said. "We distrust everyone else."

"Including your old neighbor Willy?"

"Especially him," Soames spat out. "He'd cut my throat the minute we turned up the gems."

"What about Helen Ester? Don't you trust her?"

"Hell yes."

"Hell no," Caroline said with enough heat to turn my Wonder bread to toast.

Soames shrugged. "There you have it. Besides, Helen wouldn't be much help in the mountains."

"Does she know about the jewels?"

"No," Soames said. "You're the only one we've told."

"And suddenly I'm your partner."

"It's not suddenly. Me and Caroline have been talking it over for the past few days. You're the only one involved who's got more on his mind than the Lochemont jewels—namely, trapping whoever killed Meacham."

"Rueben Archuleta," I said.

"Whoever," Soames said and gave me a wry smile. "But he's probably the same man Caroline saw following her. You can protect us and save your skin at the same time."

Soames was right about one thing: When the jewels surfaced, so would Archuleta. And then would be my best chance to nail him.

"There's another little problem," I said. "Legally, those gems belong to National Insurance."

"Legally, hell!" Soames yelled, startling Caroline. "I paid for those jewels with twenty years of my goddamn life." His eyes blazed for a moment, then the fire went out and the brief flush ebbed from his face, leaving it prison-gray. He stared down at his beer can. "Twenty goddamn years. That's a third of a man's life, Lomax, gone forever, and no amount of money can bring it back."

"Grandpa . . ."

Soames gave her a weak smile.

"Sorry, honey," he said, then to me, "You're right about the jewels, Lomax. Besides, if word got out that I had them, there'd be nowhere for me to hide."

With a fortune in gems I could think of a few good places. Not that I'd try it. Not much.

"So we'll turn them over to the insurance company," Soames said magnanimously, "and collect the ten percent reward. Which is another reason we need you. National wouldn't give me a dime, and Caroline neither, being my kin. But they'd have to pay you. Ten percent of five million is half a million bucks, of which we'd let you keep ten percent—fifty grand."

I could have explained to them that a dishonest partner might keep the entire five hundred thousand for himself, maybe even the entire five million. But why start a partnership on the wrong foot?

"When do we begin?"

"Tomorrow," Caroline said.

We talked over a few of the details, then Caroline cleared the table. Soames didn't speak until we heard her running water in the kitchen sink.

"Quite a girl, eh?"

"She's nice," I said.

"Nice? That's all you think about her?"

"I think she's nice," I said. "I like her."

"You like her. Do you think other men like her?"

"What are you getting at?"

"Other men *do* like her. They call her and ask her out on dates, but she won't go. I met one of them, a young fellow she works with, a real nice guy, good manners, good-looking. But she won't give him the time of day. The others neither. Know why?"

I shook my head.

"Because I'm the only man in her life," he said bitterly. "She wants to take care of me. And the truth is I can't even get a job, since nobody's going to hire an aging ex-con. Since she can't support us both on what she makes now, she's been talking about getting a second job and working nights." Soames drank some beer, wiped his mouth with his hand, and wiped his hand on his pants. "Before she told me that, I wasn't sure I'd even look for the jewels."

"Come on."

"It's true," he said. "It was enough for me to know that nobody else would get them. But not now. Those jewels are for her, for what they'll buy her. A life, Lomax. Something I got robbed of. Do you understand what I'm saying?"

I was beginning to.

25

When I got home, there was a furniture truck parked in front of the apartment. Two beefy dudes were hauling my new stuff inside and shoving it into the proper rooms. I told them not to worry about being too careful, since I liked that used look. They obligingly banged the shit out of the doorframes.

After they'd gone, I gave my new couch a trial run—I stretched out on it and fell asleep during the second half of the Broncos' game. The phone woke me.

"Meet me at your office right away."

It was a man's voice, vaguely familiar.

"Who is this?"

"Can't talk now," he said and hung up.

I tried putting a face with the voice. The closest I could come was Detective O'Roarke, although I couldn't imagine why he'd act so mysteriously. I guess I'd have to ask him.

But neither O'Roarke nor anyone else was waiting anxiously outside my office. I went in and checked my machine for messages. There was one from Helen Ester, asking me to call. She answered on the first ring.

"I've been trying to reach you all day," she said. "I've decided to leave town."

"You can't," I said, keeping my voice calm. "I need you in court with me on Thursday."

"I know."

Someone began pounding on my office door. I covered the mouthpiece and yelled at whoever it was to wait a minute, then I spoke softly to Helen.

"You promised you'd be there. If you're not, things could go badly for me."

"I know, Jacob, and please don't worry. I'll be there. But ever since Archuleta threatened me, I haven't felt safe in Denver, so—"

Suddenly the office door burst open, kicked in by big Tom Two Hawks. He charged in, followed closely by his father and brother. Young Mathew pointed a gun at me, and Willy closed the busted door. I finally put a face on the urgent and mysterious caller: Mathew Two Hawks.

I showed them all the phone. "Be with you in a minute, guys."

"What is it, Jacob?" Helen said in my ear.

Before I could answer, Tom came around my desk and ripped the phone cord out of the wall.

"That just unplugs, you know."

Willy sat in the visitor's chair, his dark shades in place, his chin whiskers awry.

"Don't open any desk drawers." he said.

"Don't worry about it, the cops have all my guns."

"Who's worried, hombre?" Mathew said and waggled his revolver. It was a .22-caliber Colt Peacemaker with a nickel finish and a long barrel. Some people don't get nervous around .22's, but I'm not one of them. When I was on the force, I knew cops who said they'd rather get shot with a .38 than a .22. One in particular, a Sergeant Mobley, explained to me that with a .38 at least you're either dead right away and out of your misery or else wounded in one particular spot that the doctors can patch up. But a .22 slug is so fast and light that it can bounce around inside you like a steel ball in a pinball machine, ringing bells and racking up points. Ironically, a few weeks after

Mobley told me that, he entered a liquor store during a holdup and some punk kid shot him with a .22 rifle. The bullet hit Mobley in the collarbone, ricocheted down through his left lung and kidney, hit another bone, and exited through his lower abdomen. He was in surgery for six hours and died the next day. I'm sure Mathew Two Hawks had never heard of Sergeant Mobley, but he was aiming at my collarbone.

"Are you boys here for a chat?" I asked. "Or did you want to play Cowboys and Indians?"

"Don't get smart with Pop," Tom said, and slapped me hard across the back of the head.

I guess I'd had my fill of being hit in the head, because without even thinking I swiveled around and came out of my chair, driving my shoulder into Tom's midsection, knocking him off balance into the wall. I stayed close to him and hit him a few short chops under the ribs while he hammered me on the back. Willy was screaming and Mathew stepped up and shoved the muzzle of his Western-style gun in my face. "Sit down!" he yelled as Tom came off the wall with a huge right that I tried to duck. It caught me on the ear and knocked me back into my chair.

Mathew got between me and Tom and trained his dandy six-shooter on my midsection. I considered making a grab for it, but I didn't want it accidentally going off and reaffirming Sergeant Mobley's theory of vectors.

"Everybody just settle down," Willy said. "We came here to talk."

"Lucky for me."

"He's a smart ass, Pop. Let me knock his fucking head off."

"You keep still, Tom, or you can go sit in the car."

Tom pouted. Willy smiled from behind his shades and shook his head.

"You shouldn't rile that boy," he told me. "Sometimes I can't hold him back."

"I'll try to keep it in mind." Which wouldn't be too tough, since my throbbing ear felt as big as Tom Two Hawks' fist.

"Do that," he said, "because this is the last time I'm going to tell you to stay away from Charley Soames."

"Why? I like Charley. He's a fun guy."

"You're begging for trouble, Lomax."

"Can't I spend time with my new pal?"

"You're after the jewels," Mathew put in. "Just like the rest of us."

"I think my boy's probably right."

"There are no jewels," I said, trying to sound convincing.

Willy grinned. "Oh, there's jewels, all right. And Charley Soames knows right where they are."

"If that's true, Willy, then why hasn't he dug them up?"

"Because he's having trouble with his recollection, maybe on account of too many people hanging around. Or maybe on account of that damn granddaughter of his. He listens to her too much, if you ask me. Either way, he knows where they are."

"You're wasting your time," I said. "Rueben Archuleta got away with the jewels twenty years ago. You can look it up."

Willy snorted, fluttering his chin whiskers.

"Hell, I spent eight years in the cell next to Charley and talked to him every day and listened to every damn detail of his life. I heard it all so many times I could tell when he was lying and when he was telling the truth. He knows where he dumped that satchelful of gems. Maybe not the exact spot, but close enough to find it. He just won't admit it, at least not yet. But when he finally digs it up, he's going to give a fair share to his old pal Willy. And no son of a bitch like you is going to mess things up."

"Is that what you told Lloyd Fontaine?"

"Who?"

"He was hanging around Soames when somebody shot him in the head with a twenty-two just like Mathew's."

"Mathew never shot nobody," Willy said indignantly. "Tom neither."

"Then maybe it was you."

"I don't even know this Floyd whoever."

"Lloyd Fontaine."

"Whoever. Which ain't to say I never killed no one before." He cocked his forefinger at me.

"Is that what you did time for, Willy?"

Willy shrugged. "It was a fair fight. The jury just didn't see it that way. But we're talking about you, and I'm telling you now, one last time: Stay the fuck away from Charley Soames."

"Or what? You tell your son to commit murder?"

Mathew swallowed hard and glanced at his father.

"I'd take care of that job myself," Willy said.

"Then you're dumber than I thought. If you kill me, Soames is worthless to you."

"Huh?" Willy's eyebrows arched up from behind his shades.

"Pay attention, Willy," I said, making it up as I went along. "The police think I killed Zack Meacham on orders from Soames because Meacham was threatening him. They're keeping an eye on both of us. Anything happens to me and they'll be on Soames like ticks on a dog. You won't be able to get within ten feet of him without stepping on a cop."

Willy chewed the inside of his cheek. My confidence rose.

"With me gone, the cops won't have anyone to pin Meacham's murder on but Soames. And since he's already a convicted murderer, a jury will take about twenty minutes to send him back to Canon City. And that would put an end to your fantasy treasure hunt."

"Don't listen to him, Pop," Tom said from behind me. "Let's finish him now."

"No, I think maybe he's got a point."

I saw Mathew relax, and I breathed a bit easier.

"Now you're getting smart," I said to Willy.

"You're right, Lomax, we don't want any bodies lying around attracting cops. Besides, we don't have to kill you to keep you away from Charley Soames. We can just cripple you."

"Now you're talking, Pop," big Tom said. He sounded as excited as a kid ready to climb on an amusement park ride.

26

Willy Two Hawks came around the desk and took the pistol from Mathew.

"Put your hands behind your chair, Lomax. Tom, hold him."

Tom stood behind me and held my wrists tight enough to cut off the circulation.

"What're you going to do, Pop?" Mathew asked, worry in his voice. Simple assault was one thing, but whatever was about to happen was out of his league.

"I'm just gonna put him out of commission for a while," Willy said. He stood before me and pointed the gun like an accusing finger. "You hurt me today, Lomax. My neck is still sore. I don't forget things like that."

He lowered the gun, aiming at my right knee.

Tom twisted my wrists tighter. "Hold it right up against him, Pop, so's you don't miss."

"I know what the hell I'm doing, boy. You know, Lomax, when I was in Canon City, me and another dude busted up a guy's knees. He was in casts for two months, and when he got them off, he walked stiff-legged as a geek, probably still does."

He pressed the barrel against my kneecap, thumbed back the hammer, and squeezed the trigger. I jerked my leg as the gun fired. The bullet creased my pants and plowed into the floor.

"Goddammit," Tom said, and yanked at my wrists.

Willy chuckled into his chin whiskers. "You might as well be still, Lomax. The sooner this is over, the better for everyone. Come here, Mathew, and grab onto his leg."

"What's going on here?"

We all looked up to see Helen Ester standing in the doorway. She wore a tweed skirt and jacket and an expression of mild outrage, like a teacher who'd just walked in on a roomful of unruly students.

"Run!" I yelled. "Call the poli——"

Willy smacked me across the mouth with the barrel of the pistol—not hard, or I would have been choking on broken teeth, but hard enough to split my lip and give me the taste of blood.

"Get her, Mathew."

Mathew grabbed Helen Ester by the arm and pulled her into the room.

"Get your hands off me." She shoved her purse into Mathew's chest. "Jacob, what's going on?"

"They're the Indians and I'm the wagon train and you're the cavalry."

"Shut up," Willy said. "And you, missy, just stand there and be quiet and you won't get hurt. We're not going to do much here except slow down your friend."

"It's out of control now, Willy," I said. "There's a witness."

"It don't matter," he told me, lowering the gun to my kneecap.

"No!" Helen shouted and started forward, but Mathew wrapped his arms around her waist.

Willy looked up. "Just hold her still, son. And you," he said to me, "move that leg again and the lady gets hurt."

I tried not to look down. I watched Helen Ester struggling in Mathew's arms. She pulled something out of her purse and held it under his chin.

"Stop," she said.

Willy thumbed back the hammer.

"Right now, I mean it, tell him." She sounded scared but determined.

"Pop, I think she means it," Mathew said.

"What?"

"Don't shoot," Mathew said.

It wasn't clear whether Mathew meant Willy or Helen. Both were pointing guns. The nod went to Helen, though, because although her gun was smaller, a double-barreled Derringer, it was shoved under Mathew's jaw. Her left arm was hooked around the back of his neck to prevent him from pulling away. Willy straightened up. He looked mildly amused, but when he spoke, his voice was so cold you could almost see his breath.

"Put down the gun now, missy, and maybe I won't shoot your boyfriend."

"No," Helen said, swallowing hard. "You let him go." She pushed the fat little Derringer harder into Mathew's throat.

"Pop?" Mathew was sweating it.

"She's bluffing, son, she won't shoot."

"The hell I won't."

Even *I* was beginning to believe her.

"Jesuschrist, Pop!" Mathew cried.

"Okay, okay," Willy said and let his pistol hang down at his side. "Just put away the piece and the three of us will leave quietly, no problem."

"First let him go," Helen told Tom.

Tom tightened his grip on my arms. "She's bluffing, Pop."

"Let him go now or I swear to God I'll pull the trigger."

"Tom, Jesus." Mathew's face was pale.

"Take it easy, missy," Willy said, his voice as smooth as a snake's belly. "Tom, you do like she says."

"But, Pop—"

"Do it, goddammit!"

Tom let go. I stood up, rubbing feeling back into my wrists, then held out my hand. Willy gave me his gun. Helen released

Mathew, and he began taking deep breaths, nearly collapsing from relief.

"Party's over, guys," I said. "I'll send you a bill for the door."

The three men solemnly retreated—braves defeated by a woman. Willy gave me a whiskery smile.

"See you again real soon," he said. "You, too, missy."

He kicked a piece of splintered doorframe from his path and walked out.

"Oh, Jacob, I—"

"Wait."

I made sure Willy and his sons walked all the way down the hall, then I watched from the window as they drove off in Willy's battered green Chevy. There was a cab parked at the curb, lights on, motor idling. Helen huddled against me.

"I've never been so frightened in my life," she said.

I put down Willy's gun and held her in my arms.

"I thought you did fine."

"It was all an act, Jacob. Inside I was scared to death."

"Maybe so, but your timing was outstanding."

"Thank God," she said. "I'd heard a terrible crash, and then when we were disconnected and I was unable to get through, I knew something was terribly wrong. I took a taxi right over."

"Lucky for me. Let me see your gun."

It was a small-caliber piece, stainless steel with fancy engraving and worn rosewood grips. I handed it back and she put it in her purse.

"When did you start carrying that?"

"I bought it yesterday after Archuleta attacked us. The man at the gun store called it a 'purse gun,' and I thought I'd feel safer with it, but I don't, not really. I suppose it was foolish of me."

"It is loaded, isn't it?"

She smiled. "God, I *think* so. The man at the store showed me how to use it and said it was ready to go." She reached in her purse, I thought for the weapon. Instead, she pulled out a cigarette and a lighter. Her hands were shaking.

I sat her down, then got out the Jack Daniel's and a couple of glasses and poured us each three fingers. Helen sipped it like she would a liqueur.

"You said on the phone you were leaving town."

She nodded. "I'm not safe here, Jacob. Archuleta called me last night."

"What?"

"Actually, it was three in the morning. He warned me again to stay away from Charles. I'm getting out, Jacob. I'm scared to death of that man."

"Where will you go?"

"I have a place in the mountains," she said, blowing smoke at the ceiling. "It belonged to my late husband, and we stayed there occasionally."

"It's essential that you be with me in court on Thursday."

"Please don't worry. I fully intend to be there. But I can't stay in Denver, not with Archuleta around."

"Have you told Soames you're leaving?"

"Yes, and he agrees it's probably best, at least for now. I gave him the rural route number, should he feel the urge to write."

"That seems a bit cold."

She stubbed out her cigarette in the ashtray.

"There's no phone. Besides, even before Archuleta showed up, it was becoming difficult for me to be around Charles."

"Why?"

"Because of Caroline. She hates me, and she makes no secret about it. She thinks I have ulterior motives for wanting to be near her grandfather."

"She's just a kid," I said, as if that mattered.

Helen shook her head sadly. "If it wasn't for your hearing coming up, I might leave for good, go back to San Francisco."

"You still love him, don't you."

"I . . . I'm fond of him, Jacob. It's you I . . ." She stood up abruptly. "I should go. In fact, I was packing when you phoned."

"You're leaving Denver now?"

She nodded gravely, then gave me a brief smile.

"I'll be back Thursday."

"Call me Thursday morning," I said. "If you can't reach me, meet me at the City and County Building before one o'clock."

She hugged me, her head against my chest.

"I'll be glad when this is all over," she said. Her voice was so soft and sweet that I had trouble picturing her holding a gun to the throat of Mathew Two Hawks.

27

On Monday morning Caroline Lochemont answered her door wearing an oversized flannel shirt, hiking boots, and shorts. Her legs were tan and smoothly muscled. When she saw Willy Two Hawks' pistol stuck in my belt, she told me to get rid of it.

"We may need it," I said.

"No guns."

I looked at Soames for help, but he merely shrugged.

"This may seem like a romp in the woods to you," I said to Caroline, "but if Rueben Archuleta shows up, things could get ugly."

Caroline finally agreed, reluctantly, and since she and Soames had already loaded up her Toyota Land Cruiser, the three of us set out at once—Caroline driving, Soames beside her, and me in the back with the gear. The sun was bright, the fall air was clean and crisp, and the traffic was light. We rode in silence, the car filled with a sense of quiet apprehension. As we climbed I-70 into the mountains, I found myself looking over the seat, checking the scattering of cars behind us. Twice I thought I saw a familiar tan Ford, but I couldn't be sure.

When we got to Idaho Springs, Caroline took the second turnoff and headed away from the town, south toward Mount Evans. The two-lane blacktop twisted up the narrow canyon cut by West Chicago Creek, which flowed cheerfully by on our left.

The slopes were steep and rocky and heavily wooded. They were cut by smaller canyons and draws. The floor of the main canyon widened in places, and there were houses—some old, some new. After a few miles Caroline slowed down as if to turn onto a dirt road that climbed up a side canyon to the right.

"Go to the shack first, honey. I want Lomax to get into the spirit of things." Soames's tone was sardonic.

Caroline stayed on the asphalt road for several more miles, then pulled into the weeds and stopped before a dilapidated one-room building featuring gray weathered wood, boarded windows, and a swaybacked roof.

"Kinda cozy, ain't it, Lomax?" Soames said. "Ed Teague had a lot of fun in there a few decades ago. Back over here and up that ravine was where I ran for my life, a few million dollars in gems in my hands and the Angel of Death at my heels, blasting merrily away with a twelve-gauge shotgun." He shook his head and scratched his gray chin. "It don't look quite like I remember it, but things change after twenty years."

There was something about seeing the murder shack that bothered me, something I couldn't quite put my finger on.

Caroline made a U-turn and took us back to the dirt road. It was steep and rough, but passable even in two-wheel-drive. Barely passable. After half an hour of teeth-jarring and kidney-shaking, Caroline stopped on a level area and shut off the engine. Soames and I hustled out and stood for a few thankful minutes behind our respective trees. By the time we returned to the Land Cruiser, Caroline already had the gear out—two backpacks, canteens, a shovel, and a brush hook. She unfolded a U.S.G.S. quad map. It showed densely placed brown contour lines on a green background.

"Here we are," she said.

Her finger tapped the intersection of a twisting pair of dashed lines, supposedly a road, and a contour line marked "9000." The few square miles around us on the map were peppered with tiny Y's and half-blackened squares—mine tunnels and shafts, according to Caroline.

"Down that ravine a couple miles is the shack." Soames was pointing to our left. "There's a half-dozen mines between here and there that we've already checked. Now we go upslope."

"How far?"

"All through here," Caroline said, drawing her finger across four or five miles on the map.

"Great. That doesn't look like more than fifty or sixty mines."

"What'd you want me to do, Lomax, paint a sign on it?"

"Great."

"Let's get going," Caroline said and picked up the larger of the two packs.

"I'll take that one," I said, big, gallant guy that I was.

"Whatever." She loosened the shoulder straps and helped put it on my back. It was heavier than it looked.

"What've you got in here?"

"Climbing equipment, lanterns, a first-aid kit, and so on. I'll carry it if you like."

"Hey, gimme a break."

Caroline took the map, a canteen, and the other pack and led the way uphill. I followed Soames and carried a one-gallon canteen, the brush hook, and the shovel. We started off in chilly mountain shadows but soon walked into sunlight. Caroline moved easily ahead of me and Soames, sometimes out of sight. She would frequently come back to see how we were doing, then move out again, not even breathing hard. I guess her twisted ankle was all better now.

It wasn't long before the altitude started getting to me. I was huffing for air and sweating freely. The straps on the pack dug into my armpits. My heels were moving around in my hiking boots, and even though I wore two pairs of socks, I knew blisters were growing. And if fighting the steepness of the slope and the weight of the backpack weren't enough, I was constantly helping

Soames over every little bump in the ground. After a while, though, I was glad he was there to slow things down. Caroline let us rest now and then and fed us water and trail mix.

At ten o'clock we found our first mine. The entrance was almost overgrown with brush, but it was plainly marked by tailings and timbers.

Caroline pointed it out on the map, then drew a small circle around it. It was one in a group of seven tunnels in the immediate vicinity—the vicinity being acres of hillside.

Caroline began clearing the entrance to the mine with the brush hook, swinging the long-handled blade in big lazy arcs, slashing through the overgrowth. By the time I'd gotten my pack off, she was nearly finished. I dragged her cuttings out of the way, and when I moved a rotted six-by-six timber that lay diagonally across the entrance, dirt and small rocks sprinkled down.

"Now what?" I asked.

"We go in."

"I was afraid you'd say that."

We carried lanterns and proceeded single-file into the dark wound in the mountainside, with Caroline leading the way.

The tunnel was about four feet on a side, which meant we had to stoop over, then bend lower still to get under some of the overhead timbers. It was cool and damp inside. Water ran in tiny rivulets at our feet, and I could hear it dripping from deep within the mountain. I began to feel a tightness in my chest—partly from walking stooped over, but mostly because I felt the weight of the mountain on my back. I fought the urge to run outside.

Soames stopped, and I nearly bumped into him.

"This is far enough, don't you think, honey?" he said. "We should have come to it by now."

"Come to what?"

"The shaft, Lomax, the shaft."

"Stay there," Caroline said. "I'll check ahead a little more."

"Be careful."

We watched her silhouette move down the tunnel.

"If she collapses," Soames said, "take a deep breath and go get her and drag her out fast. And don't breathe in between."

"What the hell are you talking about?"

"Mine gas, bad air, whatever you want to call it."

I sniffed.

"You can't smell it," Soames said. "It just lacks oxygen. That's why miners in the old days used to bring in canaries in cages. When the birds dropped dead, the miners ran out."

"Terrific."

Caroline was outlined by her lamp fifty feet away. I took a few deep breaths and wondered if I could get to her and drag her to the entrance without breathing. Then her light hit us in the face as she started back toward us.

Outside, I filled my lungs with sweet mountain air, raised my face to the sun, and tried not to think that this was only our first mine.

Half an hour later, we entered our second. This mine, unlike the previous one, was as dry as dust. We found no shaft. Once outside, Caroline opened her backpack on a large, flat rock and we ate lunch in a small circle, cross-legged like movie Indians.

"What will you do with the reward money?" I asked Caroline between bites of bologna. Christ, is that all these two ate? Maybe that's all they could afford.

"Reward . . ."

"The insurance reward," Soames said, patting Caroline on the knee. "Remember, Lomax has to turn in the jewels for us, since the insurance company wouldn't give me or you a cent."

"Oh."

"Well?"

"Oh, well, we'll go . . . we'll probably move out of Denver, someplace where it's warm most of the time."

"And where there's plenty of beach," Soames said. "Salt air's the thing." He crumpled up his sandwich wrapper and tossed it aside. Caroline picked it up and put it in her pack.

"What about you, Lomax?" Soames said. "You should come away with about fifty grand. Maybe you could buy a new car."

"I like the old one."

"Or hell," he said, "an upright citizen like you, you could always give your share to charity."

"We've got to find the jewels first."

"Oh, we'll find them," Soames said.

But we didn't, not after searching five more tunnels. Each one had its own design, its own personality, dug by miners of varying degrees of expertise who followed elusive veins of ore. Some mines were simple straight bores into the mountain, while others had side tunnels or shafts. But they all had one thing in common: Each and every one scared the hell out of me. I kept waiting for the mountain to wince and close its open sore with me inside.

By now Soames was exhausted, and I wasn't far behind. We made our way down to the dirt road as the sky went from blue to purple and the air turned cold. The Toyota Land Cruiser was exactly where we'd left it. But parked behind it was the ubiquitous beat-up green Chevy of Willy Two Hawks.

28

Mathew Two Hawks was leaning against the side of the Chevy, a .30-30 Winchester lever-action rifle cradled in his arms. He looked like he was watering his pony and keeping an eye out for soldiers. When he saw us, he leaned toward the side window.

"Here they come, Pop."

Willy and big Tom climbed out of the car. Willy finished his Bud and tossed the can in the dirt with a half-dozen other empties.

"Hiya, Charley," Willy said. "Find anything interesting up there?"

"Lots of rocks and trees."

"Let's have a look in that pack."

"We ate all the sandwiches," I said.

"Tom."

Tom obeyed his father and stepped up to me, ready to rip the pack off my back and maybe an arm with it. I unshouldered it, and he took it from me.

"You've got no right, you goddamn ape," Caroline said angrily.

"Oh, let him be, hon," Soames said.

"Your kid's got spunk," Willy said.

"She's not my kid, Willy. She's my grandkid."

"Same difference."

Soames shook his head in resignation. "You got any more beer?"

"Hell yeah. And you, Lomax, I want my gun back."

"I sold it."

"Then you owe me a hundred bucks."

The two ex-cons climbed in the Chevy. Meanwhile, Tom had jammed the zipper and couldn't get the pack open.

"At least let me—"

Before Caroline could finish, Tom whipped out a hunting knife from his belt and slashed open the pack.

"Goddamn you." Caroline started forward, and I grabbed her arm.

"Don't worry about it."

"You're going to let these jerks do whatever they want?"

"We'll get you a new pack," I said.

Tom dumped everything out of the pack and pawed through it on the ground. "Nothing," he said, then yelled to the car, "There's nothing, Pop!"

He straightened up and held the knife loosely at his side.

"Now let's see your pack, babe."

"Fuck off, asshole."

Tom threw back his head and whooped.

"Hear that, Mathew? This squaw has got spit." He came forward, and I stepped in front of Caroline. Tom raised the knife to waist level. The blade glinted in the dying light. "You could die right here," he said. He meant it.

With some effort I turned my back to him.

"Give me your pack," I said to Caroline.

"Goddammit, Jake, why do—"

"Just give it to me."

She glared at me for a moment, then stepped around me, pulling off her pack. She unzipped it and dumped the contents on big Tom's boots. Then she threw the empty pack at his face. He caught it easily and whooped again. He was good at it.

"Maybe I should search you, babe," he said. "Right down to the short hairs."

She moved behind me.

"That's enough," I said.

Tom went into a semicrouch and flipped his knife from hand to hand. "Maybe you think you could stop me." His voice was a low rumble.

"Hey, Tom, lay off," Mathew said. Good old Mathew. "You know what Pop said."

Tom's eyes never left mine.

"When this is over," he said, "I'm going to skin you like a rabbit."

"Then can we be friends?"

Tom gave me his fiercest warrior look, spit in the dirt, and went back to the car.

"You'd better not poke him too hard," Mathew said.

"I figured you'd stop him," I said. "Isn't that what the rifle's for?"

Soames got out of the Chevy and came over to Caroline.

"I'm going to ride back to town with Willy."

"No," she said. "You come with us."

"Don't worry about it. I want to talk a few things over with him."

He gave her arm a squeeze, then climbed in the back of the Chevy with Willy. Mathew slid into the driver's seat, spun the tires in the dirt, and drove up the road and around the curve. A few minutes later, they came back down and roared past us in a cloud of dust. Caroline stared after them.

"He'll be all right," I said lamely.

She didn't bother to reply.

We gathered our things off the ground, then drove up the narrow road to a place wide enough to turn around. I saw a truck parked off the road behind some trees—a big blue Dodge pickup with fat tires, a chrome roll bar, and spotlights mounted on the roof. There was no one in sight. Caroline turned the Land Cruiser around, and we headed down the road and out of the mountains.

"Do you think your grandfather will tell Willy where he hid the jewels?" I asked. "I mean, about the mine shaft."

"No, I . . . I don't know. I don't think so."

"If he does, then—"

"I said no, didn't I?" Her knuckles were white on the wheel.

"I'm sure you're right," I said, "since he wants to use the reward money to take care of you."

She glanced at me, then back at the road, smiling.

"He said that? And here I thought I was going to take care of him."

"Your grandfather wants you to be free from that obligation, Caroline. He wants you to have a life of your own, get married, whatever."

She nodded, slowly, sadly. "You know, before my grandfather got out of prison, I was practically engaged to a boy I work with. Jeffrey. But not many people want to be around an ex-con." Her tone was bitter. "I haven't seen any of my friends for weeks. I still see Jeffrey at work, but, I don't know, it's not like it was before. And maybe I don't blame him. All I know now is I want to find those jewels and take my grandfather far away from here, away from people like Willy Two Hawks and the rest, someplace where we can both start over." She smiled. "And five million dollars should give us quite a start."

"The reward will be about half a million," I corrected.

"Oh, right. Half a million." But her smile didn't fade.

When we got to Caroline's house, she drove around to the back and parked in the garage. I walked her to the door. All the house lights were out.

"He probably went to a bar with them," she said.

"Do you want me to wait till he gets home?"

"No." She went in without saying good night.

When I got to my apartment, I looked through Lloyd Fontaine's newspaper clippings until I found a photo of the murder shack. Ever since Soames had insisted I see it, something had bothered me. The picture I held was faded with age, but it more or less resembled the shack Soames had pointed out. But something was definitely wrong.

And then it hit me.

I dialed Caroline's number.

"We were searching the wrong area," I told her.

"What? But my grandfather is certain—"

"He's wrong. I'll pick you up tomorrow and we'll get it straightened out."

Tuesday morning I picked up Caroline at her house.

"Where's your grandfather?"

"He didn't come home last night." She sounded more angry than worried. "He's probably sleeping off a drunk with Willy. Now, what's this about us searching the wrong area?"

"You've been starting at the wrong point," I said. "The wrong shack."

"What do you mean? You saw the old building."

"I saw *an* old building. Someone told me the murder shack had been torn down."

I took U.S. 6 rather than the interstate, because its grade was gentler and the old Olds could do without the added strain. Even so, cars were passing us whenever the road straightened out enough to lose its solid yellow line. That was how I spotted the tan Ford a quarter mile behind us. He was hanging back, keeping his distance, letting cars go around him when they could. But he temporarily created long stretches of empty road between us. Caroline saw me watching the mirror.

"What's wrong?"

"We've got company."

She turned in the seat. "The brown car?"

"I think he's working with Archuleta," I said.

Caroline sat up rigidly and stared straight ahead.

"Can we outrun him?" she said nervously.

"Probably not."

"Then what do we do?"

"We keep going. I doubt he'll try anything."

"What if he does?"

"Willy's gun is in the glove compartment."

Caroline pressed back in her seat, away from the dashboard—as if "gun" meant "snake."

Somewhere before Idaho Springs, the Ford dropped back out of sight. I took the first turnoff into the town and parked near the *Gazette* building.

Gladys Hicks led us to Witherspoon's office. He was on the phone, and he waved us to a seat. There weren't any. I moved a pile of paper from a chair and let Caroline sit.

"Jacob Lomax," he said, hanging up the phone. "I thought I might see you again."

"Why?"

"Just a newsman's instinct. Hello," he said to Caroline.

"Caroline Lochemont, Harry Witherspoon."

Witherspoon reached over the mess on his desk and shook her hand. His eyes twinkled at me. He knew something was up.

"How busy are you?" I asked.

"I'm always busy."

"Maybe we should come back later."

"And I can always take time off. What can I do for you?"

"Show us the site of the murder shack," I said.

"You changed your mind, eh? What is it, historical curiosity?"

"You might call it that."

Witherspoon stood and rolled his sleeves down over sinewy forearms. He was in good shape for a guy in his fifties, and he obviously did more than sit behind a desk all day. When we got in my car, he squeezed into the front seat so he could rub knees with Caroline. She didn't seem to mind. I did.

I drove up West Chicago Creek canyon. Caroline leaned forward when we approached the swaybacked shack.

"That's not it," Witherspoon said. Then, "So that's why . . ."

"Why what?"

"Nothing," he said.

After two or three miles on the curving road, Witherspoon pointed to an asphalt driveway. I pulled into it. The drive led to a wrought iron gate and beyond to a ranch-style home with a shake-shingle roof and three Dobermans that were as motionless as statues, except for the saliva dripping off their bone-crushing teeth. We climbed out of the Olds. One of the dogs barked to tell us not to come closer. We didn't.

"The shack was right where the house stands now," Witherspoon said.

"Are you sure?"

He looked at Caroline. "Sure I'm sure. I was here with the cops and took pictures of the whole bloody mess. This is the spot."

Caroline's eyes moved above the house and up the ravine beyond. Witherspoon watched her and smiled, as if he were in on some big secret. I was beginning not to like him.

"Let's go," I said.

I drove back to the *Gazette*.

"Thanks for the tour," I told Witherspoon.

"Believe me, it was my pleasure."

What bothered me was that he sounded like he meant it.

29

I drove us out of the mountains, checking the mirror all the way. The tan Ford didn't show itself. Caroline seemed pleased, but not about that.

"If it hadn't been for Harry Witherspoon," she said, "we might never have figured out the right area to search."

"Maybe not. But we've got another serious problem."

"What?"

"The Two Hawks family," I said.

"Oh. You're right."

"Of course, we can keep them off our backs temporarily."

"How?"

"We make sure they're with your grandfather. Like now."

She looked puzzled. I suppose because she couldn't imagine doing anything without Soames.

"You and I would be free to search the mines," I explained.

"I don't know. . . ."

"Why not? You know what to look for, don't you?"

"I suppose." She chewed her lip.

"Unless you've got a better idea."

"No," she said. "You're probably right. But Willy might get suspicious when you and I drive off in my four-wheel-drive loaded with gear."

"So we leave it all in your garage and buy whatever we need."

She gave me a big smile. "Have you got any money?"

"Hell, I've got plastic."

Caroline found most of what we needed at a mountaineering store on Bannock Street—Perlon ropes, oval snap links called carabiners, slings and harnesses, descenders and ascenders, wired nuts, and a backpack to carry it all—pushing my Visa card to the limit. We picked up the hand tools at Target.

When we got to Caroline's house, we saw Willy's Chevy parked out front.

"They're back," I said. "You want me to go in with you?"

"No."

"Are you sure your grandfather's all right?"

"I'm sure," she said sadly. "He's done this before—gone drinking with Willy and sons, slept it off at Willy's house, then come back here the next day to start over with beers from the fridge." She shook her head, and for a moment I thought she might cry. "He's still influenced by that . . . that scum."

"Influenced enough to tell them what we're up to?"

"Absolutely not," she snapped.

"Okay," I said gently. "Just checking."

I drove around to the garage. While Caroline dug through her gear for the quad map, I removed the Land Cruiser's rotor and put it under the front seat.

"If Willy's still here in the morning," I said, "tell him your car won't start, then phone me for a ride to work. If he's not here, tell your grandfather to stay home and give Willy the same story, if he shows up. Can you get someone at work to cover for you in case Willy checks there?"

"Jeffrey will."

"Good. Then I'll see you in the morning."

She put her hand on my arm as I turned to leave.

"Thanks for helping," she said.

"Hey, don't thank me. I'm only in it for the money."

She smiled at my little joke. I think it was a joke.

* * *

On Wednesday morning Willy's Chevy was still parked in front of Caroline's house. I honked and Caroline came out carrying a purse as big as a shopping bag. She'd smuggled out her hiking boots and a change of clothes.

"Willy wanted us all to go treasure hunting today," she said. "But I told him I had to work, and then, of course, my car wouldn't start. Also, my grandfather isn't feeling well."

"Did Willy buy it?"

She nodded, unhappily. "But truly, my grandfather isn't well. It's the pressure. Everyone's hounding him for the jewels. And I . . . I suppose I'm the worst."

"Don't blame yourself," I told her, and stopped myself from ending with, "I'd do the same in your position."

I drove her to Summer Sky Bicycles and waited in the car while she went in to establish her cover. Then we headed for the hills. As far as I could tell, no one followed us. We didn't stop until I'd turned up West Chicago Creek. Caroline traced a path on the quad map from the site of the murder shack, up a ravine, to a scattering of mines—perhaps a dozen or so.

"It's probably one of these," she said. "We can drive up this way." She pointed to a snaky dashed line on the map.

"That's not much of a road."

"You're right. Maybe this old bucket can't make it."

"Please don't call her a bucket," I said. "Cars have feelings, too, you know."

She smiled. "Sorry."

We drove several miles past the site of the murder shack and nearly missed the road we wanted because it was so overgrown with scrub brush. It soon deteriorated to a trail. The old Olds didn't like it one bit. She lurched and groaned and scraped her bottom with a screech, while I struggled to avoid oil-pan-ripping rocks.

I stopped near some huge boulders that blocked the trail. With Caroline's Land Cruiser we could have driven around the rocks, up through the trees, and back down to the trail. But the Olds would have none of it, so I shut her off.

The mines were scattered over several miles of mountainside, and by the time we got to the first one, the stiffness from Monday's climb had worked itself out of my legs. Caroline and I searched the mine in vain. And the second. The entrance to our third mine had suffered a small rockslide. We spent the rest of the day digging through the entrance—only to find that a few yards farther in the entire tunnel had collapsed. Whether one year ago or fifty, it was impossible to tell.

"What if this is the one?" I asked Caroline.

"I don't know. When we've searched the rest, I guess we could come back."

"With what? Dynamite and power shovels?"

"I said I don't know!" she shouted, then stomped out of the mine. I followed her through the trees and the deep afternoon shadows all the way down to the car. I backed the Olds down off the mountain and stopped at a gas station in Idaho Springs so Caroline could wash up and change clothes. When she climbed back in the car, she looked shiny clean and mollified.

"Sorry I got mad," she said.

"No problem."

"It's just so frustrating."

"Tell me."

We drove back to the city in silence. When we got to Caroline's house, Willy's car was still parked out front.

"Tomorrow?" she asked.

"I suppose."

"We'll find it," she said. It was a plea. "We've got to."

"I'll pick you up at seven-thirty," I said.

She smiled, then scooted over and gave me a quick kiss on the cheek, and immediately looked embarrassed, which surprised me. She hurried out of the car and practically ran up the walk to her house. Until then I'd been thinking of her in an avuncular way, and I'd assumed she'd been doing the same. I sat there for a few minutes wondering if maybe I'd been missing something, if maybe Caroline and I . . . But no, I told myself, forget it. She's just a kid. A sweet, generous, pretty kid. Although nicely developed. Niece, Lomax, think niece.

Thursday morning I called Abner Greenspan at his home and his office and got recordings at both places. I stopped by my office to check my machine for word from Helen Ester. Nothing. I phoned Greenspan again and left messages on both his machines that Helen Ester had promised me she'd be at the courthouse at one o'clock today to testify on my behalf and thereby blow the case of Dalrymple and Krenshaw right out of the water and, oh, yes, that I would be unavoidably detained.

I picked up Caroline at her house. Willy's car hadn't moved.

"He spent the night on my couch," she said with disgust and, I think, fear. "I'm not sure how much longer he'll buy the story about my car."

"We'll take care of that," I said. "One way or the other."

I left the Olds at the same spot as yesterday, where boulders blocked the trail. Caroline and I shouldered our gear and headed off, each of us fighting a nagging sense of futility.

We searched most of the day for a mine that appeared plainly on the map but that we were unable to locate. Either the map was wrong, or else the mine's entrance was completely buried.

By three-thirty we'd given up and moved on to the next mine on the map. The sky had clouded over, and a cold breeze slapped our faces. I wondered how things had gone with Greenspan and Ester and Dalrymple at my preliminary hearing. Or maybe since I hadn't been there, Greenspan had gotten it postponed.

Caroline and I entered the mine. It was high enough for me to walk nearly erect under the sagging timbers. After we'd advanced thirty or forty feet, there were fewer timbers—the tunnel now bored though mostly solid rock. After a hundred feet, I stopped, even though our lanterns showed the tunnel extending deeper into the mountain. This was the distance Soames remembered encountering the shaft.

"Far enough, right?" The tunnel walls seemed too damn close, and I could feel their pressure.

"Wait," Caroline said.

She shone her lantern on some boards on the tunnel floor just ahead. We moved closer and saw that the boards partially covered a black, gaping hole.

"My God," she said. "This might be it."

She knelt down and began pulling boards away from the hole.

"Be careful," I cautioned, feeling like a coward for not going nearer the hole.

After a few minutes she'd completely uncovered the mouth of the shaft. It was rectangular, about three feet wide by six feet long—the size of a grave. It ran lengthwise along the tunnel, leaving enough room to walk past. Caroline lay flat on her stomach and shone her light into the inky black pit.

"It's pretty deep," she said, "but I think I see something down there. Bring your lantern."

I crawled forward like a baby, lay down beside her, and shone my light down the shaft, illuminating dust motes. The walls of the shaft were vertical and cut from solid rock. The miners had probably used a winch, long gone, to lower and raise men and ore. There was something at the bottom, a good eighty feet below us. It looked like a dark, lumpy rock, but it was too far away to be certain.

"I'll be right back," Caroline said, and she was gone before I could run out with her.

I scooted away from the shaft, then took in long slow breaths, trying not to panic in the dark, trying not to dwell on the time when I was a child of five and the bully on the block and his friend rolled me up in a discarded rug in a vacant lot and left me alone with my arms pinned to my sides and my eyes in darkness and my nose pressed against the musty, stifling carpet and I couldn't unroll myself or even move and if someone didn't save me I would die, I would suffocate, I would starve, and I was trapped in there for hours and days, it seemed. Finally I was set free by a neighbor lady. She said I'd been trapped for only a few minutes. I still say it was days.

Caroline returned with a three-pronged grappling hook attached to a coil of rope. She shone her light on me.

"You okay?"

"Couldn't be better. Now what?"

"I'll try to snag whatever is down there," she said. "If I can't, well . . ."

"Well what?" I knew what.

"I'll have to climb down."

"Great."

"It's not that big a deal, Jake. Give me some light."

Caroline sat near the edge of the abyss, knees up and feet apart, and lowered the hook over the side, the rope uncoiling beside her. She stopped when she'd played out about eighty feet. Then she lay down, peeking over the edge. She gently swung the rope and tugged, and swung it again and tugged.

"Got it," she said triumphantly.

She sat back and began pulling up the rope, hand over hand, grunting with the effort. I aimed my lantern over Caroline's shoulder and waited for the treasure to be hauled up—a satchelful of precious gems.

"It's heavier than I thought," Caroline said and pulled her catch up into the light.

It wasn't a satchelful of gems.

It was a partially clothed, age-blackened, desiccated corpse—its wild-haired skull agape in a death grin.

Caroline screamed and lurched back, knocking the lantern from my hand. By the time I'd recovered the light, the mummified remains had dropped back down the shaft, taking our hook and rope with it.

30

We stood outside the mine in the chill shadow of the mountain. Caroline was shivering, but not from the cold.

"What . . . I mean who . . ."

"Probably a treasure hunter who got too close to the edge."

"My God."

"Whoever it is, he's been down there a long—" I stopped. I'd seen movement on the mountain's slope, fifty yards above us.

"What's wrong?" Caroline asked.

"Someone's up there."

We stood perfectly still, staring up at the dark pines, listening to the wind sift through the branches.

"Maybe it was nothing," I said. "Let's get out of here."

"But I'm sure the satchel is in that shaft."

"We'll come back tomorrow. You need a drink and so do I."

We went to the Buffalo Bar in Idaho Springs. I'd been in there once years before, and I remembered shot-and-beer drinkers, high-backed wooden booths, and the heads of bisons mounted on the walls. Now there were skylights, hanging plants, and big-screen TV's. At least they'd left one buffalo head. I left Caroline under its glassy-eyed gaze, and used the pay phone in the back. It was nearly six, but Abner Greenspan was still at his office.

"Where the hell are you?" he said. "No, don't tell me. Better that I don't know. Why weren't you in court today?"

"It couldn't be helped. What happened?"

Greenspan sighed audibly. "You bought yourself a lot of grief is what happened. Judge Sanchez issued a bench warrant for your arrest for jumping bail. In effect, you've waived your right to a preliminary hearing. You're to be held without bond and bound over for trial."

"Goddammit, Abner."

"Hey, Jake, I *told* you to be there. I did all I could, but—"

"What about Helen Ester?"

"What about her?"

"Didn't she tell Sanchez that Dalrymple forged those statements against me?"

"She wasn't there."

"What? Why not?"

"How should I know?"

"Didn't she call you?"

"No."

"Something's wrong."

"No shit, Sherlock. Look, my advice to you is to surrender yourself to the court forthwith. It will look better at your trial."

"You've got to find her, Abner. She can straighten out Sanchez. She probably left a message on the answering machine at my office. Check it out. Vaz has an extra key, or hell, just kick it down, everyone else does."

"Are you coming in or not?"

"Not until I get my hands on Rueben Archuleta."

"Who?"

"He killed Meacham."

"Can you prove that?"

"I can make him confess, believe me."

"This is wrong, Jake. You've got to turn yourself in."

"Find Ester."

"As your attorney I would advise—"

"Just find her."

"Yeah, yeah, sure." He hung up.

When I got back to the table, Caroline had already ordered burgers and onion rings, and she was filling two glasses from a pitcher of beer. I told her about my phone call with Greenspan.

"The best way to make Archuleta show himself is for us to get the jewels."

Caroline nodded in agreement. "We'll do it tomorrow," she said.

She'd said "we," but she was the one who'd descend into the pit with a shriveled corpse waiting for her at the bottom.

"There's one small problem," I said. "I can't go back to Denver tonight. The cops will be watching my apartment and office, and there's probably an all-points out on the Olds."

"So what do we do?"

"Spend the night up here."

She frowned for a moment. "Okay," she said. "I'll call my grandfather and let him know."

"Willy Two Hawks might be there."

"I'll think up some good lie."

I paid the check, then waited while Caroline used the phone in the back. Getting the jewels tomorrow would be one thing, but using them as bait for Rueben Archuleta would be something else. I'd have to wait for him to make his move, and avoid the cops while I did so.

Caroline returned. "I have to go home. Now." She looked upset.

"What is it?"

"My grandfather said he'd explain when I got there. He told me he was all right, but . . . I just have to go."

"You can't take my car. The cops might pick you up and hold you for questioning."

"Then I'll rent one."

"In this town? Forget it."

"Then what?"

"We'll borrow one."

We drove to the *Gazette* building. Closed. At the corner drugstore I looked up Witherspoon, H. R., in the local directory. I started to dial, then changed my mind. It was always easier to say "no" over the phone.

"Let's find his house," I told Caroline.

We did. It was an old Victorian frame built before the turn of the century, with a steeply peaked roof, a wide porch supporting narrow columns, and a profusion of wood filigree. Warm yellow light spilled through the lace curtains. When Witherspoon answered the door, he looked alarmed. But he recovered immediately and gave us a big smile.

"You folks really took me by surprise," he said. "Come in, come in."

The interior of the house featured hardwood floors, faded floral patterns on the furniture and rugs, and iron lamps with leaded glass shades. A woman was sitting in the parlor. She was tight-lipped and as faded as the room. Her patterned shawl perfectly matched her chair, and she seemed to blend into the surroundings. The only thing out of place in the house was Harry Witherspoon in blue jeans, flannel shirt, and stockinged feet.

"I'd like you to meet my wife," he said. "Myrna, this is Jacob Lomax and his friend Caroline."

Myrna nodded to acknowledge our presence, then went back to her book, its cover threadbare and devoid of color. When she turned the page, it crackled with age.

"Let's talk in my den," Witherspoon said.

Caroline and I followed him down a hallway and into a good-sized room, which had an enormous old desk at one end and a seven-foot-tall stuffed grizzly at the other. Caroline started when she saw the bear.

"That's Ben," Witherspoon said and sat behind his desk. "Would you believe I bought him at a garage sale?"

The walls were cluttered with bookshelves and framed photographs of Witherspoon——here holding a string of rainbow trout, there showing off a brace of freshly shot pheasants, over there smiling with a group of sunburned, parka-clad folks atop a snowy peak. Myrna wasn't in any of the pictures. I wondered what she and Witherspoon had in common. Then I remembered he'd told me her father had owned the *Gazette*. Myrna probably owned it now.

"What brings you folks up here?" Witherspoon asked. The light gleamed on his steel-framed glasses.

"We're in a jam," I said, "and we need a favor. Two favors, actually."

"Are they illegal or will they cost me money?" he asked with a grin.

"Neither."

"Then let's hear them."

"Caroline needs a ride into Denver, and I need a place to spend the night."

"No problem," he said without hesitation. "You can sleep there on the couch." He looked at Caroline. "Can you drive a stick shift?"

"Of course."

"Then you can borrow my wife's car."

"She won't mind?"

"She won't even know," Witherspoon said in a mock whisper. "She rarely drives anymore. Just have the car back by eight or nine tomorrow morning."

"I really appreciate it," Caroline said. "I'll pay you whatever you—"

Witherspoon stopped her with a wave of the hand.

"Then I'd like to leave now, if it's okay."

"No problem," he said and dug out a set of keys from a desk drawer.

We followed him down the hallway, past the kitchen, and

out the backdoor. He flipped on an outside light, illuminating a tiny backyard jammed against the hillside. The yard could barely accommodate a carport, which covered a shiny blue Dodge pickup and a dull brown four-door Rambler. Witherspoon didn't have to tell us which vehicle belonged to his wife.

I'll see you in the morning," Caroline said to me.

She climbed in the Rambler and drove down the narrow driveway along the side of the house to the street. Witherspoon and I went back to his den.

"You're very generous," I told him.

"I like you folks."

"Don't you even want to know what's going on?"

"Not unless you want to tell me," he said. "You want a drink? All I keep in here is bourbon."

We sipped Wild Turkey out of shot glasses. Witherspoon said being a private eye must be a most exciting profession and I said the same thing about running a newspaper. We stayed up most of the night swapping tall tales, trying to prove the other guy right.

When I rolled off the couch at seven the next morning, my head hurt and my stomach was queasy.

I tiptoed around the house, looking for a bathroom. There was no sign of Witherspoon or his wife. After I'd thrown some water in my face and brushed my teeth with my finger, I went out the backdoor to wait for Caroline. Witherspoon must have started off early for work, because the carport was empty. The sky was clear and blue, but the town was still deep in mountain shadows and the morning air was cold. I shuffled my feet and beat my arms and wished I hadn't locked the backdoor behind me. I also regretted not having pillaged the kitchen, and I promised myself that when Caroline got here, we'd find a nice, cozy, warm restaurant before we climbed to the mine.

Then I heard a car.

Myrna's Rambler came up the driveway and stopped under

the car canopy. Caroline sat behind the wheel. She didn't get out or shut off the engine.

"Are you okay?" I asked.

Caroline just looked at me, her eyes wide with fear. Then a man sat up from where he'd been crouched, hiding behind her in the backseat. He was wearing a nice leather jacket and he pressed a gun to Caroline's head.

It was Rueben Archuleta.

31

Rueben Archuleta, alias Anthony Villanueva, had one hand on Caroline's shoulder and the other wrapped around a 9mm Beretta. No doubt it was the same gun he'd used to pistol-whip me in my office and shoot at me outside the Frontier Hotel and under the Westin Hotel—the same gun he'd used to blast holes in Zack Meacham. Its muzzle was now buried in Caroline's hair.

"Nice to see you again, Lomax," he said smiling, his teeth white against olive skin.

"Let the girl go."

"Why would I want to do that?" he asked pleasantly, then in a colder voice, "Get back."

I moved away from the Rambler as the left-hand doors swung open. If I'd had Willy Two Hawks' gun, I might have yelled at Caroline to drop and then shot it out with Archuleta. But Willy's pistol was in the glove compartment of the Olds.

"We'll take your car," Archuleta said. "Unless sweet cakes here was lying about the ropes and gear in your trunk."

"He knows everything, Jake. I . . . I'm sorry."

"It doesn't matter," I told her. "Look, Archuleta, why don't you let her go? I can take you to the jewels."

"Who's Archuleta?"

"You can cut the act," I said. "I know who you are."

"Move it."

We walked down to the street and got in the Olds, me behind the wheel, Caroline and Archuleta in the backseat. I took Thirteenth Street over the interstate and headed up West Chicago Creek.

"What happened last night?" I asked Caroline, trying desperately to find a way out of this.

"I lost my patience with you people," Archuleta answered. "Soames could have died of old age before he got around to digging up the gems. So I went to his house last night and knocked him around until he told me everything. And then sweet cakes here phoned. I waited for both of you to show up, but since she came alone and since I'd already tucked Gramps away for the night, well, me and my sweety got real intimate."

I looked at Caroline in the mirror and she lowered her eyes.

"You son of a bitch."

"Hold that thought, Lomax. It'll remind you that I won't hesitate to kill her."

I considered slamming on the brakes and going for the gun in the glove box. Of course, Archuleta would only have time to shoot me four or five times before I got to it, assuming he didn't shoot Caroline first.

"Why did you kill Meacham?" I asked, guessing the answer.

"He was threatening to whack Soames before Soames dug up the satchel. So I whacked him first."

"And Lloyd Fontaine?"

"My partner took care of him."

"Your partner. He's the skinny blond character driving a tan Ford, right?"

Archuleta laughed. "And here I thought you were stupid. Anyway, Fontaine was a threat, too. He had a diary and some incriminating photographs. And then *you* had them. I should have killed you the first time we met."

I thought about Helen not appearing in court.

"What have you and your pal done with Helen Ester?"

Archuleta said nothing. My grip tightened on the wheel.

"You killed her, didn't you?"

"Just shut up and drive," he said.

If Caroline hadn't been with us, I might have slammed us both into the next big tree. After a few miles I turned off the blacktop and onto the dirt road. The old Olds squeaked and groaned in protest as we bounced along.

"Take it easy," Archuleta said.

"Can't help it," I said, steering for every rock and rut in the trail. I coaxed the Olds over a small boulder, then winced when she screamed in pain, bleeding oil onto the dirt and rocks behind us. By the time we got to the boulders blocking the trail, the oil pressure had dropped to almost zero and the water temperature was into the red. But instead of stopping, I gave her the gas. The Olds swung up the slope, leaving aqua-and-white door paint on a pine tree, then slammed back down onto the trail.

"Take it easy!" Archuleta yelled.

The engine started to clank. I shut it off.

"We walk from here," I said. And all the way back down the mountain.

"You mean *you* walk. Me and sweet cakes are staying in the car while you go get the satchel."

"No," Caroline said.

"What's wrong, babe, don't you like me anymore?"

"It'll take two people to retrieve the satchel," she said. "Wait for us here, if you want to."

Archuleta was silent for a moment.

"Okay, we'll all go," he said.

I shouldered the pack and we all started up the trail.

It was several miles to the mine, and Archuleta made us stop a few times along the way. His Gucci loafers weren't made for this terrain. Neither were his legs. But one thing that never got tired was his gun hand—he kept the weapon pointed at Caroline. Nevertheless, I'd have to try for him before we brought up the satchel, because at that moment he'd have no further use for us.

Two hours later we reached the mine. The sun was well up, but the air was crisp, almost cold. Despite the chill and the meager protection of his thin leather jacket, Archuleta was sweating profusely. He brushed dirt from his cream-colored slacks and waved his gun at the mine entrance.

"Is this it?" he asked, panting from the climb and the altitude and the thought of what lay inside.

"Go ahead on in," I said, unshouldering my pack. "We'll stay out here and keep the bears away."

"Very funny."

"Hey, tell it to *that* big brown bastard," I said, looking behind him.

He glanced to his left and I swung the pack at his head and started to follow it in, but he ducked it, quick as a snake, then fired his automatic so close to my ear that I felt the bullet buzz past. I stopped dead in my tracks. The muzzle of the Beretta stared at my chest.

Archuleta kicked at the pack. "Pick it up," he said. "One more stunt like that and I'll shoot you both. Now let's go."

"We'll need a length of timber," Caroline said.

"For what?"

"To lay across the shaft."

We hunted around and found a six-by-six that looked long enough. Caroline and I carried it into the mine, with Archuleta right behind. Pretty soon my lantern picked out the opening of the shaft. It gaped like a mouth. Caroline took the pack from me and emptied out the gear.

Archuleta's light moved nervously from her to me. He didn't like being underground any more than I did.

Caroline doubled up one rope, put a loop in the middle, and slipped it over the timber. While she held the coil of rope, and while I tried not to look down, we set the timber across the center of the abyss. Then Caroline searched the tunnel walls near the shaft, located a crack in the solid rock, and wedged in a wired nut. She attached a sling to the nut with a carabiner.

"We'll hook you up to this," she said to me.

"What for?" Archuleta asked.

"It will help him belay me as I go down."

"You're not going down the shaft," Archuleta said and shone his light in my face. "Lomax is."

"But he doesn't know anything about climbing," Caroline protested.

"He's going down and that's it."

"But I'm more qualified to—"

"Shut up!" Archuleta was edgy enough to shoot. "Lomax goes down and you stay up here with me."

"It's all right," I told Caroline.

"But, Jake—"

"Show me what to do."

We put on our harnesses—little more than leg and waist straps—and Caroline hooked me to the belaying rope. She attached a figure-eight descender to my harness, then pushed the climbing rope through the descender and lowered it into the dark guts of the mountain, down to where Mr. Bones was patiently waiting.

"Your left hand holds the rope in front like this," she said, "but it's just for balance. It's your right hand that prevents you from falling and holds the rope down and behind you like this. Don't let it go."

"Wouldn't dream of it."

"I'll keep the slack up on the belaying rope, so even if you slip, you won't fall more than a few feet. Okay?"

"If you say so," I said.

She handed me a pair of clamplike ascenders and showed me

how to use them to climb up the rope after I'd retrieved the satchel.

"I'll help you up with the belaying rope," she said. She hooked a lantern to my belt with a carabiner. "Ready?"

"Unless he'd rather go."

"Move it," Archuleta said.

I sat on the tunnel floor and moved forward until my legs hung over the edge of the grave-shaped pit. Then I pulled up the slack on the climbing rope, took a deep breath, and rolled off the edge. My body swung gently beneath the timber, which creaked from the strain. Below me was dead, black air. Archuleta looked on, amused.

"Having fun yet?"

"How does it feel?" Caroline asked.

"Okay, I guess."

I let the rope slide slowly through the descender and lowered myself into the pit. The pressure on my ears increased as I went lower, or maybe it was my imagination. When I'd gone down about forty feet, Archuleta leaned over the edge, shining his light and pelting me with a shower of tiny rocks.

"Are you almost there?"

"Get back." Caroline's voice was angry.

Archuleta moved away, leaving a pale, empty rectangle above me. My lantern swung at my side, lighting only my feet and a small section of the rock wall. Below me was blackness. I sank into it.

Forty feet later, I reached the bottom. My lantern revealed Mr. Bones resting in a tangled mass of rope, the grappling hook still stuck through the top of his chest. His head had broken free and now lay in the corner of the pit—eye sockets and nose holes agape, toothy mouth fixed in a sardonic grin.

"Are you there yet?" Archuleta sounded far away.

"Wait a minute!" I shouted up, my voice deadened by the high, steep walls.

I moved the desiccated corpse aside, then kicked through the loose rocks and boards until I found the solid rock bottom of the shaft. No satchel.

"It's not here."

"What?"

I frisked the corpse—a morbid task, but maybe his pockets were stuffed with jewels. All I found were loose coins, a car key, and a leather wallet dried shut with age. There was a dusty Bulova watch on an expansion band around his wrist.

"There's no satchel and no jewels!" I shouted at the distant rectangle of light above me.

"You're lying."

"There's nothing down here but a dried-up corpse."

"Listen to me, Lomax!" Archuleta yelled. "Unhook your belaying rope and tie it to the satchel of jewels."

"I'm telling you there's no satchel."

"Do it now!"

"Goddammit, take a look!" I pulled the watch off the corpse's bony, leathery wrist and held it up. "The only jewels down here are in this guy's watch. I'll bring it to you for a keepsake."

I shoved the watch in my pocket, hooked up the ascenders, and tugged on the rope.

"You're not coming up until I see the jewels!" Archuleta yelled.

"There are no jewels, you stupid son of a bitch!"

I slid the right-hand ascender up the rope, then stepped into the sling that hung from it, putting my weight on my right foot. Then I raised the left-hand ascender, shifted my weight to my left foot, and began "walking" up the rope.

Suddenly Caroline cried out from above. When I looked up, I could see Archuleta silhouetted against the mouth of the shaft. He was leaning on the timber that held my rope. I took a few more steps upward, when all at once the rope let go and I fell to the bottom of the shaft, landing beside the mummified corpse. Eighty feet of doubled rope piled down on top of me.

"This is your last chance, Lomax!" Archuleta yelled. "Tie the satchel to the belaying rope or I'll cut it and leave you down there."

"There's no satchel, goddammit!"

"You're lying."

"Okay, Archuleta, wait a minute." I fought to keep the panic from my voice. "Look, I know where the jewels are. Just let me come up and I'll show you."

"Where are they?"

"I'll have to show you."

"Tell me now, Lomax, I mean it."

"No, I'll climb up and—"

The other rope came piling down on top of me.

"Wait a minute!" I shouted.

I struggled to untangle myself from the ropes. When I was free, I aimed my light up the sides of the tomb to the top, eighty feet away.

"Archuleta!"

Silence.

"Caroline!"

I was alone.

32

I switched off the lantern, surrounding myself in thick darkness. When I looked up and tried to make out the mouth of the shaft, everything was uniformly black. Archuleta had gone and taken Caroline with him.

The question was should I sit down and conserve energy for a day or three until a rescue party found me, or should I try to climb out. The answer was simple: Unless Caroline got away from Archuleta, assuming she was still alive, there would be no rescue party.

With the lantern back on, I searched the steep walls of the shaft but saw nothing resembling a toehold. There was plenty of rope down here, and even a grappling hook, but it would be impossible to throw it eighty feet straight up and snag the top edge of the shaft.

And yet there might be a way out.

I removed my harness and hooked the lantern to my belt. Then I leaned against the long side of the shaft and pressed the sole of my boot to the opposite wall. When I pushed, I could exert pressure against my lower back. With shoulders forward, arms down at my sides, and palms flat against the rock, I planted my left foot next to my right. I had climbed completely off the bottom of the shaft. Well, three feet off. Only seventy-seven more to go.

I inched my butt up the shaft, then my right foot, then my

left. Nothing to it. Except that after ten minutes and eight feet of climbing, my muscles were starting to ache from maintaining constant pressure. Also, the lantern dangling from my belt was pulling me off balance. I started to unhook it.

Then I slipped and fell.

I went headfirst onto tangles of rope, breaking a few bones in the process. Luckily, they weren't mine. But if the fall had been eighteen feet instead of only eight . . .

I placed the lantern next to the corpse, shining across the ropes to give me a visual reference, then pressed my back and boots against opposite walls and started up the shaft.

After what seemed like an hour, my arms and legs and back were on fire. The bottom of the shaft was visible thirty or forty feet below me. I was barely halfway up and already exhausted. If I continued upward, my muscles might let go before I reached the top—in which case I'd take a neck-snapping plunge to the bottom and join Mr. Bones in a long, cold sleep. But if I climbed safely down now, I'd probably learn what it felt like to die of dehydration.

I struggled upward.

Without looking up or down, I watched my boottops in the near darkness and tried not to think about falling and dying alone in a pit but concentrated on the pain and pushed one foot up and then the other and then my back and hours passed and days and my hands were wet with blood and I almost slipped and then again and I knew I'd never make it and couldn't go any farther but I did anyway just one more step one more step.

And then my head bumped the timber across the mouth of the shaft.

It surprised me so much I almost let go. I got one arm over the timber and then the other, swung my legs up, and then I was on the tunnel floor, lying flat on my stomach, trembling with fatigue.

After a while I got to my feet, stumbled out of the mine, and hugged the nearest tree. The sun was bright and yellow and the sky was bright and blue and the trees were lush and green. There was fresh air and good, clean rocks and a wind that stung my eyes, making them tear. I'm sure that's why they teared.

There was no sign of Caroline or Archuleta.

I started down the mountain, a bit shaky at first, letting the slope and gravity do most of the work, but I felt better with every step. An hour later I reached the Olds. Archuleta had turned it around, smashing a taillight into a tree. That was as far as he'd gone before the engine had seized up for want of oil. There were dirty handprints on the trunk where he'd tried to push it, and the keys were still in the ignition. I started down, then stopped. Handprints on the trunk?

When I leaned in to get the keys, I heard Caroline's muffled voice from behind the backseat. She was curled up in the trunk, trembling and gasping for air. There was a nasty bruise on her head. I helped her out. She clung to me and cried.

"I thought I was going to die there in the dark," she said.

"Believe me, I know the feeling."

"He hit me when I tried to stop him from cutting the rope. When I came to, he was dragging me down here. But how . . ." She held me at arm's length. "How did you get out of the shaft?"

"Would you believe a mighty leap?"

I told her about it as we hiked down the mountain. Then she told me that Archuleta had said he believed she and Soames and I had lied about the location of the jewels. He'd taken the keys to Myrna Witherspoon's car and was driving to the city. If Soames didn't tell him the truth this time, Archuleta had said, he would shoot him and leave Caroline in the trunk to suffocate.

We went straight down the ravine to the big house on the site of the murder shack. The lady of the house, a salt-and-pepper-haired woman with sporty clothes and a midwestern twang, calmed her three Dobermans and let us in. The four of them escorted us to the phone. I called Witherspoon at the *Gazette.*

"We've got big trouble, Harry, and not much time." I told him where we were. "Can you come get us?"

"I'll be there in ten minutes."

"Have you got a gun?" I asked, kicking myself for not remembering to take Willy's pistol from the glove box of the Olds.

"Hell yes, I've got a gun," he said. "This is America, isn't it?"

Witherspoon picked us up in his big blue Dodge pickup. There was a Western Field twelve-gauge double-barrel shotgun wedged in the rack behind our heads.

"Will that do?" Witherspoon asked good-naturedly.

"If we hurry, we may not need it," I said.

We roared down to I-70 and swung east. I told Witherspoon about Rueben Archuleta.

"He thinks Soames can tell him where to find the Lochemont jewels," I said. "If Soames doesn't, he'll kill him."

"Shouldn't we call the police?"

We should, but I wanted time alone with Archuleta, time to talk to him at length about Helen Ester and maybe a mine shaft and one or two other things—time with no cops around to interrupt me.

"If you step on it," I said, "we'll be there in fifteen minutes. By the time we explained it all to the cops . . ."

But Witherspoon was already jamming down the highway, passing cars right and left.

Along the way, I felt something jabbing my leg—the Bulova watch in my pocket. When I took it out, Caroline asked me what it was.

"It belonged to our friend at the bottom of the shaft."

She made a face and turned away. I wiped the crystal and twisted the stem, and the damn thing started ticking. The back was stainless steel, and after I buffed it with my thumb, it shone. There was an inscription. It took me a moment to realize exactly what the words meant. I shoved the watch back in my pocket.

When we got to Caroline's house, Myrna Witherspoon's Rambler was parked at the curb, and Willy Two Hawks' beat-up green Chevy was parked right behind it. We piled out of the truck and I leaned back in for the shotgun. Witherspoon beat me to it.

"You'd better let me," he said. "The triggers are kind of touchy."

We hurried up to the house and peeked in the front windows. The living room was deserted, but I could see someone lying in the kitchen. Caroline unlocked the door and we crept through the front room. She gasped when she saw Willy Two Hawks lying on his back near the kitchen sink. His mouth was open, his dark glasses were in place, and his shirt was soaked with blood.

We heard a muffled scream.

"Grandpa!" Caroline said in a loud whisper.

She started toward the basement door, but I pulled her back and went down the stairs with Witherspoon right behind me.

Charles Soames was tied to a kitchen chair under a naked light bulb. His shirt was off and there were burn marks on his gray, wrinkled skin. Rueben Archuleta stood before him. A cigarette dangled from his fingertips.

"We've got all day, Pops."

"No, you don't," I said.

Archuleta spun around, his hand on the automatic pistol in his belt, his eyes as wide as if he were staring at a ghost.

"Raise your hands," Witherspoon said from behind me.

Archuleta looked from me to Witherspoon. Slowly, he seemed to relax. He smiled and shrugged in resignation. I stepped down off the last stair, and suddenly Archuleta dove to his right, went into a tuck and roll, and came up with the Beretta pointed at me. Witherspoon let go with both barrels, the blast nearly rupturing my eardrums. The buckshot caught Archuleta full in the chest, exploding it in shreds of leather and fabric, tissue and blood. He was slammed back into the wall like a rag doll. He slid to the floor, dead.

33

The basement was filled with the smell of gunpowder and death. I untied Soames, while Caroline cried over the old man and rubbed his face. Witherspoon was pale as a fish's belly. He kept looking over his shoulder at the bloody heap in the corner.

"It's okay, Grandpa," Caroline said. "It's okay."

Soames nodded but didn't try to speak.

"Let's take him upstairs," I said. My voice sounded odd—my ears were still ringing from the shotgun blast.

Witherspoon and I got Soames to his feet and helped him up the stairs, past the body of Willy Two Hawks on the kitchen floor, and into his bedroom, where we eased him back onto the bed. Witherspoon went quickly into the bathroom and passed Caroline coming out with cotton pads and the tube of ointment. He shut the door, and we heard him throwing up.

Caroline dabbed at her grandfather's first-degree burns. They looked painful but not serious. Soames's tormentor had touched the glowing tip of his cigarette to the old man's neck and chest, as he'd done to Lloyd Fontaine a few weeks ago.

"He . . . he killed Willy." Soames's voice was weak, as if he'd just finished a marathon, which in a way he had.

"Don't try to talk," Caroline said.

"He heard Willy picking the backdoor lock and . . . and he went up and shot him."

"Did he say anything about Helen Ester?" I asked.

"Helen? No. What do you mean?"

I shook my head. "I guess it doesn't matter. Not now. I only wish I'd've had the chance to get him to tell me what he'd done with . . . to tell me about her."

"What are you saying, Lomax?"

I felt sick inside and figured I might as well share it with someone. "I'm afraid our friend downstairs killed Helen."

"What? There's no way. Helen told me she was leaving town, staying up at her place in the mountains where she'd be safe."

"I have a bad feeling she came back and ran into him."

"No." Soames looked from me to Caroline.

She squeezed his hand. "You're safe now, Grandpa, and that's what counts."

Witherspoon stepped out of the bathroom. Some of the color had returned to his face.

"No." Soames was shaking his head at us. "No."

"Just rest now, Grandpa. Everything's all right."

"It sure as fuck is *not* all right," I said, getting everyone's attention. "For one thing, we still have the blond man in the Ford to contend with—Villanueva's partner."

"Villanueva?" Caroline said. "You mean Archuleta."

"No, I don't."

"Shouldn't we call the police?" Witherspoon said. He glanced nervously at the door, as if he expected a dead man with no chest to walk in looking for him.

"Who is he, Soames?" I asked. "Who's the blond guy working with Villanueva?"

"How the hell should I know?"

"There's plenty you know that you haven't told us."

"What the hell's that supposed to mean?" His anger had revived him and he started to get up, then winced, and Caroline tried to hold him back.

"Can't you see he's in pain?" she said to me, disgust in her voice.

I took out the watch I'd retrieved from the corpse in the mine and handed it to Caroline.

"Read the inscription on the back," I said.

She did, then looked from me to Soames.

"What does it say?" Witherspoon asked.

" 'To Rueben from Gloria with love,' " I said. Witherspoon didn't get it. "Gloria is the name of Rueben Archuleta's wife. Widow, I mean. That's Archuleta's dried-up body at the bottom of the mine shaft."

"What?"

"You want to tell us about it, Soames?"

Instead of answering, he sat up with Caroline's help and asked her to bring him a shirt.

"Archuleta's been down there since the day of the Lochemont robbery, hasn't he?"

Soames looked at me, then lowered his eyes and nodded slowly.

"Yes," he said.

"But, Grandpa, how . . ." Caroline wasn't sure she really wanted to know.

"What happened back then?" I said.

Soames's frail chest rose in a sigh. "You already know most of it," he said and began buttoning his shirt. "Except that when I ran away from Teague, Archuleta ran with me."

"You mean he ran *after* you, don't you, Grandpa?"

Soames shook his head. "And there's something else I never told anyone. When Ed Teague first approached me, he used more than threats to get me to help him rob Lochemont Jewelers—he offered me a share of the take. I accepted. And they accepted me as one of them."

"No," Caroline said. "You must have just *pretended* to join them. You were never one of them."

Soames reached out for her hand.

"Maybe I was only pretending," he said. "Maybe not. There was an awful lot of money involved."

"So you were a willing partner," Witherspoon said.

"No, he wasn't!"

Caroline wasn't ready to accept that as fact, and neither was I.

"You couldn't have been stupid enough to trust Teague and the others," I said.

"No, I guess not. But either way, I had to go along. It was Teague's show. Teague and whoever was giving him orders."

"Whoever masterminded the robbery," Witherspoon said.

Soames nodded. "Teague told me someone else was running things, someone I never met."

"The blond guy in the Ford."

"I suppose so," Soames said. "Anyhow, that's why I couldn't go to the police before the robbery—this guy was in the background waiting to kill me and my family if anything went wrong during the robbery."

"What happened *after* the robbery?" I asked him.

"We drove to the shack near Idaho Springs to split the jewels and then, supposedly, to leave in three cars—Teague in one, Buddy Meacham and Robert Knox in another, and me and Archuleta in the third. But Teague killed Knox and Meacham before anybody knew what was going on, then came after me and Archuleta. Archuleta grabbed the satchel of jewels, and the two of us ran for it. We ran for hours, then stumbled into the mine opening. It was pitch black in there, and all of a sudden Archuleta crashed through some boards and fell down the shaft, taking the jewels with him. My momentum almost carried me in after him." Soames stared at nothing, remembering. "After that, well, you know everything that happened. I didn't tell anyone about Archuleta, because it would have implicated me in the robbery. Of course, as it turned out it didn't matter."

"How did Villanueva get involved?" Witherspoon asked.

Soames shrugged.

"The blond guy probably hired him," I said. "He's been using Villanueva to do his dirty work, just as he used Ed Teague twenty years ago."

"Maybe the blond guy found the jewels," Witherspoon said.

"I doubt it. Otherwise, Villanueva wouldn't still be hanging around. Which means we may see Blondy again."

"Surely he's not a threat to us now," Caroline said.

"He is if he thinks we have the jewels."

But I had a more pressing issue—surrendering to the cops. First I got everyone to agree on a little white lie, one that didn't stretch the truth too much, one that would save me a lot of grief later. When everyone had it straight, I went to the front room to make the call. Someone had saved me the trouble. There were police cars in the street and policemen crouched behind them, each displaying his favorite firearm. One red-faced sergeant put down his riot gun and picked up a bullhorn. He gave me some friendly advice:

"COME OUT WITH YOUR HANDS UP!"

The cops weren't taking any chances—not with one of Caroline's neighbors calling to report us creeping into the house with a shotgun and then minutes later hearing it go off, not with corpses in the kitchen and the basement and the smoking guns to go with them, not with a convicted murderer in one room and an accused murderer in another. They arrested us all on suspicion, read us our rights, and hauled us downtown.

We were separated and each given our personal inquisitor. Lucky me, I got Dalrymple. We had a nice chat and he rarely used his rubber hose. I spoke openly and freely without my attorney, and I hardly lied at all. When Greenspan finally showed up, we conferred alone.

"Have the police found Helen Ester?" I asked, dreading the answer, guessing what Villanueva and his pal had done. "I mean, have they found her body "

"Her body?" He shook his head, frowning. "Look, Lomax, you're in a lot of fucking trouble here. Now talk to me, goddammit, and don't leave anything out."

I told him the whole truth and nothing but. Never lie to your lawyer, they say, because you'll only hurt yourself. Let him do the lying. That's what he gets paid for.

The cops cut loose Caroline and Soames and Witherspoon late Friday afternoon. There was no reason to hold them, since their stories and the physical evidence all pointed to one thing: Witherspoon had shot Villanueva in self-defense. Me, however, they kept locked up overnight.

And I remained in jail all day Saturday while they ran a background check on Anthony Villanueva and a ballistics check on his gun. I sat and waited, confident of the results. Fairly confident. Lieutenant Dalrymple was not to be underestimated. Or, I feared, trusted.

On Sunday afternoon Greenspan showed up with a turnkey.

"I'm wasting my talents on you," Greenspan said as the guard let me out. "You're a free man."

We shouldered our way through the crowded cop station and into the sunlight. I felt like I'd just climbed out of another mine shaft.

"What happened?" I asked.

"The lab tests proved Villanueva's gun killed both Zack Meacham and Willy Two Hawks. Also, with a bit of prompting from me, Detective Healey showed Villanueva's picture to the people at the Frontier Hotel, and guess what? The desk clerk remembered seeing him the night Meacham was murdered. The D.A. decided his case against you was too weak. He dropped the charges."

"That's great, Abner. No doubt Dalrymple's pissed."

"No doubt."

"What about my jumping bail and not appearing in court?"

Greenspan waved his hand to show me it was nothing, really.

"Judge Sanchez dismissed your arrest warrant after I sold him on your lie."

The lie was that Caroline and I had been prisoners of Villanueva all day Thursday and Friday, while he forced us to search for the jewels. I couldn't be in court, Your Honor, because some fool was pointing a gun at me.

"I'm in your debt, Abner."

"Don't worry, I'll let you know exactly how much."

"Just one more favor."

"What, for chrissake?"

"I need a ride to Lakewood."

"For chrissake, Lomax."

"Hey, I'll give you gas money."

"My car's a diesel."

We rode in his Mercedes—dark-tinted windows, power everything, and Mozart drifting from six speakers—and I asked him if the cops had dug up anything on Villanueva.

"Yes, as a matter of fact," Greenspan said. "Four years ago he was a suspect in a murder case in California."

"Oh?"

"He was a chauffeur for some rich old dude named Parmody, who died under suspicious circumstances. Villanueva was charged with murder, but the case was dropped for lack of evidence."

And I was dropped at Caroline's house, where Greenspan left me standing in a thin cloud of diesel smoke.

Charles Soames let me in the front door. He looked grayer than ever. And for good reason: He'd been beaten and burned, and his girlfriend was still missing and presumed dead.

"How you feeling?"

"My chest hurts," he said.

No shit. "I want to thank you and Caroline for helping me out with the cops with the story—"

"Caroline's out back. Go thank her."

So he didn't feel sociable. So what? Or maybe he was just grumpy because the jewels were gone. I wasn't too happy about that myself. I went out through the kitchen. The basement door was closed tight and the kitchen floor looked freshly washed and waxed. Caroline had tried desperately to scrub away the memory of Willy Two Hawks and Anthony Villanueva.

She was raking leaves between a pair of peach trees under the warm October sun. Several black trash bags lay near by, stuffed full as balloons. When she saw me she smiled and rested her hands on top of the rake. Her forehead glistened with sweat.

"You're free?"

"I am that." I told her about Greenspan's efforts.

"That's great news, Jake. So everything's okay?"

"Almost. I seem to have a car stuck up on a mountain."

She laughed. "I'd forgotten. You'll need a tow."

"Tell me."

"There's a towrope in the Land Cruiser. We've got time to do it today, if you want."

"Honest, I didn't come here to ask—"

"Sure you did," she said, and gave me a playful punch in the arm. "I'll see if my grandfather wants to go for the ride."

A few minutes later she came out the backdoor with her oversized purse and no grandfather. We took I-70 west toward Idaho Springs. The afternoon traffic was light and we cruised along with everybody else, about ten miles over the speed limit. Snow had brushed the high country last night and all the peaks were dusted white.

"I hope it didn't snow on the Olds," I said. "It's going to be tough enough to get it out of there without slipping and sliding all over the place."

Caroline didn't respond.

"You know what I mean?" I said, turning toward her.

She was staring horrified at the rearview mirror.

"What's wrong?"

"Oh, my God," she whispered. Her face was pale.

When I looked back, I saw why. Sneaking through the thin traffic behind us was the blond man in the tan Ford.

34

"**W**hat are we going to do?" Caroline sat rigidly behind the wheel, gripping it with both hands.

The blond guy kept the Ford ten or twelve car lengths behind us. He might have been Anthony Villanueva's boss, and he might have murdered Helen Ester, and he might or might not have masterminded the Lochemont robbery, but one thing was certain: He didn't have the jewels. Otherwise he wouldn't be after us.

"Just keep driving," I told Caroline.

"Is . . . is it him?"

"It's him."

"God, Jake, if he was working with Villanueva . . ."

"Don't worry, we've got a little surprise for him."

We drove to Idaho Springs and turned up West Chicago Creek. Our friend stayed with us. When Caroline left the pavement and started up the road to my car, the Ford pulled onto the shoulder a hundred feet back and stopped. Maybe he thought we were finally going to retrieve the jewels and he'd get us on the way out.

Caroline steered up the mountain to the boulders blocking the road, then put the Toyota in four-wheel drive and easily maneuvered around the rocks and through the trees. She stopped beside the old Olds. It looked pathetic and out of place.

I got Willy's long-barreled .22 revolver from the glove box and snapped open the cylinder. Six shiny brass eyes winked back at me.

We turned around and drove down the trail. Caroline let me off before we reached the paved road.

"Give me twenty minutes," I told her.

I moved on foot through the trees and brush, picking a course parallel to the asphalt road and a few hundred feet above it. When I spotted the Ford, I circled behind it and came down to the gravel shoulder.

Blondy was still sitting at the wheel with his elbow out the window and his head on his hand. He'd shut off the engine and now watched the road ahead and behind, occasionally checking his outside mirror.

I kept low and to the right edge of the shoulder, out of sight of his mirrors. As I reached the Ford's rear bumper, I could hear the muffled pulsing of a Top Forty tune. God, I hate that music.

I yanked open the passenger door and shoved Willy's pistol in Blondy's face. Obviously too young to have been involved in the Lochemont robbery, this guy was in his late twenties with a narrow nose and close-set pale blue eyes, wide with surprise and fear. He wore a cheap suit and a fifties haircut, and his thin-lipped mouth was sucking air.

"Holy shit," he said.

"Put your hands on the wheel and—"

Before I could finish, he popped open his door and literally fell backward out of the car onto the pavement in a tangle of long, skinny limbs, then scrambled to his feet and took off down the road, his suit coat flapping on him like a ripped mainsail.

I ran after him and considered shooting at his legs, but before we'd gone more than a hundred yards, he pulled up short, holding his side. I grabbed his collar, yanked him across the gravel shoulder, and shoved him against a dead tree at the bottom of the mountain slope.

"P-please," was all he could manage. His face was pale and

twisted in pain, and I wondered if he was having a heart attack, not that I cared much. I patted him down. He wasn't armed.

"Please," he said, gasping for breath and clutching his side. "Please don't kill me."

"Who are you? And what've you done with Helen Ester?"

"I'm only doing my job, honest, I—"

I shook him by the lapels and he rattled inside his clothes like a gunnysack full of bones.

"Was Villanueva working for you?"

"No, no, I work for the insurance company and—"

"What?"

Caroline was coasting down the road, looking for us. I waved her over.

"My name is Neal Ullman. I work for National Insurance as an investigator and—"

"You're a lying sack of shit."

Caroline made a U-turn and parked on the shoulder. I shoved the guy in the backseat and went in after him.

"Who is he? What does he want?" Caroline looked ready to bolt from the car.

"My name is Neal Ullman and I work for—"

"Shut up," I told him. "Give me your wallet."

He fumbled with his wallet, dropped it, picked it up, dropped it again, so I took it from him. He had thirty-seven dollars in cash and a Colorado driver's license identifying him as Neal N. Ullman. There were a few other things with his name on them, including a picture ID from National Insurance Company: Neal N. Ullman, Investigator.

"Jesuschrist."

I tossed Ullman his billfold and asked him what the fuck was going on.

"I was assigned to the case by Mr. Carr after—"

"What case?"

"The Lochemont Jewelers case," he said. "Mr. Carr reopened it after you told him about Lloyd Fontaine and inquired about the reward for recovering the jewels. He thought it would be worthwhile to stick someone on your tail. Me."

I told Caroline to find a phone in Idaho Springs.

Ten minutes later I was shoving Ullman into a phone booth near a gas station on the edge of town. I dialed the number for National Insurance and after talking to a receptionist and a secretary, I got Mr. Carr on the line. When I asked him if he had someone following me, he hemmed and hawed.

"I've got him in a phone booth right now, Carr, with a gun stuck in his ribs. He says his name is Ullman."

"Oh."

"Well?"

"Yes, he works for me."

"What does he look like?"

Carr accurately described Ullman, right down to his two-tone wing tips, then asked to speak with him. I gave the phone to Ullman. He mumbled a lot of yes, sirs and no, sirs and then hung up.

"He's not too happy you spotted me," he said dejectedly.

"Things are tough all over."

We got back in the Toyota.

"He is what he says he is," I told Caroline.

"Then why are you still following us?" she asked him.

"The Lochemont jewels. Why else?"

"The jewels are long gone, Ullman," I said. "We found the mine, but someone got there first."

He shook his head and smiled. "That's not true and you know it. You just haven't found the right mine yet."

"What makes you think that?"

"I don't think it, I *know* it."

"How?"

He just smiled, the smug bastard.

"Talk to me, Ullman, or you'll be limping back to your car on two broken legs."

"Are you *threatening* me?" he asked with mock fear.

"Goddamned right."

He looked me in the eye for a few seconds, trying to decide just how serious I was. Then his Adam's apple bobbed up and down, as if he were trying to swallow an olive.

"Okay," he said, "you might as well know. I've had someone helping me up here. I phoned him each time you drove to the mountains, and he followed you while you searched the mines. He told me just yesterday that you two hadn't given up and that I'd better stick close."

"Who is it?" Caroline asked, but I knew even before Ullman answered. I remembered now seeing the big blue Dodge pickup on the mountain the first day that Caroline and Soames and I searched the mines—then again parked behind a Victorian house in Idaho Springs—and again when Caroline and I got a lift into Denver after escaping death at the hands of Anthony Villanueva.

"Harry Witherspoon," Ullman said.

"Witherspoon?" Caroline looked from Ullman to me. "But why would he cooperate with this clown?"

"Why do you think?" I said. "Remember when we came out of the mine after hauling up the remains of Archuleta?"

She shuddered. "How could I forget?"

"There was someone above us on the hillside. Witherspoon. He knew then that we'd found the right mine."

"What the hell are you two talking about?" Ullman wanted to know.

"Witherspoon's got the jewels, you stupid son of a bitch," Caroline said, venting her outrage on the hapless investigator. She flipped the key, and the engine roared to life.

"He's probably left the country by now," I said.

"Not necessarily," Caroline said emphatically. "There are, I mean, there would be a dozen details to take care of—finding a safe place to run to; getting there without leaving a trail for the cops or anyone to follow; and probably changing identity, which means a fake passport and other ID. And fencing a bagful of stolen jewels isn't easy. I don't think Witherspoon just ran off, not if he's got any brains." Caroline sounded as if she'd given this a lot of thought.

"You may be right," I said. "Unless Witherspoon's been planning this for twenty years."

They both looked at me.

"Don't forget, someone organized the Lochemont robbery, and it wasn't Teague or Archuleta."

"But *Witherspoon?*"

"He's been around since then," I said. "And he sure didn't hesitate to blow away Villanueva."

"Jesus, Jake, if you're right, then *he's* the one responsible for my grandfather going to prison."

"If he's got the jewels," Ullman said, "they belong to National Insurance."

Caroline ignored him. "The paper or his house?"

"Try the paper first."

A few minutes later we screeched to a stop near the front door of the *Gazette*. The late Willy Two Hawks' beat-up green Chevy was parked across the street. Caroline and I exchanged glances.

"Maybe you'd better wait out here."

"Bullshit," she informed me.

There was a "Closed" sign in the window, which seemed out of place on a Saturday afternoon, even for a newspaper this small. The door was ajar. We went in. The counter was empty and the desks were deserted.

"Witherspoon?" I called out.

Suddenly big Tom Two Hawks rose up from behind the counter, looking like a Sioux warrior confronting Custer's last troopers. His braids were undone and his thick black hair fell behind him like a mane. He pointed his .30-30 lever-action Winchester at my chest and gave me some bad news.

"You whites killed my father," he said, "and now I'm gonna kill you."

35

"**D**rop the gun," big Tom told me, and I did.

Ullman pushed past Caroline and tried to get out the door. Tom fired into the wall above his head, blasting out a big hunk of plaster and wood, knocking a hole through the first layer of bricks and mortar, and setting everybody's ears ringing. Nobody moved.

Mathew Two Hawks came running out from the back room. He stopped short when he saw us.

"More scalps," Tom said and roared like a bear.

"Holy shit," Ullman said.

"Take it easy," I told Ullman. "Nobody's going to do anything."

I stepped to the counter, bold as hell. Tom levered another round into the chamber and casually aimed at my sternum.

"You're gonna die."

"Relax, Chief," I said, trying to relax. "Obviously, you and your brother don't have all the facts. You want vengeance for Willy's murder, and vengeance has already been, ah, wreaked."

"No, it hasn't," Mathew said. He picked up his father's pistol from the floor.

"Haven't you talked to the cops? Villanueva shot your father, and Witherspoon shot Villanueva."

"That's what the cops told us, all right." Tom's voice was a growl. "Only we don't think it was that simple. We think you and Witherspoon teamed up to murder Pop."

"Don't be stupid," I said. "Your father stumbled onto Villanueva while he was torturing Soames. That's why Villanueva killed him. It's over. Except for the jewels. And the man who planned the heist twenty years ago."

Tom shook his head, his ears closed to further discussion.

"We looked for you this morning," he said. "When we couldn't find you, we came up here for Witherspoon. But it looks like things worked out after all."

"What about the jewels?" Mathew asked me.

"Before I kill you," Tom said to me, "I'm gonna take off your kneecaps. Just the way Pop wanted to a week ago."

"Wait a minute, Tom. Let him tell us about the jewels."

"Fuck the jewels. Back away from the counter, Lomax. Do it now or I'll kill you where you stand."

Some choice. I backed up. Tom raised the rifle to his cheek and took careful aim at my right leg.

"No!" Caroline yelled.

"Wait a minute, Tom, goddammit. Let him talk first."

"You'd best listen to your brother," I said. "Unless you want to be poor all your life. What's left of your life, that is, before they shut you in the gas chamber."

"Let him talk," Mathew said. "I mean it, Tom."

Tom's aim wavered. He lowered the rifle.

And I talked, telling them absolutely everything that had happened since Lloyd Fontaine walked into my office three weeks ago. It took me the better part of an hour, but when I was through, Mathew was more or less on our side—ready to shake Witherspoon until a confession came out, along with a bag of jewels, which we'd turn in for a share of the reward. Tom was still ready to shoot somebody, anybody.

"Let's go find Witherspoon," he said.

"What about the others?" Mathew asked.

I looked at Mathew. "What others?"

"Witherspoon's employees. We've got them tied up in back."

"And that's where they stay," Tom said. "Nobody's going to call the cops or warn Witherspoon."

So the five of us squeezed into Caroline's Toyota, drove to Witherspoon's house, and piled out on the sidewalk. I took Caroline's arm, led the war party up to the front porch, and knocked on the door. Witherspoon parted the curtains. He smiled at me and Caroline and started to open the door. Then he saw Ullman standing behind us and the Two Hawks brothers behind Ullman, and his jaw dropped about a foot. He disappeared.

"Now what?" Caroline asked.

"Let's bust it in," Tom said.

He shoved me and Caroline out of his way. Then we heard an engine cough to life. I jumped off the porch onto the driveway—right in line with Witherspoon's big blue Dodge truck roaring from behind the house toward the street. Witherspoon swerved to miss me, lost control, and crashed into the side of the house. I yanked open the truck's door, forgetting about his shotgun. But the only thing he had was a briefcase.

"Almost made it," he said, smiling sheepishly.

Tom and Mathew crowded around, waving their firearms.

"Put down the guns," I said, taking the briefcase. Its contents felt heavy and loose. "Let's go inside."

We trooped through the empty house to Witherspoon's den. Ullman gave a start when the saw the dead grizzly standing at the end of the room. I set the briefcase on the desk, and Witherspoon gave me the key. The others circled around, like members of an occult religion preparing for worship. When I clicked open the locks of the case, everyone stared, transfixed. Everyone, of course, but Witherspoon. He already knew what was inside. The Lochemont jewels.

They dazzled, even in this artificial light—five million sparkles reflecting in everyone's eyes.

There were heavy handfuls of diamond rings, tangles of diamond necklaces, piles of diamond bracelets. And emeralds, like rare spring clovers, pushing up through the miniature drifts of snowy diamonds. And here and there, rubies and sapphires buried in heaps of loose diamonds.

We gazed on the fortune and dreamed our own dreams, perhaps *the* dream—a lifetime of freedom and ease.

Caroline reached in for a solitaire diamond ring. The flawless stone must have weighed five carats. She stared into it the way a bird stares into the eye of a snake, then she returned it, carefully, reluctantly, to the heap of jewels in the briefcase.

"And this," Ullman said, lifting out a necklace and laying it on the green desk blotter.

The choker was made up of scores of half-carat flawless white diamonds, the lot of them shamed by the central ruby, as large as a small hen's egg, its color as deep and rich and red as new blood. Baby Doe Tabor's blood stone shone with an intense inner light that held us all like flamestruck moths.

Ullman broke the spell and put the necklace back in the briefcase. I turned to Witherspoon.

"When did you get the jewels?" I asked him.

"Thursday night, after you and Caroline left the mine."

"But we came here after we left the mine," Caroline said.

"Not right away," I said. "We spent time at the Buffalo Bar, remember?"

"I'd been watching you from the hillside," Witherspoon continued. "My truck was already loaded with climbing gear and everything else I could think of that I might need." He rubbed his chin and glanced down at the briefcase. "But it was pretty hairy, let me tell you. I hadn't done any climbing for a few years. Never anything like that, never in the dark. I went down and up as fast as I could, scared every foot of the way. I wasn't back home more than ten minutes before you and Caroline showed up."

"No wonder you looked shocked to see us."

"Hell, I hadn't even taken the jewels out of the old black satchel. It was right under this desk, Lomax, not ten feet from where you slept that night."

"Terrific."

Witherspoon shrugged.

"Why didn't you run after you got the gems?" Ullman asked.

"There was no hurry," Witherspoon said. "No one would suspect I'd found the satchel." He looked from me to Caroline. "At least I didn't think they would. So I started getting my affairs in order, the newspaper and so on."

"And your wife?" Caroline asked.

"Enough of this crap," Tom Two Hawks said. "I want to know about you and Villanueva."

Witherspoon ignored him and spoke to Caroline. "My wife can get along very well without me. As it is, she spends half her time in Boston with her blue-blooded friends. She's there now."

Tom reached over and poked Witherspoon in the chest with the muzzle of the rifle.

"Tell me how you and Villanueva killed my pop."

"Take it easy," I told Tom, pushing the gun aside, gently, so it wouldn't accidentally blow Witherspoon in half. "What about it, Harry? What was the connection between you and Villanueva?"

"What?"

"Was he working for you?"

"What?" Witherspoon was smiling now, as if he couldn't believe we were all so stupid, and I was beginning to wonder about it myself. "What the hell are you talking about?"

"Your involvement with the Lochemont robbery," I said, and the idea suddenly seemed ludicrous to me.

"Jesus H. Jones," he said, a pained look on his face. "What do you think I am, Lomax, an archcriminal? You're giving me too much credit. I was a kid back then, living in a small town, and I barely knew my ass from my elbow. And I sure as hell have never been more than what I am at this moment—just a goddamn newspaperman."

He was right and I knew it. Unfortunately, the braves weren't convinced.

"You're a liar," Tom said.

Witherspoon just smiled at me and shook his head.

"You'd better talk now," Mathew said, raising his father's pistol, not exactly aiming, just waving it for emphasis. "Tell us about you and Villanueva."

"Read my lips. There *is* no 'me and Villanueva.' And since Ullman is here," he said dejectedly, "there's no 'me and the jewels.' You might as well take them and leave. I'm going to see about my truck."

He started toward the door, but Tom hustled around the desk and blocked his way, leveling the rifle at Witherspoon's midsection.

"I oughta shoot you right now for what you did to Pop."

"I didn't do *anything* to him, you dumb fucking Indian."

Big Tom hit Witherspoon in the chin with the butt of the gun, knocking him bleeding and groaning to the floor. Then Tom raised the gun and I jumped on his back and down we went. He rolled and twisted and tried to shake me loose, then arched up on all fours and tried to buck me off, like kids playing "horsy," so I did my bronc rider imitation and hung on for dear life. Tom rose to his knees and then to his feet and I put a stranglehold on him and he tried to swing back and hit me in the ribs with the butt of the rifle, inadvertently pulling the trigger and blasting a big furry chunk out of the leg of the stuffed grizzly while Mathew was yelling and pointing his father's gun at us and Ullman came up behind him with a heavy oak-and-bronze plaque he'd taken from the wall—"Twenty Years of Community Service to the City of Idaho Springs Presented to H. R. Witherspoon"—and smacked Mathew across the back of the head, knocking him cold, just as I hooked my leg around

Tom and tripped him and we crashed into the grizzly. One of its claws caught him in the face, making him yelp in pain and drop the rifle. I untangled myself from the Indian and the bear, picked up the rifle by the barrel, and swung it like a baseball bat, nailing a home run right up the middle of big Tom's forehead, ending the game: Sleuths 2, Braves 0.

36

Caroline, quiet through it all, came from behind the desk and helped Witherspoon into a chair. She took a wad of Kleenex from her big purse and pressed it against his chin.

"Maybe you need a doctor," she said.

"I can take care of it myself. There's some stuff in the bathroom." Witherspoon left the room.

The Two Hawks brothers began to come to. Ullman and I kept them under our guns, but his hand was shaking so badly I took Willy's pistol from him.

"Now what?" he asked.

"Get your boss on the phone."

"But it's Sunday."

"Then call him at home," I said. "Tell him we're bringing in the jewels. Have him arrange security and maybe an accountant or a notary or whatever it takes to verify what we've got and how much the reward will be."

"You're not cutting us out," Mathew said. He was sitting up on the floor and rubbing the back of his head.

"Don't worry, you'll get a fair share," I said. Although I could foresee a major hassle trying to figure out who'd get what.

Witherspoon returned with a gauze pad taped to his chin. Tom struggled to his feet, glowering at me, ignoring the blood running down his own forehead and dripping off the end of his nose. I thought he might try to attack, but instead he helped his brother to his feet.

"What's to keep you from running with the jewels?" Mathew wanted to know.

"It's simple," Caroline said, locking the hefty briefcase, bringing it around the desk, and handing it to big Tom. "He carries the case, Ullman carries the key, and we all drive back to Denver together."

Ullman didn't like the idea of letting big Tom handle the briefcase. Neither did I, but we worked out a compromise. Then Ullman called his boss at home and explained what was going on.

"Mr. Carr will be waiting for us at his office," he said after he'd hung up. "Everything's being arranged, but it may take a couple of hours."

Before we left, I got a rural route number near Vail from Caroline and tried calling Detective Healey. There were some very important questions I had to ask him concerning a Mr. Parmody. But the cop I talked to said Healey was off duty until tomorrow morning, and he refused to give me his home phone.

Caroline shouldered her purse and led us out the door to her Land Cruiser. We all squeezed in and drove to the *Gazette*, where we freed Mrs. Hicks and young Lois and Jimmy. Witherspoon calmed them down and explained what was going on, while Mathew took Ullman up West Chicago Creek to get his car. When they returned, we headed into Denver—me and Caroline and big Tom in the Toyota with the briefcase full of gems, Ullman following in his Ford with the key, and Mathew and Witherspoon in Willy's beat-up Chevy bringing up the rear.

There was an armed guard waiting to let us in the Republic Plaza. Caroline stopped me at the door.

"This could take hours," she said. "All I want is to go home and be with my grandfather. We both trust you enough to see that we get our share of the reward."

She kissed me on the cheek, climbed in her Toyota, and drove off. The rest of us followed the guard up the elevator to the ninth floor and the offices of National Insurance.

It was an hour and a half before all the proper parties arrived—a gemologist; an accountant with a camera; a couple more armed guards; and Mr. Carr's boss, a fat man, I swear, named Tubb. Tom Two Hawks handed Tubb the briefcase, and Ullman gave him the key.

When Tubb opened the case, we all stared in silence at the contents.

There were two paperweights, a stapler, a brass pencil cup, pens and pencils, and a bone-handled letter opener, all from Witherspoon's desk—plus a jar of hand lotion, a roll of Certs, ChapStick, a pocket mirror, a hairbrush, a Swiss Army knife, a checkbook, a handful of loose change, and other assorted junk, all from Caroline's purse.

"Holy shit," Ullman said.

Witherspoon thought it was funny as hell.

"She pulled a switch on us," he said with a laugh. "While we were all knocking heads in my den, she was dumping a fortune into that big purse of hers."

Carr picked up the phone. "I'm calling the police."

"We're leaving now," Ullman said, heading for the door. "By the time you explain it to them and they get to her house, she and the old man will be long gone."

So they mounted up and headed for Lakewood—Ullman, Witherspoon, Tom and Mathew Two Hawks, and all three armed guards. I went along to make sure the posse didn't get out of control.

Caroline's house was dark when we arrived. Ullman wanted to break in, and I was arguing against it when Tom overruled me by kicking down the door. We searched the house and found no trace of Caroline or Soames or the jewels. None of the dresser drawers was empty, and there were few empty hangers in the closets, so apparently the two fugitives had left with little more than the clothes on their backs. Of course, with five million in gems, they could buy necessities along the way.

Ullman reported to Carr on the phone and we all left, closing the splintered door behind us. Ullman gave me a ride home.

"They won't get far," he told me. "The police are in on it now and they'll be watching the airport, the train station, and the bus depot. Also, there's an APB out on Caroline's Toyota. They won't get far," he repeated.

"Probably not."

"Even if they get out of the state," he said, "they've still got a problem with the jewels. They've got to fence them, which is not such an easy thing to do for the average guy—I mean, do it and not get ripped off or busted."

"You're probably right."

Except Soames wasn't an average guy—he knew about jewels and he'd been in criminal college in Canon City for twenty years. And with Caroline along to help him . . .

Maybe I was hoping, perhaps perversely, that they'd get away. Realistically, though, I didn't give them much chance. In a way I felt sorry for them.

On Monday morning I tried three times before I reached Detective Healey. I asked him about the background check the police had run on Anthony Villanueva.

"What do you want to know?" he asked.

"Abner Greenspan told me Villanueva beat a murder rap in California. A guy named Parmody."

"Right. It was San Francisco, to be exact. Villanueva was Parmody's chauffeur."

"Was Parmody married at the time?"

"I'd have to look it up, but I think so, yeah. Why?"

"Just curious," I said, keeping my voice amazingly calm. "Did the Parmodys own mountain property in Colorado?"

"How the hell should I know?"

"If I were you, I'd check on it," I said. "I'd also find out Parmody's wife's maiden name."

Healey was silent for a moment.

"Do you know something I don't?" he said.

"I'm afraid I do."

I hung up. On my way down the stairs, I ran into Vaz coming out of his apartment. He looked as upset as I felt.

"Jacob, where have you been for the past few days?"

"Later, Vaz, I . . . later."

"But we need to talk about Lloyd Fontaine's journal. There are things that—"

"Later, Vaz, please," I said and pushed past him.

I rented a car and drove to Vail.

37

By the time I got to Vail, the day had turned cold and the sky promised snow.

I asked directions from eight or ten people—giving them the rural route number I'd gotten yesterday from Caroline—before I found the narrow dirt road leading to the house belonging to Helen Ester's late husband. Or as the locals called it, the Parmody place. It was an A-frame tucked away on twenty acres of aspen and pine. Parked in front of the house was a new maroon Chrysler New Yorker. The last place I'd seen it had been the parking garage of the Westin Hotel.

I left my rental car blocking the road. Flakes of snow began to fall from the dead gray sky.

Helen Ester opened the front door before I could knock. She wore buff-colored chamois pants and a white cashmere turtleneck. Her reddish-brown hair fell loosely to her shoulders. She looked older than the last time I'd seen her. And not quite so attractive.

"Hello, Jacob. What a pleasant surprise."

"I'll bet it is."

The house appeared larger than it had from the outside—the ceiling peaked two stories above us, and the second floor was a loft tucked to the rear. The furniture had deep cushions and wooden arms. A new made-to-look-old wood-burning stove stood in the corner flanked by insulated windows, which were becoming spotted now by melting flakes of snow.

"I would have been here sooner," I said, "but I thought you were dead."

"Dead? You must be joking."

"When you didn't show up in court last Thursday, I thought the worst."

"I can explain about that, Jacob, I—"

"Right. I need a drink."

"It's a bit early for me. . . ." The concern in her voice was buried under a smile.

"Bourbon, if you've got it."

I sat on the couch while she poured my drink.

"Soames and Caroline got away with the jewels."

"They what?" She nearly dropped my glass.

"At least temporarily," I said.

She sat near me on the couch, and I put away half the bourbon, trying to kill the pain in my gut. I told her how Witherspoon had retrieved the satchel and how Caroline had pulled a switch. Helen's eyes were bright, and she barely suppressed her delight. I could see the wheels whirring in her head.

"You think Soames is going to send for you, don't you?" I said. "Maybe mail you money from Rio and say, 'Come on down.' That's why you're still here waiting."

She smiled smugly. "Charles Soames still loves me," she said. "Of *course* he'll send for me."

"Don't count on it."

"Your coming up here may complicate things a bit, Jacob, but otherwise nothing has changed."

"Try this for a complication. Prison."

Her smile faded a shade or two. "Whatever are you talking about?"

"You and Anthony Villanueva," I said. "You two have been together in this from the beginning."

"Jacob, that's nonsense. I don't know—"

"You can stop lying," I said, loud enough to make her flinch. I tossed back my drink and got up to get another. My hand shook a bit, but I didn't spill a drop.

"I should have suspected you long ago, but it didn't start to sink in until I learned that Villanueva had been charged with murdering his wealthy employer in California four years ago, which was the same time, according to you, that your husband died in San Francisco. Mrs. Parmody."

"Villanueva must have followed me out here when—"

"You don't quit, do you? Admit it, for chrissake. You and Villanueva bumped off your old man and lived the good life off the inheritance. I have a hunch the money was running low when you learned Soames was being released from prison. So you came back to Denver."

"I don't have to sit here and listen to this."

"You sure as fuck do."

"There's no need to get vulgar, Jacob."

She reached in her purse and brought out a cigarette and a lighter.

"You stayed close to Soames, waiting for him to dig up the jewels, while Villanueva watched from the background. When Meacham threatened Soames, you two killed him and tried to frame me for it."

"That's simply not—"

"When I went up to talk to Meacham that night, while you waited in the car, I heard a horn honk. At the time, I thought maybe you were trying to signal me. You were signaling, all right, but it was to Villanueva."

Helen opened her mouth to protest, then decided not to waste the effort. She lit her cigarette and blew smoke toward the distant ceiling.

"And before Meacham," I said, "there was Lloyd Fontaine. He was snooping around, getting in your way, so you killed him."

"He was trying to blackmail me," she said.

Her voice was as cold as a tomb. More chilling, though, was the realization that she was speaking the truth, finally and without remorse.

"Fontaine was a fool," she went on. "I asked him to give me the photos and his journal, but—"

"Asked. You mean you burned holes in his flesh until he told you and Villanueva that I had what you wanted. Then you put two bullets through his head."

She said nothing.

"Fontaine had you figured out, didn't he? He knew it was you who'd masterminded the Lochemont robbery twenty years ago."

The cigarette stopped in midflight to her lips.

"It was no great deduction," I said, "just a process of elimination. Soames sure as hell wasn't the leader and neither was Archuleta. And it couldn't have been Teague, because whoever was behind things wasted him. And Villanueva entered the picture later, so it wasn't him. I even began to suspect Witherspoon, which shows how far I was reaching. There was only one player left: you."

Helen Ester inhaled and let smoke drift like a veil before her face.

"Stop me if I get any of this wrong," I said, "because a lot of it's guesswork. Twenty years ago you worked out a plan to rob Lochemont Jewelers, with Ed Teague directing Rueben Archuleta, Robert Knox, and Buddy Meacham. You wanted to find out all you could about the store, so you seduced the manager, Charles Soames. No problem there. You must have been a real knockout back then, about Caroline's present age, and Soames was a lonely widower. The only trouble was you found you needed Soames's help, because only he could open the safe where most of the loose gems were kept, and only he could shut off the alarms."

She tipped ashes from her cigarette, carefully, precisely.

"My, you are thorough, aren't you."

"So you got Teague to coerce Soames into helping. Soames, the poor sap, never suspected that you were behind it. You planned to kill him and everyone else after the robbery."

"That was Ed's idea," she said, as if it were an important distinction.

"But Teague blew it, didn't he? He let Soames and Archuleta escape with the satchel of jewels. So you killed him."

She inhaled and tossed smoke my way. "Ed Teague was a fool," she said, "and dangerous to me."

"When it was over, you had nothing. You'd murdered your partner and lost the jewels. But it was no big deal, right? You just moved to a different state and started fresh. No sweat. You were smart and good-looking and you could always get by."

"I can do better than 'get by,' Jacob." She gave me a smile, the kind that makes little children run and hide behind their momma's skirts. "If you team up with me now," she said, "there's no telling how far we could go."

"Don't make me laugh. You used me from the beginning."

"Perhaps at first," she said, her tone soft and sincere. "When you appeared on the scene, Anthony suggested we use you to help us find Meacham."

She stubbed out her smoke and reached for my hand. Her fingertips had the chill of death.

"I know you won't believe this, Jacob, but I truly fell in love with you. I still love you. I would never have let the police send you to prison for Meacham's murder."

"You signed statements against me."

"I lied to the police to keep you out of the way, at least temporarily. You know as well as I do that those statements could never be used against you at a trial if I wasn't there to back them up. But I had to do something, because you'd become too much of a threat. You were getting too close. And

when you saw me and Anthony together in the parking garage,
t was only his quick thinking that—"

"He tried to kill me," I said.

She let go of my hand.

"Exactly what do you want from me, Jacob?"

"I'm taking you back to Denver and turning you over to
Detective Healey. He knows, or soon will, about your connection with Villanueva. At the very least they'll hang a conspiracy
charge on you for Meacham's murder. And maybe for Fontaine's."

"They can prove nothing," she said grimly. "In any case, I've
decided to leave the state. Now. I won't be seeing you again,
and I certainly won't be talking to the police."

She rose from the couch.

"I can't let you go," I said.

"You can't stop me."

She reached in her purse again, but not for a cigarette. She
brought out her shiny, squat Derringer, the one I'd seen pressed to
the neck of Mathew Two Hawks. Now it was pointed at my neck.

"I'll use this, Jacob, if you force me to."

"Is that what you shot Fontaine with? And Teague? It fires
both barrels at once, doesn't it? Some people thought Fontaine's
murder was a professional hit, two shots to the head. I guess it
was done by a professional."

She backed toward the door and kept her small, deadly gun
pointed at me.

"You'd better put on a coat," I said, moving toward her. "It'll
be a cold ride to Denver."

"I mean it, Jacob, stay back."

"You can't shoot me. You love me, remember?"

Her finger tightened on the trigger and I started to raise my
hand and the gun popped and the next thing I knew I was on
the carpet staring up at the faraway ceiling. Pain throbbed high
in my chest, and my shirt was becoming soggy. All I could
think of was Sergeant Mobley's theory of vectors.

Outside, Helen started her car.

I got to my knees and pulled myself up by the door frame. The feeling was gone from my left arm, and it hung uselessly at my side.

Snow was falling steadily now. It covered the ground like a thin white shroud. Helen tried to maneuver the Chrysler around my rental, but there wasn't enough room, and when she backed up, she dropped the right rear wheel in the ditch. I staggered to my car. When she saw me, she panicked and gunned the motor, digging the wheel deeper into the ditch. I pulled open the passenger door of the rental and got Willy Two Hawks' pistol from the glove box. Helen climbed out of her car and began hurrying away on foot.

"Stop," I said.

She did. When she turned around, her purse was open and the Derringer was out. I waited for her to snap open the gun and eject the two spent shells and fumble in her purse for two shiny fresh cartridges and put them in the chambers and click shut the gun and raise it and point it at me. Then I shot her just below her left breast. She blinked, surprised, then crumpled to the wet ground.

I shuffled over, dropped to my knees, and touched her snow-white neck. It had already begun to cool.

38

Detective Healey saved my life.

After I'd questioned him on the phone, he'd dug around until he learned that Helen Ester's married name was Parmody, which tied her to Villanueva. Then he guessed my next move and phoned the Eagle County sheriff, who knew the location of the Parmody place. The sheriff showed up, found me unconscious, and radioed for an ambulance to take me into Vail. He left Helen Ester for the county coroner.

A doctor examined me in Vail, then called Flight For Life, and less than an hour later I was flying in a big orange helicopter toward Denver. The Eagle County sheriff came along for the ride. He was afraid I'd bleed to death before he could charge me with murder.

They operated on me at St. Anthony's. One slug from Helen's nasty little Derringer had passed between my ribs, punctured my left lung, and lodged itself deep in my back. The other bullet had nicked a rib, ricocheted up toward my shoulder, and stopped at my collarbone. The medics fed me blood, dug out the lead, and sewed me up.

The next morning, right after my tepid tea and tasteless, mushy breakfast, Abner Greenspan paid me a visit.

"Stupid question, but how do you feel?"

"Like I've been shot," I said. "Like I've shot someone."

"Self-defense, Jake. You had no choice."

"There are always choices."

"Whatever. The doctor told me you'd probably be out of here tomorrow."

"Yeah, I guess."

"So cheer up, for chrissake."

"Sure." His sunny outlook was frying my nerves.

"Hey, Jake, come on. I got you off the hook."

"Meaning what?"

"Dalrymple and Healey and I explained to the Eagle County D.A. what's been going on for the past few weeks. When he learned that Ester was a murder suspect, and that when you tried to make a citizen's arrest, she shot you and you shot back in self-defense, well . . . he's not going to file charges."

"Swell."

"Hey, don't thank me," he said.

"Why don't you mind your own fucking business."

"What the hell's the matter with you?"

"The matter, Abner, is that I killed her."

"So what do you want, to be *punished*? You did it to save yourself, remember? And this after she'd murdered Lloyd Fontaine."

"Regardless. If I'd have played it differently, she'd still be alive."

" 'Regardless,' my ass. You know what the trouble is? You think she was somehow less guilty because she was a woman. Hell, maybe she even convinced you there was love in the vicinity, just waiting to happen between you two."

I said nothing.

"It's a common affliction, Jake, and you're not immune. Your glands are clouding your judgment."

"You're full of shit, Abner."

"I am, huh?" he said, raising his voice. "Then what's your problem? Straighten up, for chrissake."

"Yeah, yeah." I knew he was right, and it pissed me off. I turned away from him.

He was silent for a moment before he yelled, "And quit feeling sorry for yourself!" and nearly knocked over a nurse on his way out the door.

Wednesday at noon they released me from the hospital. Lieutenant Dalrymple was waiting for me at the front desk.

"Lomax."

"Lieutenant."

"Need a ride?"

"I was going to jog home, but if you insist."

Dalrymple drove slowly, ponderously, making every car pass us. He watched them, as if everyone out there were in a continuous police lineup. After a while, he spoke.

"You owe me an apology," he said.

"For what?"

"You called me a liar."

"*You* called *me* a murderer."

"True." A squeal started coming in on the car radio. Dalrymple turned down the volume. "She played you for a fool."

"Thanks for reminding me."

"All she ever wanted was that bag of jewels, and she would've killed anybody who got in her way." He drifted through a yellow-red light. "You should have known she was involved in Meacham's murder. Hell, *I* knew from the beginning."

"Sure you did."

"I don't mean knew as in knew. I mean knew." He rubbed a fat thumb over the pads of his fingers. "I could feel it."

"If that's true, Dalrymple, then why'd you work so hard to put me away?"

"Because I thought you pulled the trigger on Meacham. Why the fuck do you think?"

"Because you hate my guts."

He stopped in front of my apartment house.

"I do," he said. "More or less. But I get paid to apprehend perpetrators, not to toss every jerk in jail who gives me tight jaws. I'm a cop."

"I've heard rumors to that effect."

He grunted good-bye and drove away.

Vaz and Sophia were waiting to help me upstairs, whether I needed it or not. Sophia made soup and fussed like a hen over her sick chick. Vaz showed me Fontaine's original journal and the decoded version. He'd tried to tell me Monday morning that he'd broken the code, but I'd been too preoccupied to listen.

"Fontaine's code was fairly simple," Vaz said. "He wrote backward, placing a null letter in the middle of each five-letter group. Look at the last page, the one dated September fifteenth, the one I showed you before. If you start at the end and read forward, skipping over the middle letter of each—"

"Vassily, *please*," Sophia said. "Jacob needs his rest."

When they'd gone, I read through Fontaine's decoded journal. Other than one early entry that made me sit up straight, there was little in it that I didn't already know. It was clear from Fontaine's more recent entries that if he'd recovered the Lochemont jewels, he'd have tried to keep them for himself. His biggest mistake, though, had been in underestimating the viciousness of Helen Ester. But then, look who's talking.

The early entry that had caught my eye was dated nearly twenty years ago, when Fontaine was conducting his investigation for National and his loyalties were still with the company.

Spoke again today with Trenton Lochemont, Sr. Still extremely upset over the death of little Emily Sue Ott during the robbery. Actually cried, saying he felt guilty. Then confessed to me that he'd discussed the possibility of saving his faltering business by robbing his own store, but that it had never been more than "bedroom talk." When I asked what his wife's reaction had been to such talk, he said he hadn't meant his wife. Then he regained his composure and refused to speak further on the matter. He swore he would deny he'd admitted anything to me.

I had a fair idea who old man Lochemont had been sleeping with on the sly. Helen Ester had covered every angle before the robbery.

Later that day I phoned Neal Ullman at National Insurance to get the latest word on Soames and Caroline.

"We've found no trace of them," he said. "Yet. They've no doubt left the state, but I guarantee they won't get out of the country."

"Don't be too sure," I said, trying not to grin.

"You sound like you *want* them to get away."

"Maybe I do."

"They're *thieves*, Lomax. They have no right to those jewels."

"No? Then tell me, Ullman, what price would *you* put on twenty years of a man's life?"

He muttered something, then slammed down the phone.

Harry Witherspoon dropped by on Thursday. He'd found the negatives of the shots taken twenty years ago in Idaho Springs—the ones of Ed Teague arguing with a cop beside his car. He'd made a pair of eight-by-ten glossies, reprints of the ones Fontaine had had with him the night he'd been murdered. The passenger in Ed Teague's car, blocked from view in the photos I'd found in Fontaine's manila envelope, was clearly revealed here. Of course it was Helen Ester. She looked young and beautiful and unafraid. Invulnerable. Perhaps that image would eventually replace the one I carried of her lying in the snow. Perhaps after my chest wounds healed.

* * *

A few days later a shoebox-sized package arrived in the mail. It noticeably cheered me up. It was full of money.

I counted it out twice and got the same number both times: fifty thousand dollars. Also in the box, wrapped in wads of tissue paper, was Baby Doe Tabor's ruby necklace. With it was a note, unsigned and handprinted on cheap paper:

> Here's your commission like we agreed on before. Keep it or give it away or do whatever the hell you want with it. The necklace belongs to the museum.

The package was postmarked Seattle. At least they'd gotten that far. Maybe that's where Caroline would find her young man and Soames would find his beach. I hoped so. The only trouble was, it got pretty cold up there. And it was too close to here.

Soames was right about one thing, though: The necklace belonged to the museum. The money was another matter. I began to wonder if I should turn over the fifty grand to National Insurance. Then I thought about how broke I was and how many unpaid bills I had and how my poor crippled Olds was still stuck on the side of a mountain and how I'd been beat up and shot at and shot, and I stopped wondering. I could try to claim the reward money for the necklace, but this was better. And more certain. And like the man said, money won smells twice as sweet as money earned.

I took Baby Doe Tabor's necklace to the folks at the state historical museum. They couldn't accept it.

The problem was that legally the necklace belonged to National Insurance, who had settled long ago with Lochemont Jewelers for six hundred thousand dollars, half of which Trenton Lochemont, Sr., had returned to the museum, since that was the amount for which the museum had the piece insured. The other half, of course, had gone into old man Lochemont' pocket. But with the return of the necklace, no one was quite sure what to do. National owned it and would sell it for no less than six hundred thousand dollars. The museum couldn't come up with that kind of money.

There was talk that National might auction off the piece to private collectors.

And then, to the surprise and gratitude of the museum and the insurance company and the public at large, Trenton Lochemont, Jr., bought the necklace from National Insurance and donated it to the museum.

Lochemont refused to be interviewed about his magnanimous act, so the media quickly produced three theories about why he'd been so generous: one, it was a tax write-off; two, it was great publicity for his jewelry store; and three, it simply made him feel good. I know it made *me* feel good, especially since no one suggested that Lochemont had been shown a certain entry from a certain dead private eye's journal concerning his late father's duplicity and that he'd been assured he'd read that entry in the local newspapers if he didn't perform his good deed.

A month later, around the middle of November, while the city was suffering through its first big snowstorm of the year, the necklace was put on display behind heavy glass at the state historical museum. On that same day I received a postcard from sunny Australia. There was no written message.

The picture on the front showed a young man and woman astride horses on a beach. The sky was clear, the ocean was blue, and the water lapped at the horses' hooves. The animals were healthy and eager and bursting with life. So was the young couple. They were pointing at someone who was little more than a dot, far up the sunny coastline. They were smiling.

Sizzling Fred Carver Mysteries by Edgar Award-Winning Author John Lutz

KISS

70934-1/$3.95 US/$4.95 Can

When asked to look into the mysterious death of a Florida retiree, ex-cop Fred Carver finds that the life expectancy for the residents of the Sunhaven Retirement Home is shockingly brief.

TROPICAL HEAT

70309-2/$3.95 US/$4.95 Can

Fred Carver thinks he's got every problem under the Florida sun. When he's hired to investigate a suicide *without* a body, he *knows* he does!

SCORCHER

70526-5/$3.95 US/$4.95 Can

Florida private investigator Fred Carver burns for revenge when his son is horribly killed during a robbery. He goes undercover and finds a psychopathic murderer with a homemade flame thrower.